...ght © 1985 by David Drake and Karl Edward Wagner

...hts reserved, including the right to reproduce this book
...rtions thereof in any form.

...aen Book

...aen Enterprises
...-10 W. 36th Street
New York, N.Y. 10018

First printing, January 1985

ISBN: 0-671-55931-1

Cover art by David Mattingly

Printed in the United States of America

Distributed by
SIMON & SCHUSTER
MASS MERCHANDISE SALES COMPANY
1230 Avenue of the Americas
New York, N.Y. 10020

IT WAITED IN ITS BURROW BENEATH THE RIVER BANK

Waited patiently for its wounds to heal—
patiently, for it watched the boats pass up
and down the Tiber, and it knew it was only
a short matter of time before its red dreams
were fulfilled.

It had learned a great deal from observing
the soft-skinned bipeds who appeared to be
the dominant race of this world. To an extent,
it no longer regretted its capture during its
initial few hours after the crash, dazed and
injured. The bipeds had sheltered and fed the
phile—or lizard-ape, as they named it in their
various tongues. They posed no real threat,
except in their numbers. The phile had already proven to itself how easily they died.

The phile shook with rage as it remembered that one biped who had pursued it this
last time. It had touched that biped's aura,
recognized that this one was different from
the others—another species, perhaps, and
trained to kill for its master as the phile itself
had been trained.

Perhaps this one hunter would offer combat again. The phile hoped it would.

DAVID D

KILLER

A BAEN BOOK

DEDICATION

To Gary Hoppenstand and Michel Parry—

And super heroes come to feast
To taste the flesh not yet deceased
And all I know
Is still the beast is feeding—

Richard O'Brien,
The Rocky Horror Show

from the mud. His huge head hung loose, and his
had gleamed for an instant. Blood spurted up a

EPIGRAPH

The gates of mercy shall be all shut up,
And the flesh'd soldier, rough and hard of heart.
In liberty of bloody hand shall range
With conscience wide as hell....

William Shakespeare, *Henry V*

CHAPTER ONE

Rain was again trickling from the greyness overhead, and the damp reek of the animals hung on the misty droplets. A hyena wailed miserably, longing for the dry plains it would never see again. Lycon listened without pity. Let it bark its lungs out here in Portus, at the Tiber's mouth, or die later in the amphitheater at Rome. He remembered the Ethiopian girl who had lived three days after a hyena had dragged her down. It would have been far better had the beast not been driven off before it had finished disembowelling her.

"Wish the rain would stop," complained Vonones. The Armenian dealer's plump face was gloomy. "A lot of these are going to die otherwise, and I'll be caught in the middle. In Rome they only pay me for live delivery, but I have to pay you regardless."

"Which is why I'm a hunter and you're a dealer," chided Lycon without overmuch sympathy. "Well, it won't ruin you," he reassured the dealer. "Not at the prices you pay. You can replace the entire lot for a fifth of what they'll bring in Rome."

The tiger whose angry cough had been cutting through the general racket thundered forth a full-throated roar. Lycon and the Armenian heard his heavy body crash against the bars of his cage. Vonones nodded toward the sound. "There's one I can't replace."

"What? The tiger?" Lycon seemed surprised. "I'll grant you he's the biggest I've ever captured, but I brought back two others with him that are near as fine."

"No, not the tiger." Vonones pointed. "I meant the thing he's snarling at. Come on, I'll show you. Maybe you'll know what it is."

Vonones put on his broad felt hat and snugged up his cloak against the drizzle. Lycon followed, not really noticing the rain that beaded his close-cut black hair. He had been a mercenary scout in his youth, before he had sickened of butchering Rome's barbarian enemies and turned instead to hunting animals for her arenas. A score of years in the field had left the beastcatcher as calloused to the weather as to all else.

For the beasts themselves he felt only professional concern, no more. As they passed a wooden cage with a dozen maned baboons, he scowled and halted the dealer. "I'd get them into a metal cage, if I were you. They'll chew through the lashings of that one, and you'll have hell catching them again."

"Overflow," the Armenian told him vexedly. "Had to put them there. It's all the cages I've got, with your load and then this mixed shipment from Tipasa getting here at the same time. Don't worry.

They move tomorrow when we sort things out for the haul to Rome."

Beasts snarled and lunged as the men threaded through the maze of cages. Most of the animals were smeared with filth, their coats worn and dull where they showed through the muck. A leopard pining in a corner of its cage reminded Lycon of a cat he once had force-fed—a magnificent mottled-brown beast that he had purchased half-starved from a village of gap-toothed savages in the uplands of India. He needed four of his men to pin it down while he rammed chunks of raw flesh down its throat with a stake. That lithe killer was now the Empress' plaything, and her slavegirls fed it tit-bits from silver plates.

"There it is," Vonones announced, pointing to a squat cage of iron. The creature stared back, ignoring the furious efforts of the tiger alongside to slash his paw across the space that separated their cages.

"You've got some sort of wild man!" Lycon blurted with first glance.

"Nonsense!" Vonones snorted. "Look at the tiny scales, those talons! There may be a race somewhere with blue skin, but this thing's no more human than a mandrill is. The Numidians called it a lizard-ape in their tongue—a sauropithecus."

After that first startled impression, Lycon had to agree. The thing seemed far less human than any large ape, which it somewhat resembled. Probably those hairless limbs had made him think it was a man—that and the aura of malign intelligence its stare conveyed. But the collector had never seen anything like it, not in twenty years of professional hunting along the fringes of the known world.

Lizard-ape, or sauropithecus to render the word into Latin, seemed as good a name as any for the beast. Lycon could not even decide whether it was mammal or reptile, nor even guess its sex. It was scaled and exuded an acrid reptilian scent, but its movements and poise were feline. Ape-like, it walked erect in a forward crouch, and its long forelimbs seemed adapted for gripping and climbing. It would be about man-height if it straightened fully, and Lycon estimated its lean weight close to that of a big leopard. Its face was cat-like, low-browed and triangular of jaw. A wedge-shaped, earless skull thrust forward upon a snaky neck, and it had no more nostrils than a lizard did. Its eyes looked straight forward with human intensity, but were slit-pupiled and showed a swift nictitating membrane.

"This came from the Aures Mountains?" Lycon questioned wonderingly.

"It did. There was a big lot of gazelles and elephants that one of my agents jobbed from the Numidians. This thing came with them, and all I know about it is what Dama wrote me when he sent the shipment: that a band of Numidians saw a hilltop explode and found this animal when they went to see what had happened."

"A hilltop exploded!"

The dealer shrugged. "That's all he wrote."

Lycon studied the cage in silence.

"Why did you weld the cage shut instead of putting a chain and lock on it?"

"That's the way it came," Vonones explained. "I'll have to knock the door loose and put a proper lock on it before sending it off tomorrow, or those idiots at Rome will wreck a good cage trying to smash it open, and never a denarius for the damage. I guess the Numidians just didn't have a lock—I'm a little surprised they even had an iron cage."

Lycon frowned, uncomfortable at the way the beast stared back at him. "It's its eyes," he reflected. "I wish all my crew looked that bright."

"Or mine," Vonones agreed readily. "Oh, I make no doubt it's more cunning than any brute should be, but it's scarcely human. Can you see those claws? They're curled back in its palms now, but—there!"

The lizard-ape made a stretching motion, opening its paws—or were they hands? Bones stood out—slim, but like the limbs themselves hinting at adamantine hardness. The crystalline claws extended maybe a couple of inches, so sharp that their points seemed to fade into the air. No wild creature should have claws so delicately kept. The beast's lips twitched a needle-toothed grin.

"Fortune!" Lycon muttered, looking away. There was a glint of bloodlust in those eyes, something beyond natural savagery. Lycon remembered a centurion whose eyes had held that look—an unassuming little man who once had killed over a hundred women and children during a raid on a German village.

"What are they going to pit this thing against?" he asked suddenly.

Vonones shrugged. "Can't be sure. The buyer didn't say much except that he didn't like the thing's looks."

"Can you blame him?"

"So? He's supposed to be running a beast show, not a beauty contest. If he wants pretty things, I should bring him gazelles. For the arena, I told him, this thing is perfect—a real novelty. But the ass says he doesn't like the idea of keeping it around until the show, and I have to cut my price to nothing to get him to take it. Think of it!"

"What's the matter?" Lycon gibed. "Don't tell me that you so dislike its looks that you'll unload it at a sacrifice!"

"Hardly!" the dealer protested, defending his business acumen. "Animals are animals, and business is business. But I've got a hundred other beasts here right now, and *they* don't like the thing. Look at this tiger. All day, all night he's trying to get at it—even broke a tooth on the bars! Must be its scent, because all the animals hate it. No, I have to get this thing out of my compound."

Lycon considered the enraged tiger. The huge cat had killed one of his men and maimed another for life before they had him safely caged. But even the tiger's rage at capture paled at the determined fury he showed toward Vonones' strange find.

"Well, I'll leave you to him, then," the beast-catcher said, giving up on the mystery. "I'm crossing over to Ostia to see my old mate, Vulpes. Tomorrow I'll be by to pick up my money, so try to stay out of reach of that thing's claws until then."

"You could have gone on with it," Vulpes told him. "You could have made a fortune in the arena."

Lycon tore off a chunk of bread and sopped it

with greasy gravy. "I could have got killed—or crippled for life."

He immediately regretted his choice of words, but his host only laughed. The tavern owner's left arm was a stump, and that he walked at all was a testament to the man's fortitude. Lycon had seen him after they dragged him from the wreck of his chariot. The surgeons doubted Vulpes would last the night, but that was twenty-five years ago.

"No, it was stupidity that brought me down," Vulpes said. "Or greed. I knew my chances of forcing through on that turn, but it was that or the race. Well, I was lucky. I lived through it and had enough of my winnings saved to open a wine shop here in Ostia. I get by.

"But you," and he stabbed a thick finger into Lycon's grey-stubbled face. "You were too good, too smart. You could have been rich. A few years was all you needed. You were as good with a sword as any man who's ever set foot in the arena—fast, and you knew how to handle yourself. All those years you spent against the barbarians seasoned you. Not like these swaggering bullies the crowds dote on these days—gutless slaves and flashy thugs who learned their trade in dark alleys! Pit a combat-hardened veteran against this sort of trash, and see whose lauded favorite gets dragged off by his heels!"

Vulpes downed a cup of his wares and glared about the tavern truculently. None of his few customers was paying attention.

Lycon ruefully watched his host refill their cups with wine and water. He wished his friend would let old memories lie. Vulpes, he noted, was getting red-faced and paunchy as the wineskins he sold here. Nor, Lycon mused, running a hand over his close-cropped scalp, was he himself as young as back then. At least he stayed fit, he told himself—but then, Vulpes could hardly be faulted for inaction.

Tall for a Greek, Lycon had only grown leaner and harder with the years. His face still scowled in hawk-like intensity; his features resembled seasoned leather stretched tightly over sharp angles. Spirit and sinew had lost nothing in toughness as Lycon drew closer to fifty, and his men still talked of the voyage of a few years past when he nursed an injured polar bear on deck, while waves broke over the bow and left a film of ice as they slipped back.

Vulpes rumbled on. "But you, my philosophic Greek, found the arena a bore. Just walked away and left it all. Been skulking around the most forsaken corners of the world for—what is it, more than twenty years now? Risking your life to haul back savage beasts that barely make your expenses when you sell them. And you could be living easy in a villa near Rome!"

"Maybe this is what I wanted," Lycon protested. "Besides, I've got Zoe and the kids to come home to in Rome—maybe not a villa, but we do all right." He tried to push away memories of sand and sweat and the smell of blood and the sound of death and an ocean's roar of voices howling to watch men die for their amusement.

Vulpes was scarcely troubling to add water to their wine. "*Maybe* what you wanted!" he scoffed. "Well, what *do* you want, my moody Greek?"

"I'm my own master. Maybe I'm not rich, but

I've journeyed to lands Odysseus never dreamed of, and I've captured stranger beasts than the Huntress ever loosed arrow after."

"Oh, here's to adventure!" mocked Vulpes good-humoredly, thumping his wine cup loudly.

Lycon, reminded of the blue-scaled creature in Vonones' cage, smiled absently.

"I, too, am a philosopher," Vulpes announced loftily. "Wine and sitting on your butt all day make a good Roman as philosophic as any wander-witted Greek beastcatcher." He raised his cup to Lycon.

"And you, my friend, you have a fascination for the killer trait, a love of deadly things. Deny it as you will, but it's there. You could have farmed olives, or studied sculpture. But no—it's the army for you, then the arena, and what next? Are you sick of killing? No, just bored with easy prey. So now you spend your days outwitting and ensnaring the most savage beasts of all lands!

"You can't get away from your fascination for the killer, friend Lycon. And shall I tell you why? It's because, no matter how earnestly you deny it, you've got the killer streak in your own soul too."

"Here's to philosophy," toasted Lycon sardonically.

Lycon had done business with Vonones for many years, and the habitually morose Armenian was among the handful of men whom the hunter counted as friends. Reasonably honest and certainly shrewd, Vonones paid with coins of full weight and had been known to add a bonus to the tally when a collector brought him something exceptional. Still, after a long night of drinking with Vulpes, Lycon was not pleased when the dealer burst in upon him in the first hour of morning in the room he shared with five other transients.

"What in the name of the buggering Twins do you mean getting me up at this hour!" Lycon snarled, surprised to see daylight. "I said I'd come by later for my money."

"No—it's not that!" Vonones moaned, shaking his arm. "Thank the gods I've found you! Come on, Lycon! You've got to help me!"

Lycon freed his arm and rolled to his feet. Someone cursed and threw a sandal in their direction. "All right, all right," the hunter yawned. "Let's get out of here and let other people sleep."

The stairs of the apartment block reeked of garbage and refuse. It reminded Lycon of the stench at Vonones' animal compound—the sour foulness of too many people living within cramped walls. Beggars clogged the stairs, living there for want of other shelter. Now and again the manager of the block would pay a squad of the Watch to pummel them out into the street. Those who could pay for a portion of a room were little cleaner themselves.

"Damn it, Vonones! What is it!" Lycon protested, as the frantic Armenian took hold of his arm again. He had never seen Vonones so shaken.

"Outside—I can't. . . . That animal escaped. The sauropithecus."

"Well," Lycon said reasonably. "You said you didn't get much for the thing, so it can't be all that great a loss. Anyway, what has it to do with me?"

But Vonones set his lips and tugged the hunter down the stairs and out onto the cobbled street, where eight bearers waited with his litter. He pushed Lycon inside and closed the curtains before speaking in a low, agitated voice. "I don't dare let word of this get about! Lycon, the beast escaped only a few miles out of town. It's loose in an estate now—hundreds of those little peasant grainplots, each worked by a tenant family."

"So?"

"The estate is owned by the Emperor, and that lizard-ape thing killed one of his tenants within minutes of escaping! You've got to help me recapture it before worse happens!"

"Lady Fortune!" swore Lycon softly, understanding why the loss of the animal had made a trembling wreck of the dealer. "How did it get loose?"

"That's the worst of it!" Vonones protested, in the tone of someone who knew he would be called a liar. "It must have unlocked the cage somehow—I checked the fastenings myself before the caravan left. But nobody will believe that—they'll think I was careless and didn't have the cage locked properly in the first place. And if our lord and god learns that one of his estates is being ravaged . . . ."

"Domitian shows his displeasure in interesting ways," Lycon finished somberly. "Are you sure it isn't already too late to hush this business up?"

Vonones struggled for composure. "For now it's all right. The steward is no more interested in letting this get out than I am, knowing the Emperor's temper. But there's a limit to what he can cover up, and. . . . It won't take very much of what happened to that farmer to exceed that limit. You've got to catch the thing for me, Lycon!"

"All right," Lycon decided. The sane voice of reason warned that he was plunging into a situation that might call down Domitian's wrath on all concerned, but his own voice was edged with excitement. "Let's get out to where the lizard-ape escaped."

CHAPTER TWO

The caravan was still strung out along the road when they arrived in Vonones' mud-spattered carriage. There were thirty carts, mostly loaded with only a single cage to avoid fights between the bars. Despite wind, rain and jostling, the beasts seemed less restive than in the compound. Perhaps there was a reason. The third cage from the end stood open.

Lycon stepped between a pair of carts—then ducked quickly as a taloned paw ripped through the bars at him. Disappointed, the huge tiger snarled as he hunched back in his cage.

The hunter glanced to be certain his arm was still in place. "There's one to watch out for," he cautioned Vonones. "That one was a man-killer when we captured him—and out of preference, not just because he was lame or too old to take other prey. When they turn him loose in the arena, he'll take on anything in sight."

"Maybe," muttered Vonones. "But he'd like to start with that lizard-ape. I never saw anything

13

drive every animal around it to a killing rage the way it does. Maybe it's its scent, but at times I could swear it was somehow taunting them."

Lycon grunted noncommittally.

"Suppose I should let the rest of the caravan go on?" Vonones suggested. "They're just causing comment stopped here like this."

Lycon considered. "Why not get them off the road as much as you can and spread out. Don't let them get too far away though, because I'll need some men for this. Say, there aren't any hunting dogs here, are there?"

Vonones shook his balding head. "No, I don't often handle dogs. There's a small pack in Ostia for the local arena though. I know the trainer, and I think I can have them here by noon."

"Better do it, then," Lycon advised. "It's going to be easiest just to run the lizard-ape down and let the dogs have it. If we can pull them off in time, maybe there'll be enough left for your buyer in Rome."

"Forget the sale," Vonones urged him. "Just *get* that damned thing!"

But Lycon was studying the lock of the cage. It clearly had not been forced. There were only a few fine scratches on the wards.

"Any of your men mess with this?"

"Are you serious? They don't like it any better than the animals do."

"Vonones, I think it had to have opened the lock with its claws."

The merchant looked sick.

Twenty feet from the cart were the first footprints of the lizard-ape, sunk deeply into the mud of the wheat field beside the road. In the black earth their stamp was as ambiguous as the beast itself. More lizard than bird-like, Lycon decided. Long toes leading a narrow, arched foot, but with a thick, sharp-spurred heel.

"First I knew anything was wrong," explained the arm-waving driver of the next cart back, "was when this thing all of a sudden swings out of its cage and jumps into the field. Why, it could just as easy have jumped back on me—and then where would I have been, I ask you?"

Lycon did not bother to tell him. "Vonones, you've got a couple of archers in your caravan, haven't you?"

"Yes, but they weren't of any use—it was too sudden. The one in the rear of the column aimed where he could see the wheat waving, but he didn't really have a target. If only the thing *had* turned back on the rest of the caravan, instead of diving through the hedges! My archers would have skewered it for sure then, and I wouldn't be in this fix. Lycon, this creature is a killer! If it gets away . . ."

"All right, steady," the beastcatcher growled. "Going to pieces isn't going to help." He rose from where he knelt in the wheat.

"You won't be so self-assured once you've seen the farmer," Vonones warned.

The tenant's hut was a windowless beehive of wattle and daub, stuck up on the edge of his holdings. Huddled in the doorway, three of his children watched the strangers apathetically, numbed by the cold drizzle and their father's death.

The farmer lay about thirty yards into the field. A scythe, its rough iron blade unstained, had fallen near the body. Blank amazement still showed in his glazed eyes. A sudden, tearing thrust of the creature's taloned hands had eviscerated the man— totally, violently. He lay on his back in a welter of gore and entrails, naked ribs jagged through his ripped-open chest cavity.

Lycon studied the fragments of flesh strewn over the furrows. "What did you feed it in the compound?"

"The same as the other carnivores," Vonones replied shakily. "Scrap beef and parts of any animals that happened to die. It was always hungry, and it wasn't fussy."

"Well, if you manage to get it back alive, you'll know what it really likes," Lycon said grimly. "Do you see any sign of his lungs?"

Vonones swallowed and stared and stared at the corpse in dread. The archers held arrows to their bows and looked about nervously.

Lycon, who had been following the tracks with his eye as they crossed the gullied field, suddenly frowned. "How's your bow strung?" he asked sharply of the nearest archer.

"With gut," he answered, blinking.

Lycon swore in disgust. "In this rain a gut string is going to stretch like a judge's honor! Vonones, we've got to have spears and bows strung with waxed horsehair before we do anything. I don't want to be found turned inside out with a silly expression like this poor bastard!"

Lycon chose a dozen of Vonones' men to follow the dogs with him. After that nothing happened for hours, while Vonones fumed and paced beside the wagons. At the prospect of extricating himself from his dilemma, the Armenian's frantic fear gave way to impatience.

About mid-afternoon a battered farm cart creaked into view behind a pair of spavined mules. The driver was a stocky North Italian, whose short whip and leather armlets proclaimed him the trainer of the six huge dogs that almost filled the wagon bed. Following was a much sharper carriage packed with hunting equipment, nets as well as bows and spears.

"What took you so long, Galerius!" Vonones demanded. "I sent for you hours ago—told you to spare no expense in hiring a wagon! Damn it, man—the whole business could have been taken care of by now if you hadn't come in this wreck!"

"Thought you'd be glad I saved you the money," Galerius explained with dull puzzlement. "My father-in-law lets me use this rig at a special rate."

"It doesn't matter." Lycon headed off the quarrel. "We had to wait for the weapons anyway. How about the dogs? Can they track in this drizzle?"

"Sure, they're real hunting dogs—genuine Molossians," the trainer asserted proudly. "They weren't bred for the arena. I bought them from an old boy who used to run deer on his estate, before he offended Domitian."

Vonones began to chew his ragged nails.

At least the pack looked fully capable of holding up its end of things, Lycon thought approvingly. The huge, brindle-coated dogs milled about the wagon bed, stiff-legged and hackles lifted at the babble of sounds and scents from Vonones' caravan. Their flanks were lean and scarred, and their massive shoulders bespoke driving strength. Their trainer might be a slovenly yokel himself, but his hounds were excellent hunting stock and well cared for. With professional interest, Lycon wondered whether he could talk Galerius into selling the pack.

"Don't you have horses?" the trainer asked. "Going to be tough keeping up with these on foot."

"We'll have to do it," Lycon snorted. The trainer's idea of hunting was probably limited to the arena. Well, this wasn't just some confused animal at bay in the center of an open arena. "Look at the terrain. Horses'd be worse than useless!"

Beneath grey clouds, the land about them was broken with rocky gullies, shadowy ravines, and stunted groves of trees. Gateless hedgerows divided the tenant plots at short intervals, forming dark, thorny barriers in maze-like patterns throughout the estate. There were a few low sections where a good horse might hurdle the hedge, but the rain had turned plowed fields into quagmires, and the furrows were treacherous footing.

Lycon frowned at the sky. The rain was now only a dismal mist, but the overcast was thick and the sun well, down on the horizon. Objects at a hundred yards blurred indistinctly into the haze.

"We've got one, maybe two hours left if we're going to catch the lizard-ape today," he judged. "Well, let's see what they can do."

Galerius threw open the back gate of the wagon, and the pack bounded onto the road. They milled and snarled uncertainly while their trainer whipped them into line and led them past the remaining wagons. As soon as they neared the open cage, the hounds began to show intense excitement. One of the bitches gave a throaty bay and swung off into the wheat field. The other five poured after her, and no more need be done.

They hate it too, mused Lycon, as the excited pack bounded across the field in full cry. "Come on!" he shouted. "And keep your eyes open!"

Taking a boar spear, the hunter plunged after the baying pack. Vonones' men strung out behind him, while the dogs raced far ahead in the wheat. Too out of condition for a long run, Vonones held back with the others on the road. Fingering a bow nervously, he stood atop a wagon and watched the hunt disappear into the mist. He looked jumpy enough to loose arrow at the first thing to come out of the woods, and Lycon reminded himself to shout when they returned to the road. Vonones was a better than fair archer.

Already the dogs had vanished in the wheat, so that the men heard only their distant cries. Trailing them was no problem—the huge hounds had torn through the grainfield like a chariot's rush—but keeping up with them was impossible. The soft earth pulled at the men's legs, and sandals were constantly mired with clay and straw.

"Can't you slow them up?" Lycon demanded of the trainer, who panted at his side.

"Not on a scent like this!" Galerius gasped back. "They're wild, plain wild! No way we can keep up without horses!"

Lycon grunted and lengthened his stride. The trainer fell quickly back, and when Lycon glanced over his shoulder, he saw that the other had paused to clean his sandals. Of the others he saw only vague forms farther behind still. Lycon wasted a breath to curse them and ran on.

The dogs had plunged through a narrow gap in

the first hedge. Lycon followed, pushing his boar spear ahead of him. Had the gap been there, or had their quarry broken it through in passing? Clearly the lizard-ape was powerful beyond proportion to its slight bulk.

The new field was already harvested, and stubble spiked up out of the cold mud to jab Lycon's toes. His side began to ache. Herakles, he thought, the beast could be clear to Tarantum by now, if it wanted to be. If it did get away, there was no help for Vonones. Lycon himself might find it expedient to spend a few years beyond the limits of the empire. That's what happens when you get involved in things that really aren't your business.

Another farmhouse squatted near the next hedgerow. "Hoi!" the beastcatcher shouted. "Did a pack of dogs cross your hedge?"

There was no sound within. Lycon stopped in sudden concern and peered through the open doorway.

A half-kneaded cake of bread was turning black on the fire in the center of the hut. The rest of the hut was mottled throughout with russet splashes of blood that dried in the westering sun. There were at least six bodies scattered about the tiny room. The sauropithecus had taken its time here.

Lycon turned away, shaken for the first time in long years. He looked back the way he had come. None of the others had crawled through the last hedgerow yet. This time he felt thankful for their flabby uselessness.

He used a stick of kindling to scatter coals into the straw bedding, and tossed the flaming brand after. With luck no one would ever know what had happened here. As Vonones had said, there was a limit. They had better finish the lizard-ape fast.

The pack began to bay fiercely not far away. From the savage eagerness of their voices, Lycon knew they had overtaken the lizard-ape. Whatever the thing was, its string had run out, Lycon thought with relief.

Recklessly he ducked into the hedge and wormed through, not pausing to look for an opening. Thorns shredded his tunic and gouged his limbs as he pulled himself clear and began running toward the sounds.

No chance of recapturing the beast alive now. Any one of the six Molossians was nearly the size of the blue creature, and the arena would have taught the pack to kill rather than to hold. By the time Vonones' men arrived with the nets, it would be finished. Lycon half regretted that—the lizard-ape fascinated him. But quite obviously the thing was too murderously powerful to be loose and far too clever to be safely caged. It was luck the beast had kept close to its kill instead of running farther. The pack was just beyond the next hedgerow now.

With an enormous bawl of pain, one of the hounds suddenly arched into view, flailing in the air above the hedge. A terrified clamor broke through the ferocious baying of the pack. Beyond the hedge a fight was raging—and by the sound of it, the pack was in trouble.

Lycon swore and made for the far hedge, ignoring the cramp in his side. His knuckles clamped white on the boar spear.

He could see three of the dogs ahead of him, snarling and milling uncertainly on the near side of the hedge. The other three were not to be seen.

They were beyond the hedge, Lycon surmised—and from their silence, dead. The lizard-ape was cunning; it had lain in wait for the pack as the dogs squirmed through the hedge. But surely it was no match for three huge Molossians.

Lycon was less than a hundred yards from the hedge, when the blue-scaled lizard-ape vaulted over the thorny barrier with an acrobat's grace. It writhed through the air, and one needle-clawed hand slashed out—tearing the throat from the nearest Molossian before the dog was fully aware of its presence. The lizard-ape bounced to the earth like a cat, as the last two snarling hounds sprang for it together. Spinning and slashing as it ducked under and away, the thing was literally a blur of motion. Deadly motion. Neither hound completed its leap, as lethal talons tore and gutted—slew with nightmarish precision.

Lycon skidded to a stop on the muddy field. He did not need to glance behind him to know he was alone with the beast. Its eyes glowed in the sunset as it turned from the butchered dogs and stared at its pursuer.

Lycon advanced his spear, making no attempt to throw it. As fast as the sauropithecus moved, it would easily dodge his cast. And Lycon knew that if the beast leaped, he was dead—dead as Pentheus after his sisters rent him in their fury. His only chance was that he might drive his spear home, might take his slayer with him—and he thought the beast recognized that.

It crouched like a wrestler advancing upon a foe, its lips drawn in a savage grin—and then it vaulted back over the hedge again.

Lycon tried to make his dry mouth shape a prayer

of thanks. Eyes intent on the hedge, he held his spear at ready. Then he heard feet splatting at a clumsy run behind him.

Galerius puffed toward him, accompanied by several of the archers in a straggling clot. "That hut back there caught fire!" he blurted. "Didn't you see it? Just a ball of flame by the time we could get to it. Don't know if anyone was there, or if they got out or . . ."

He caught sight of the torn bodies of the hounds, and his puffing excitement trailed off. His voice drawled in wonder: "What happened here?"

Lycon finally let his breath out. "Well, I found the lizard-ape we were supposed to be hunting— while you fools were back there gawking at your fire! Now I think Vonones owes you for a pack of dogs."

Lycon waited long enough to make certain the lizard-ape no longer lay in wait beyond the hedge. After seeing the hounds, no one had wanted to be first to wriggle through to the other side. Thinking of those murderous claws, the beastcatcher had no intention of doing so either. There was a gap in the hedge some distance away, and he sent half the men to circle around. There was no sign of the beast other than three more mutilated hounds. In disgust Lycon hiked back to the caravan, letting the others follow as they would.

As he reached the road a shrill voice demanded, "Who's there!"

Lycon swore and yelled before nervous fingers released an arrow. "Don't loose, damn you! Fortune, that's all it would take!"

Vonones thumped heavily onto the roadbed from

his perch on the wagon. His face was anxious. "How did it go? Did you get the sauropithecus? Where are the others?"

"Dragging-ass back," Lycon grunted wearily. "Vonones, there isn't one of your men I'd trust to walk a dog."

"They're wagon drivers, not hunters," the dealer protested. "But what about the lizard-ape?"

"We didn't get it."

And while the others slowly drifted back, Lycon told the dealer what had happened. The damp stillness of the dusk settled around the wagons as he finished. Vonones slumped in stunned silence.

Lycon's weathered face was thoughtful. "You got ahold of something from an arena, Vonones. I don't know whose arena or where it came from— maybe the Numidians raided it from some kingdom in the interior of Africa. But the way it moves, the way its claws are groomed—the way it kills for pleasure. . . . Somebody lost a fighting cock, and you bought it!"

Vonones stared at him without comprehension. Licking his lips, Lycon continued. "I can't say who could have owned it, or what sort of beast it is— but I know the arena, and I tell you that thing is a superbly trained killer. The way it ambushed the dogs, slaughtered them without a wasted motion! And that thing moves fast! I'm fast enough that I've jumped back from a pit trap I didn't know was there until my feet started to go through. I knew a gladiator in Rome who moved faster than any man I've seen. He'd let archers shoot at him from sixty yards, then dodge the arrow, and I never could believe I really saw it happen. But that thing out there in the fields is so much faster there's no comparison!"

"How did the Numidians capture it, then?" Vonones demanded.

"Capture? Maybe they took its surrender! A band of mounted archers on a thousand miles of empty plains—they could have run it down and killed it easily, and that damned thing knew it! Then they welded it into an iron cage, and strong as it is, the lizard-ape can't snap iron bars."

"But it can pick locks," Vonones finished his thought.

"Yes."

The dealer took a deep breath, shrugging all over and seeming to fill his garments even more fully. "How do we recapture it, then?"

"I don't know."

Lycon chewed his lips, looking at the ground rather than at Vonones. "If the lizard-ape sleeps, maybe we could sneak up and use our bows. Maybe with a thousand men we could spread out through the hedgerows and gullies, encircle it somehow."

"We don't have a thousand men," Vonones stated implacably.

"I know."

Smoky clouds were sliding past the full moon. With dusk the drizzle at last had lifted; the overcast was clearing. A few stars began to spike through the cobwebby sky. Across the twilit fields, shadows crept out from hedgerows and trees, flowed over the rocky gullies.

"I can lay my hands on a certain amount of money at short notice," Vonones thought aloud. "There will be ships leaving Portus in the morning."

But Lycon was staring at the nearest cage.

"Vonones," the hunter asked pensively. "Have you ever seen a tiger track a man down?"

"What? No, but I've heard plenty of grisly reports about man-killers who will."

"No, I don't mean hunt down as prey. I mean track down for, well, revenge."

"No, it doesn't happen," Vonones replied. "A wolf maybe, but not one of the big cats. They don't go out of their way for anything, not even revenge. That's a human trait you're talking about."

"I saw it happen once," Lycon said. "It was a female, and one of my men had cleaned out her litter while she was off hunting. We figured later she must have followed him fifty miles before she caught up to him."

"She followed her cubs, not the man."

The beastcatcher shook his head. "He'd given me the cubs. The man was three villages away when she got him. Her left forepaw had an extra toe; there was no mistake."

"So what?"

"Vonones, I'm going to let that tiger out."

The dealer choked in disbelief. "Lycon, are you mad? This isn't the same at all! You can't . . ."

"Have you got a better idea? You know how all the animals hate this thing—that tiger even broke a tooth trying to chew his way to get at the lizard-ape. Well, I'm going to give him his chance."

"I can't let you turn yet another savage killer loose here!"

"Look, we can't get that blue-scaled thing any other way. Once it runs wild through a few more tenant holdings, Domitian isn't going to do any worse to you if you turn the whole damn caravan loose!"

"So the tiger kills the lizard-ape. Then I'm responsible for turning a tiger loose on his estate! Lycon . . ."

"I caught this tiger once. I know about tigers. This thing, Vonones . . ."

The dealer's hand shook as he turned the key over to Lycon.

Muttering, the drivers made an armed cluster in the middle of the road, watching Lycon as he unlocked the cage and vaulted to the roof as the door swung down. The tiger bounded onto the road almost before the door touched gravel. Tail lashing, he paused in a half-crouch to growl at the nervous onlookers. Several bows arched tautly.

Lady Fortune, breathed Lycon, let him scent that lizard-ape and follow it.

Turning from the men, the cat moved toward the other cage. He rumbled a challenge into the empty interior, then swung toward where the tracks stabbed into the damp earth. Without a backward glance, the tiger headed off across the field.

Lycon jumped down, boar spear in hand, and stepped across the ditch.

"Where are you going?" Vonones called after him.

"I want to see this," he shouted back, and loped off along the track he earlier had followed with the hounds.

"Lycon, you're crazy!" Vonones shouted into the night.

Even after the earlier run, Lycon had no trouble keeping up with the tiger. Cats have speed but are not pacers like dogs, like men. The tiger was moving at a graceless quick-step, midway between his normal arrogant saunter and the awesome rush that launched him to his kill. Loose skin behind his neck wobbled awkwardly as his shoulder blades pumped up and down. Moonlight washed all the orange from between the black stripes, and it seemed to be a ghost cat that jolted through the swaying wheat. He ignored Lycon, ignored even the blood-soaked earth where the first victim's corpse had lain—intent only on the strange, hated scent of its blue-scaled enemy.

Following at a cautious distance, Lycon marvelled that his desperate stratagem had worked. It seemed impossible that the great cat was actually stalking the other killer. It was pure hatred, the same unnatural fury that had maddened the dogs, that had turned the compound into a raging chaos as long as the sauropithecus had been among them.

And the men? None of the men had liked the lizard-ape either. Uncertain fear had made Vonones' crew useless in the hunt. And Vonones had unloaded the thing for a trivial sum, because neither he nor the buyer from Rome had wanted the beast around. Why then did he himself feel such fascination for the creature?

The tiger changed stride to clear the first hedgerow. Lycon warily climbed through after him, trotting toward the pall of reeking smoke that still hovered over the ruined hut. Vonones would see to things here, the hunter thought, praying that there would be no more such charnel scenes across the maze-like estate.

A dozen men passing and repassing had hacked a fair gap through the second hedge, and Lycon was glad he did not have to worm blindly through again. The tiger leaped it effortlessly and was speeding across the empty field at a swifter pace by the time he stepped through. Lycon lengthened his stride to stay within fifty yards.

More stars broke coldly through the clearing sky. The cat looked as deadly as Nemesis rippling through the moonlight. Lycon grimly recalled that he had thought much the same about the pack of Molossians. The tiger was every bit as deadly as the blue-scaled killer, and probably five times its weight. Speed and cunning could only count for so much.

The third hedge had not been trampled, and Lycon's belly tightened painfully as he dived through the gore-splashed gap where the killer had awaited the dogs. But the tiger had already leaped over the brushy wall, and Lycon disdained to lose time by detouring to the opening farther down. He pushed his way free and stood warily in the field beyond.

Here the soil was too sparse and rocky for regular sowing. Left fallow, small trees and weedy scrub grew disconsolately between bare rocks and shadowed gullies. The wasteland was a sharp study of hard blacks and whites, etched by the pale moon.

The tiger had halted just ahead, his belly flattened to the rocky soil. He sniffed the air, coughing a low rumble like distant thunder. Then his challenging roar burst from his throat—moonlight glowing on awesome fangs. Far away an ox bawled in fear, and Lycon felt the hair on his neck tingle.

A bit of gravel rattled from the brush-filled gully just beyond. Lycon watched the cat's haunches rise, quivering with restrained tension. A man-sized shadow stood erect from the shadows of the gully, and the tiger leaped.

Thirty yards separated the cat from his prey. He took two short hops toward the lizard-ape, then lunged for the kill. The scaled creature was moving the instant the tiger left the ground for his final leap. A blur of energy, it darted beneath the lunge—needle-clawed fingers thrusting toward the cat's belly. The tiger squalled and hunched in mid-leap, slashing at its enemy in a deadly riposte that nearly succeeded.

Gravel and mud sprayed as the cat struck the ground and whirled. The sauropithecus was already upon him, its claws ripping at the tiger's neck. With speed almost as blinding, the cat twisted about, left forepaw flashing a bone-snapping blow against the creature's ribs—hurling it against a knot of brush.

The cat paused, trying to lick the stream of blood that spurted from its neck. Recoiling from its fall, the blue-scaled killer gave a high-pitched cry—the first sound Lycon had heard from it—and leaped onto the cat's back.

By misjudgment or sudden weakness, it landed too far back, straddling the tiger's belly instead of withers. The cat writhed backward and rolled, taloned forepaws slashing, hind legs pumping. Stripped from its hold, the lizard-ape burrowed into the razor-edged fury of thrashing limbs.

It was too fast to follow. Both animals flung themselves half-erect, spinning, snarling in a crimson spray. A dozen savage blows ripped back and forth in the space of a heartbeat as they tore against each other in suicidal frenzy.

With no apparent transition, the tiger slumped into the mud. His huge head hung loose, and bare bone gleamed for an instant. Blood spouted in a great torrent, then ebbed abruptly to a dark smear. The tiger arched his back convulsively in death, as his killer staggered away.

Lycon stared in disbelief as the blue-scaled killer took a careful step toward him. Blood bathed its bright scales like a glistening imperial cloak. The tiger's blood or the lizard-ape's? Its scaled hide had to be unnaturally tough—else it would be gutted like a fish.

Murder gleamed joyously in its eyes. Lycon readied his spear. He knew he was fast enough to drive home one good thrust, and after that. . . .

Another step and the lizard-ape stumbled, bracing itself on the ground with one deadly hand. The other arm hung useless—its shoulder certainly broken by the tiger's mauling. The sauropithecus jerked erect and grinned at the hunter, its demon's face a reflection of death. It started to lunge for him, but there was no strength to its legs. Instead it skidded drunkenly on the gravelly soil, again groping for balance. It must have suffered massive internal injuries, but it staggered upright once again.

Lycon knew a stir of hope and dared take a step forward, advancing his boar spear. His own legs felt none too steady, but there had to be an end made of this night.

The lizard-ape spun about gracelessly, suddenly making for the farther hedge. Despite its stumbling gait, it easily pulled away from the pursuing hunter—Lycon afterward wondered if he might not have run faster—and gained the distant hedge. Too weakened to rip through the interlaced branches as before—or to vault the barrier—it darted headlong into the base of the hedge, wriggling snake-like between the rocks and roots.

Lycon hesitated, realizing his chances but not willing to abandon the hunt. From beyond the thorny barrier he heard a quick splash, then silence. Gritting his teeth, Lycon dropped to his belly and crawled after the lizard-ape, following the bloodtrail through the hedge.

Nothing lay beyond the hedge but the steep-banked Tiber, and the bloodtrail slid down the muddy slope and into the oblivion of black rushing current.

The moon glared down, drowning the stars with chill splendor, and casting light over the river's unbroken surface. Lycon shivered, and after a while he walked back to the road.

He felt old that night.

CHAPTER THREE

The starship hung in orbit like a mountain of dirty ice.

To RyRelee, watching the viewscreen as his shuttlecraft drew near, the Coran starships always called to mind a congealed comet, bereft of its tail and frozen in some ungainly posture. He loathed embarking from the firm-walled compartments of the trim shuttlecraft from his homeworld to enter the seemingly organic mazes of a Coran starship, but a summons from the rulers of the measurable galaxy was not to be denied.

Such occasional summons invariably had prefaced demands upon his considerable abilities to carry out certain tasks for the Cora as their emissary—usually without the knowledge of those to whose world RyRelee was sent. While such missions inevitably entailed deadly risks, RyRelee did not normally respond to their summons with such a sense of fatalistic dread as he now felt. While the Cora had not yet informed him of the reason for this summons, RyRelee thought he knew why, and had there been any possible alternative but to obey, he would have taken it.

The interior of the Coran ship was small improvement over the comet-like appearance it gave from the outside. It had the look of something hacked from soft stone, or foamed into shape out of the spittle of an insect. The hatch closed behind his shuttlecraft as though it were growing together by a process of greatly accelerated crystalline accretion. The efficiency of Coran science was beyond question, but the organic nature of it bothered RyRelee every time it called itself to his attention. It disturbed him that he, himself an interstellar emissary and one whose race had long ago developed its own stardrive, should nonetheless be unable to comprehend the technology of the race that ruled the galaxy.

A ragged hole dissolved in one wall of the air lock. RyRelee waited for his crew to release the hatch of the shuttlecraft, then steeled himself to disembark. Though the atmosphere within this section of the starship was breathable, it smelled musty and had overtones of old meat. It was also very cold, though RyRelee's shivering was not solely a result of that physical cause. That his shuttlecraft had orders to depart immediately after bringing him here only confirmed his fear.

He had guessed quite well why the Cora had summoned him, must have summoned him; and he had obeyed nonetheless. If the Cora required his presence, they would get it—however far he ran before they made it their business to catch him. One could be reasonably safe in ones personal projects so long as such enterprises did not come

to the attention of the Cora. If they did ... well,
there was always the chance of mercy.

The crewman who now gestured peremptorily
through the opening to RyRelee was neither a biped nor, of course, a Coran. It walked on six of its
eight flat, multi-jointed limbs. Their surface and
that of the crewman's segmented body were covered with fine yellow bristles. As RyRelee followed
down the twisting corridor, he noticed that the
carrion odor was stronger close to the crewman.
Perhaps, then, the cold temperature and musky
atmosphere were balanced for the crewmen rather
than simply being faults in a life support system
built by methane breathers for servants who required oxygen. RyRelee knew from experience that
a Coran starship might contain any number of
environments within its various sections, each
suited to the needs of any particular race of beings
that might be on board. The Cora were not the
only intelligent race to exist in an atmosphere of
liquid methane, but RyRelee knew of few others.

The crewman stopped and waved RyRelee ahead
with either a limb or a mandible. The corridor,
never more than a blue-lit wormhole in the ice,
ended ahead of him.

The emissary stepped forward to the end of the
corridor, pretending not to give any sign that he
knew the next few seconds would determine his
fate. He did not turn to watch the crystalline wall
grow shut behind him, but he felt a change in the
ambient pressure. He stood in a cell instead of a
hallway, and he did not know whether he would
ever be allowed to leave during his lifetime.

An atmosphere bubble popped into being around
him. RyRelee guessed that it was maintained some-

how by a sort of forcefield despite the presence outside either of a vacuum or a thousand atmospheric pressures. He disliked both its apparent insubstantiality as well as its further evidence of Coran technological superiority.

The wall at the end of the corridor dissolved. He was not to be entombed, then—not, at least, until he had been interrogated about his part in the fiasco. He stepped forward, holding himself tall within the atmosphere bubble as it moved with him. The lock closed behind him, leaving him alone in an immense chamber with one of the Cora.

The Coran also was huge, though it was hard to arrive at specific dimensions. Within the roiling currents of hydrocarbons, the flowing multicolored veils of the Coran's tissue both swam forward and receded beyond his view. None of its sensory apparatus was visible—or at least recognizable. The vague blue light that illuminated the atmosphere bubble pierced the sea of methane adequately for RyRelee to glimpse the Coran, but he suspected that such lighting was for his benefit alone. The Coran itself seemed to shift colors constantly as it swam above the bubble. RyRelee understood that the Cora communicated through such subtly changing veils of color; such a medium was far beyond the capabilities of his eyes to translate.

The communications node affixed behind the external tendrils of his ears began to transmit in the colloquialism of his homeworld. If RyRelee chose to relax—which he did not—he might pretend he was listening to the actual speech of some congenial high official of his own race—which of course he was not.

"We Cora thank you for answering our summons so promptly once again, RyRelee." The counterfeit voice even managed to convey an official tone of impersonal politeness. "We have a problem beyond our own physical capacities—one which is serious enough to force us to require the special talents of an emissary such as yourself."

"I have always considered it my privilege to be able to serve the Cora," said RyRelee formally, covering his surprise. While he suspected that the courtesy invariably shown by the Cora in fact masked a sneer toward the lesser races, nevertheless the galactic rulers did not indulge in sadistic jokes. If the Cora had indeed known what RyRelee had assumed they knew, they would not toy with him now. RyRelee would have been formally charged, found guilty, sentenced, and the sentence carried out—hardly a minute needed, all told.

"But you do not merely serve the Cora, RyRelee," the Coran chided gently. "Perhaps the Cora are first among equals, but we all must remember that we are parts of a confederation of equals."

After a moment's pause, the Coran resumed in a less avuncular tone. "You know, of course, that blood sports and the traffic in subjects for such perversions are a continuing stain on the civilization of our galaxy. On several occasions it has been necessary for you yourself to act as our agent in punishing those involved in fostering this disgusting practice."

RyRelee found that he was more comfortable if he focused his eyes directly ahead, than if he tried to follow the drifting majesty of the Coran itself. "Some of the so-called intelligent races of our confederation have been unable to shrug off the trappings of barbarism," he said carefully, still on dangerous ground. "Like slavery, or the use of violent force to seize power, such antisocial behavioral patterns are difficult to eradicate among certain cultures." His own, for example, RyRelee did not add.

"We can only remain firm in our resolve," said the Coran brusquely. "And vigilant. We were pursuing a vessel which we suspected was smuggling beasts—certainly destined for blood sports in the arena. It attempted to escape by diving into the gravity well of an oxygen world—a proscribed world in Class 6."

RyRelee thought carefully before asking: "You say, they attempted escape? One assumes they were therefore either captured or destroyed."

"Utterly destroyed," the Coran said. "They attempted to land using their stardrive, and the result was the predictable catastrophic failure."

There was a power in the universe greater than the Cora after all, thought RyRelee, and it had just preserved him. "I could not wish for fellow citizens of the Federation to be vaporized, of course," he temporized. "But in this case, the accidental result may have been that of justice. You perhaps would like me to make a reconnaissance of the devastated area—to ensure that no artifacts survived that might interfere in the development of a proscribed world?"

"Actually, we've taken care of that sufficiently, RyRelee," said the Cora. "As you will see."

RyRelee did *see* the events recorded next, but the images were received directly by the visual centers of his brain without being transmitted through his eyes. A landing shuttle spiralled out of a bay in the starship's hull. The image was superimposed upon that of the chamber in which he stood. It was not a purely visual effect—a hologram projected across the chamber. The blue light and the rippling Coran were no less clear than before, but the outlines of the shuttle were a stronger presence. The scenes were in his mind—a recording transmitted directly through the communications nodes affixed to his skull. RyRelee stood very still as images tumbled and the Coran waited for him to assimilate the data.

It was a blue world, a water world, he saw as the shuttle approached, passing over the oceans to focus on an arid landscape. Abruptly the image concentrated on an area of limestone hillside. The russet stone was blackened and fused to chert in a long scar whose outlines blurred like those of a rope of seaweed. The point of view held at a constant but indeterminable height as it followed the line of destruction. RyRelee had no certain scale, but they must have tracked the scar for at least a mile. Plants with fleshy, dust-colored leaves were shriveled to either side of the blackened stone, and there were occasional highlights where molten metal had splashed and coated the rock, leaving a shallow depression in the hillside. There was no sign of any artifact. The point of view rose, panning more and more of the barren landscape. Even when the full course of the smuggler's desperate attempt to land was visible as a tortured black ribbon, there was no hint of anything but total catastrophe.

"Their stardrive envelope began to collapse from the stern forward." RyRelee spoke in part to organize events in his own mind, and in part to reconstruct the situation that he sincerely desired to have transpired. "Friction eroded the hull and everything within it. They could not possibly have launched a lifeboat under those circumstances."

He paused to clear his throat before he concluded: "There is nothing here to affect the development of a world without stardrive. In fact, I don't suppose you yourselves can be sure of the identity—for that matter, of what race the smugglers were." His lips sucked in in a gesture that he would have suppressed had he been aware of it.

"Only in the second assumption are you correct," said the Coran. Its voice was made dreamlike by the other events going on in RyRelee's mind. "We did proceed to determine the opinion of the local inhabitants about the event. One cannot be too careful with a Class 6 world. But there was a delay, of course. A delay in deploying the atmosphere-shuttle in the first place, a further delay in disrupting the locality ourselves except to the extent necessary. The delays proved to be unfortunate."

The images the emissary saw this time were kaleidoscopic. They were still fully comprehensible, but muted through the sensory media of another organism. RyRelee recognized this as a recording derived through a memory scan of a living creature—presumably that of one of the planet's autochthones.

It was night. A drystone hut huddled on the plain. It was a windowless dome with its low doorway closed by a bundle of thorny brush. The corral appended to the hut was also of stones laid without mortar. More brush raised the corral wall and threatened the belly of anything attempting to leap it, herd animal or predator alike. In the near distance sprawled the ridge along which the smuggler's vessel had disintegrated.

The creatures within the hut were bipedal, half a dozen of them. They stirred like a spaded-up nest of rodents when the hut lifted into the air in a single piece. It was through the biped's eyes that RyRelee saw who the Cora had sent to make the initial survey: eight-limbed crewmen like the one who had led him into the Coran's presence.

The hive of natives collapsed in thrashing confusion. One of the crewmen had calibrated the precise setting needed to disconnect motor control without doing permanent harm to the subjects. The aborigines were not stunned, but they had no conscious control of their movements. They watched themselves being loaded onto the antigravity sled with the unceremonious care given valuable objects. The images were faultlessly accurate, though doubtless the conscious portions of the natives' minds interpreted the event as an episode of hopeless madness.

"You freed these aborigines after you had examined them?" he asked. He kept his voice as perfectly neutral as he could. There was no evidence that the Cora were aware of the inflectional subtexts of spoken words—but RyRelee did not dare chance accusing his masters of either ruthlessness or stupidity.

"Yes, although of course we wiped their memories," the Coran agreed easily. "We kept guard on the dwelling and herd for the few hours we were forced to hold the aborigines. We landed, after all, to eliminate disruption to the Class 6 natives, not to cause it."

"Yes, of course," RyRelee quickly agreed. He

recalled the summons that had snatched him from his palace and brought him here—to death or torture, for all he had known. Class 6 natives were to be protected, but he himself—he was merely a catspaw to be used by the Cora, to carry out their clandestine assignments, and if he were to be killed during his task, he would simply be replaced by a more efficient tool. In theory the Cora only acted for the general best interests of the galaxy. Such doubts as he cherished, RyRelee kept to himself. The Cora paid well.

"We took the precaution of obtaining memory scans of these and other subjects to ascertain how those aborigines who might have witnessed the starship's crash would have interpreted the event," the Coran continued. "As it happened, their intellects were too primitive to have made any technological interpretations. To them, it was simply another natural catastrophe or an act of their gods—incomprehensible in either case. It was, however, exceedingly fortunate that we made so thorough an examination of the site, as you will perceive from these next recordings."

A new series of images played through his communications nodes. This time RyRelee failed to repress a hiss of consternation—one which he hoped would be interpreted as only natural dismay. The reassurance he had only moments ago dared to hope for now melted away.

It was the same arid landscape, but something walked across it now that should never have been there. The creature was in riveted irons that must have weighed as much as the blue-scaled biped did itself—and then were only marginally adequate, RyRelee knew well.

"There was a phile on board," a voice murmured, and RyRelee could not be sure whether the Coran had spoken or whether the words came from his own throat.

RyRelee's tongues were too dry for ready speech, but he was now in conscious control again. "But, of course, that's impossible. You must be misinterpreting what the aborigines saw. It's some native species that only resembles a phile."

The clarity of the continuing series of images of the phile gave the lie to RyRelee's statement. The creature was part of a long line of native animals, forty or more of them. The phile was shackled between a pair of them—great beasts that dwarfed it and their aboriginal handlers. Hunching against the mass of its chains, the phile took three of its quick strides for every one of those of the beasts to which it was fastened. Its movements were hobbled, but it managed to keep up.

"Elephants," explained the counterfeit voice of the Coran. "Being hunted in the valleys nearby for use, I regret to say, in blood sports much like those for which the phile itself must have been intended. The recently captured elephants are shackled to pairs of domesticated beasts. The same technique appears to be sufficient to control the phile, for now."

The procession of handlers, beasts, and—no, only handlers and beasts: for all its cunning the phile was no more than a beast—drew away in the distance. The elephants became dark humps against the soft yellow dust that drifted downwind from their feet. The phile was not even that, only a memory. But it had been there; that could not be in doubt.

Uneasy, RyRelee asked: "Was a lifeboat released after all, then? Surely, the phile could not have been landed at an earlier time—could it?"

"We presume," replied the Coran, "that it was caged near the bow. As the stardrive envelope shrank and the smuggler's vessel disintegrated from the stern forward, one of the cage walls must have been destroyed a moment before the final impact. If the phile's timing were precise, it might have been launching itself toward that opening at the instant the stardrive itself was destroyed."

"Nothing could survive such a landfall," RyRelee whispered.

"Nothing but a phile," said the Coran.

Again RyRelee saw the phile as it stared at the aborigine through whose eyes the procession had been recorded. Yes, a phile was intelligent enough to seize a split-second chance of escape, quick enough to succeed in it. They were difficult to kill even with energy weapons, and their recuperative powers were uncanny. The limp with which it walked was probably the result of injury, rather than from the weight of its chains as RyRelee had first thought.

As the phile returned the aborigine's stare, its gaze was flat and black and as coldly lethal as the glitter of a falling axe.

"Precisely how it escaped destruction is unimportant," said the Coran. "The matter that concerns us is that Class 6 natives have captured a phile. They must have discovered it before it had recovered from the crash, and even then only luck could have permitted them to take it captive. How will they ever avoid the mistake that releases it?

They are not wholly without intelligence, you know, these philes."

Besides its eyes, there was only one fleck of brightness in the dusty image of the phile. It held in its forelimbs the chain tethering it to the leading elephant. The aborigine had seen, although below his awareness, that one thumb-thick link of that chain was scarred by the ceaseless abrasion of the phile's claws as it staggered forward in the solitude of its own red thoughts.

"In certain aspects," the Coran continued, "the philes are perhaps more intelligent than the natives of this planet. While the philes have never developed any sort of technology, they are quick to comprehend its applications when confronted with such. They understand the threat of a stone-tipped projectile or of an energy weapon, for example, and they recognize surface vehicles or planetary shuttlecraft as transport vessels. Moreover, there is substantial evidence of low-level telepathy. It has been suggested that while they comprehend basic mechanical principles, the philes consciously disdain their application. There was once some consideration over upgrading Zuyle to Class 6 status, but it was decided that although the philes are the dominant lifeform on their planet, their environment is too savagely violent ever to permit the development of any organized social culture."

"Perhaps that's just as well," RyRelee commented, remembering that planet. Zuyle, the homeworld of the philes, was a nightmarish cauldron of ceaseless volcanic activity and violent storms, of brief blinding-hot days and long frigid nights. The flora and fauna had evolved appropriately to so murderous an environment—poisonous flesh-eating vegetation, venomous crawling things, mammoth armored beasts. Everything that walked or swam or flew or crept or burrowed on Zuyle was adapted to survival under the deadliest of conditions, and the philes were the dominant species of that world. The focus of their evolution had been survival from one second to the next, and their intellect had developed accordingly. RyRelee thought it fortunate that their savage fight for existence had never given the philes leisure to begin the climb toward technological society.

RyRelee took a deep breath, again producing an audible hiss as the air rushed through the plates of his nostril pit. "Where is the phile now?"

"That will be for you to discover, emissary." At last the Coran was disclosing the reason for his summons. "We were able to trace the phile to a coastal port of a small sea where it was dispatched by surface vessel, apparently destined for a large blood sports arena in this civilization's principal city. Too much time has been lost, and presumably the phile will have already reached this destination—that is, if it hasn't managed to escape in transit."

"My assignment, then?"

"To pick up its trail—a cold trail, I regret. You must seek out the phile and destroy it. As it has by now quite probably penetrated the major city of this region, we must act secretly to find it and destroy it without inflicting a major disruption to their developing culture.

"As you have observed, RyRelee, you share many physical similarities to the native race of this world. You will find their gravity, atmosphere and climate quite compatible, and you will be protected against their disease strains and parasites. It will require only minor cosmetic modifications and surgical adjustments for you to pass as a native from some distant region of the planet—each civilization there is ignorant of lands and cultures beyond its own sphere of influence. We have recordings of scans acquired from several of the aborigines, so your communications nodes will be programmed with an adequate selection of native languages and customs. Of course, you will be issued the usual essential equipment for operations in the field."

RyRelee knew it was pointless to inquire further about such modifications and adjustments. He had experienced such indignities on previous assignments, and there was some comfort in knowing that Coran surgery could usually undo what it had done.

"How will I be able to destroy the phile?"

"You will be equipped with the necessary weapons, concealed within your cosmetic constructions: a device to stun the natives should the need arise, and another to destroy the phile. To the aborigines it will appear that you have only gestured with your hand; try not to be observed, but if you do arouse their curiosity, explain it as magic."

"Their cultural level is that low? I thought I was to be sent to the central region of their civilization."

"It is, after all, a Class 6 world, emissary," the Coran reminded him. But RyRelee was more aware of that than the Coran could guess.

"There is another critical matter that you must attend to," the Coran continued. "An extremely critical matter. We do not know whether the phile is male or female. You must make the necessary surgical identification once you have destroyed it. You know what happened on Doronin. . . ."

RyRelee knew the story all too well, but the Coran supplied him the images of what had taken place on Doronin—all the more to impress upon the emissary the importance of his mission.

An entrepreneur on Doronin had imported a variety of exotics for blood sports staged in defiance of Coran—of Federation—law. There had been a pair of philes, both males it had been believed, but one turned out to have been a gravid female. Because of their deadly environment, philes mated only once—after which the female continued to produce fertile eggs at regular intervals throughout life. While one gravid female had the potential to produce thousands of offspring, on their homeworld only a few chicks would manage to survive to reproduce. But that was on Zuyle, and Doronin was a placid world—or once had been.

The images were of what had been a city before it became an abattoir. RyRelee did not need the voice whispering ". . . Doronin . . ." to identify the scene. The viewpoint shifted, shuddered—blinked to a view from a thousand feet in the air of an armored antigravity raft that had been drifting down a boulevard just below the height of the tallest buildings alongside it. The raft was bucking like a fish with hooks set in its guts. When the armored vehicle yawed and overturned abruptly, the cause became clear. On the raft's belly plates was a smudge of blue which the focus sharpened instantly into a phile. The beast was gripping minute projections on the metal surface with three of its clawed limbs. With the full length of its remaining arm, it was reaching into the interior through an inspection plate that it had ripped off. Out of control, the raft clipped the side of a building and plummeted into the street.

The armor would have protected the raft's crew against the philes, except that the force of the craft's impact was enough to start seams all across the domed surface.

They poured from every building in sight, philes of every size. Some of them leaped aboard the raft even as momentum carried it cartwheeling down the street. Their timing was as flawless as that of the phile that had first leaped onto a grip on the survey craft's underside. Their numbers were staggering. Even without the chicks clinging to the backs of some of the females—of most of the females—there were thousands of the blue-scaled killers in view.

Tracks of dazzling orange began to tear pavement apart and rake the philes that leaped across its length. A phile whose legs and haunches had been vaporized continued to crawl on its elbows toward the disabled raft. The expression on its dying face could only have been delight.

Covering fire from the other survey craft could not slow the tidal motion of the philes. Waves of activity were visible in the far distance, surging toward the first chance of prey in days, weeks. And the downed craft already boiled with ravenous life even if no more philes arrived to fight for a purchase among their frenzied fellows.

Fragments of armor plate glittered in the air. The philes were tearing it away so violently that the raft seemed to have exploded. The orange energy-beams ripped a brilliant, useless circle just beyond the fallen craft. Beasts shrivelled away like insects in a flame, but if they survived at all, they survived to tear deeper into the vessel.

One of the crewmen was dragged out to dissolve in seconds among the claws and teeth of countless starving philes. It had been a bristly octopod like the one who led RyRelee to the Coran's chamber.

The survey craft disintegrated in an orange flash. The point of view rocketed upward with a suddenness that might have been simple reality instead of a result of editing the transmission. The city gleamed for a moment, purified by distance of the unchecked hordes of starving philes that now were its sole population. In another instant the exploding thermonuclear device transformed the distant city into a gorgeous pearl, expanding across the surface of the planet.

The next image was from farther away still. It took a moment for RyRelee to realize the scale. The small sun glowing against blackness had been a planet. It had been Doronin before the Cora cleansed it once and for all.

"That could be Earth in a hundred years or less," said the Coran. "You must track down the phile and destroy it, emissary. And you must act very quickly now. Should this phile be a male, then once it is destroyed our concern regarding this world will be allayed. However, should this be a gravid female like the one that got loose on Doronin. . . . Then, if there is any indication—any suspicion at all—that she may have produced a brood, our only recourse will be to sterilize the entire land mass and hope that other cultures will develop from other regions of this planet.

"So you understand, RyRelee, the extreme importance of your mission on Earth."

"Yes ...," said the emissary very softly, his thoughts already totally absorbed in his mission.

But he was thinking that fate plays strange tricks and that it was fortunate the Cora themselves lacked telepathic ability. An agent in this dangerous profession often reaped wealth from clandestine operations of his own, and there were fortunes to be made through smuggling beasts for blood sports, if one had all the right connections. The starship that had crashed on Earth had been acting under RyRelee's orders before the disaster, and RyRelee knew with certainty that the escaped phile was a gravid female.

His real mission would be to make equally certain that it was kept alive without the knowledge of the Cora. Earth would prove a perfect breeding ground, and fate had given RyRelee the chance to make good on a scheme that had almost fatally miscarried.

CHAPTER FOUR

It waited in its burrow beneath the river bank, waited patiently for its wounds to heal—patiently, for it watched the boats pass up and down the Tiber, and it knew it was only a short matter of time before its red dreams were fulfilled.

It had learned a great deal from observing these soft-skinned bipeds who appeared to be the dominant race of this world. To an extent, it no longer regretted its capture during its initial few hours on this world, when the bipeds had surrounded it, dazed and injured, and had renewed the captivity from which it had only just escaped in the explosion of the metal ship. The bipeds had sheltered and fed the phile—or lizard-ape, as they named it in their various tongues—much the same as its previous captors had done. This had given it time to regain its strength, and to assess the dangers of this new world.

The bipeds themselves posed no real threat, except in their numbers. The phile had already proven to itself how easily they died; their flesh was bet-

ter than the brief sport their struggles offered, and
their bodies should provide excellent hosts. Their
weapons were far more primitive than those of the
race who had taken the phile from its homeworld,
and considering how slowly these soft bipeds
moved, the only real danger lay in being cornered
or surrounded.

The phile shook with rage as it remembered that
one biped who had pursued it this last time. It had
touched that biped's aura, recognized that this one
was different from the other naked-skinned creatures—another species, perhaps, and trained to kill
for its master as the phile itself had been trained.
The phile was certain that this one biped had
accepted the personal challenge of stalking it—that
this one had been responsible for the lower-species
quadrupeds that had been sent in pursuit. That
last one had provided interesting sport—it was
almost the phile's superior.

The phile angrily regretted that it had not destroyed the bipedal hunter as well when chance
had twice permitted. The arrival of reinforcements
with projectile weapons had saved the hunter once,
and at their next encounter the phile's judgement
had accepted the fact that, crippled from its wounds
inflicted by the large striped creature, it would
probably have sustained fatal injury from the
biped's weapon. While it felt certain it could have
killed the biped despite such a wound, the phile
obeyed the urgency of a more basic instinct—the
only instinct more basic than its need to kill.

Perhaps this one hunter would offer combat
again. The phile hoped it would. In the mean-
time, its egg sacs were growing full within its
abdomen. It was time to seek out a secure lair—

and the other things it must have to nourish its brood.

By the second nightfall its shoulder had healed sufficiently to restore function. The phile had had to align as best it could the bones broken by the mauling it had suffered from the large quadruped. It had been enough for the fragmented ends to knit rapidly. There was pain, but the phile recognized pain without any emotional component—pain was no more than an indication that warned of momentary physical inadequacy. The phile had healed more quickly than it had dared hope—even the gashes in its scaled flesh were no more than smooth lines of scar. The unnaturally benign climate and the lighter gravity of this world made it a paradise beyond the phile's dreaming, if the phile had ever indulged in dreams beyond the need to wrest survival from every deadly moment.

It was hungry now—terribly hungry. This world's pale sun had risen and set twice now since the phile had last eaten its fill. The few insignificant life forms it had caught and devoured from its burrow could not resist starvation for a metabolism that required its weight in flesh at close intervals—even if the egg sacs were not distending its flanks, demanding sustenance.

The phile had made its plans while it rested. It had already observed that the bipeds here required more than natural means of light in order to see, once their sun had set. As one of their slow-moving surface conveyances plodded upstream in the starlight, the phile chose the moment and slithered noiselessly into the river. The currents were almost stagnant compared to those of its home planet, and it swam easily despite the physical density that would have let it sink to the bottom.

It crossed the distance as certainly as an arrow pierces the sky. Its claws easily locked into the porous substance of the vessel's hull, and for a moment the phile rested and let its senses explore the craft. There were many bipeds here, and there was not one whisper of alertness from them. That was good.

That was very good.

As silent—and as fleeting—as a shadow of a bat against the moon, the phile lifted itself over the rim of the surface conveyance, and part of the rage it felt toward the hunter who had stalked it was quickly slaked as the phile had its will with those it found on board.

CHAPTER FIVE

As he grew older, Vonones found solace in the creature comforts his slowly accumulated wealth could now furnish him. While the heavyset body of his youth might now be taking on a veneer of softness, nevertheless Vonones had not forgotten that he had attained his wealth through hard work. Thus Vonones made a point of being at his office in the main compound at dawn, whether or not a new shipment was expected.

The escape and destruction—Lycon swore it was destroyed—of the sauropithecus a few nights before had been an ordeal. But Vonones had suffered worse, and thanks to Lycon he had avoided real disaster—though he would have to increase his prices on this shipment to offset the losses for the lizard-ape and the tiger, not to mention payments to Lycon, Galerius and his men, and bribes all around. He'd come out of it with a whole skin and would still turn a good profit, and that was what really mattered, although Vonones knew he would see the lizard-ape in nightmares for the rest of his life.

What happened when Vonones reached his home on the Caelian only proved how badly that near-disaster had shaken him. The messenger Vonones had sent ahead from Portus had given his house slaves hours to prepare for his arrival. Vonones had bought a new mistress, an Egyptian, just before he left to meet the shipment at Portus. She had used the time in preparation to make Vonones' first trial of her particularly memorable.

Having quite forgotten her after the business of the lizard-ape, Vonones was not thinking of anything but bed when he walked into the bedchamber, stiff with dust and fatigue. She was waiting with one hand poised on the inlaid headboard and the other arm raised to balance the curve of the first. Light from the twelve-wick oil lamp glittered on a headdress of silk and sapphires—the only garment the woman wore. She had also donned a set of long false fingernails and dusted her limbs with lapis lazuli, thinking the blue shadowing would increase her exotic air.

Vonones screamed and ran.

Sleep had been long in coming that night, and the equally startled Egyptian—Vonones had summarily ordered his servants to wash and scrub her till her skin was a shade lighter than when he bought her—decided she would never understand the eccentric ways of Armenian merchants.

When Vonones' litter stopped in front of his office, his staff were in the midst of the job of unloading. The wagons had been brought into the courtyard by the main gate. It would remain closed until the last of the beasts had been transferred to their holding cells. Any other technique chanced the escape of a predator and bloody chaos in the streets of the neighboring Ceronian District. The dealer wanted no more such escapes, not even of a peacock. At the moment, a hundred or so ostriches that made up a major part of this shipment were being transferred to the corral in a flurry of wings and curses.

The deputy compound manager swirled toward Vonones with an entourage of clerks poised over waxed tablets of accounts. "Excellency," the deputy called, "there's a serious discrepancy here! A tiger, according to the bill of lading . . ."

"Yes, I know about the damned tiger. Cross it off," Vonones said with a scowl. "And the other one too—the sauropithecus. They both died in transit."

"The what?" said the deputy. Clerks flipped pages to find the unfamiliar term.

"Pollux, give me a moment to look the compound over before you bother me with the accounts," Vonones snapped to change the subject.

The ostriches had been bundled for transport with their legs, beaks, and wings tied shut. A nearby slave had cocked his head to listen to Vonones, intent on learning further details of the events that had sparked so many rumors. When he cut the twist of papyrus rope holding the bird's legs, he nicked a leg as well.

The bird squirmed instantly upright. It kicked sideways with its right leg, even as the handler turned his attention back to his work. The clawed toes ripped across the man's belly too suddenly for the victim to cry out.

Vonones swore bitterly. The clerks and deputy scattered like quail from the eight-foot apparition with bloody claws. The injured handler writhed on the ground with his hands pressed against his torn abdomen. His fellows sprang up from their own duties. One ran for a net.

Vonones uncoiled his whip in a fluid arc behind him. The ostrich cocked its right leg again. It stood sideways to Vonones, but one black eye glittered at him with cold purpose.

The lash snaked out and around the bird's left ankle. Setting himself, Vonones yanked back on the whipstaff. He might no longer have the shoulder muscles of his younger days, but the weight he had put on was finally an advantage to him. The ostrich flopped back onto the ground. Handlers leaped onto it from three sides.

Vonones dropped the whip when he was sure the bird had been immobilized. He backed away, breathing hard and dusting his hands. A pair of litter bearers belatedly stepped between their master and the commotion that had been a threat moments before.

"That's all right," Vonones muttered, thankful that he was still good enough to make such bodyguards superfluous. "That's all right." He felt better for the incident. It had given him an opportunity to exorcise the helpless terror caused by the lizard-ape's escape. It was uncertainty that melted a man's nerves, not simply danger. It was a relief to return to familiar tasks and familiar dangers. He turned to where his men were seeing to the injured slave's wounds. More expense . . . .

The main gate of the compound began to swing open. The deputy manager ran toward it, shouting. Vonones himself snarled toward the gatekeepers: "Not while we're unloading a shipment, damn you! I'll have you all fed to the crocodiles if so much as a rabbit escapes!"

A column of horsemen in glittering armor rode through the gateway four abreast. The deputy dodged out of their way, but the newcomers made no attempt on their part to avoid him.

There were twenty horsemen in the troop. All but their tribune were huge men whose hair was red or blond where it spilled from beneath their helmets. They dismounted. Every fourth man acted as horseholder while the remainder kept their hands on their weapons.

The officer in charge—a tribune named Lacerta whom Vonones knew by reputation—wore a breastplate of gilded bronze. In low relief upon it was molded a scene of nymphs yearning upward toward the figure of Jupiter enthroned. "You," said Lacerta, pointing toward Vonones. "Do you speak Latin, boy? Go fetch the merchant Vonones."

"I speak Latin," said Vonones. He drew himself to his full height, although he was even then no taller than the Italian-born tribune. Vonones was twice the tribune's age as well; *boy* was purely from the assumption that the man in leggings and a coarse tunic had to be a slave. At that, an aristocrat like Lacerta might have used the same form of address for a man whom he knew to be the compound's owner. "And I am Gaius Claudius Vonones." He wiped his damp hands on his thighs.

"You're wanted," Lacerta said with a quick one-fingered gesture over his shoulder and out the gate. He frowned. "Get a horse, will you? You'll slow us up too much if we have to tie you to one of the saddles and let you run."

The troop of horsemen would have silenced a human crowd, but it had little effect on the compound's normal cacaphony. Even the handlers were forced back to their normal duties by the nervous uproar of the beasts. Three men carried the blood-splashed ostrich to the corral and flung it inside with its fellows. The deputy manager and his clerks hovered between a desire to hear what was going on and a well-founded fear of being noticed. The Germanic horsemen glared about them with pale eyes and disdain for what they saw.

"I am a Roman citizen!" Vonones blurted. He managed to keep his back straight when he heard Lacerta's command, but his voice shook. He was imagining himself alone on an island. Every time his heart beat, the surf washed the shore a little higher.

"A Roman citizen, merchant?" the tribune said in an amused tone. He gestured daintily toward the big men he commanded. "These aren't, you know. And since the one whose orders we obey is divine, I don't suppose he's going to be much swayed by the fact that you became a Roman citizen when your master struck off your chains."

Amusement hardened into a sneer as frigid as the eyes of the armored Germans. "Don't try my patience, freedman. You've the count of ten to get a horse."

Lacerta leaned slightly forward and tapped the god enthroned on his breastplate. "Our lord Domitian told me to bring you alive. But I'm not sure that he'd really care."

CHAPTER SIX

Lycon's bedroom had a window on the light shaft of the apartment house, but it faced west and was six stories beneath the roofline. Lycon stretched, letting his fingers play in the pool of sunlight that had finally reached the bed. Unlike most of his contemporaries, he was used to night work and its corollary, sleeping by day. As he grew older, he required increasingly longer periods of recuperation—and a day and a night like the recent chase would have wrung anyone to exhaustion.

The door was closed, but Zoe must have heard the bronze bed creaking as her husband stretched himself on it, and she looked in to see if Lycon were awake. She was nursing their youngest, Glauce, who at three months of age was older than either of the couple's three previous daughters had lived to be—or two of the boys, for that matter. Still, they had two sons to survive infancy—Perses, who could be heard bouncing his ball in the next room, and Alexandros, who was as fine a young lad as a father could wish to have.

"Well, don't hang back there, Zoe," Lycon said, bleary-eyed. He thumped the bed beside him. "Come, let's have a look at you and our little one." Glauce had been born during his absence, and the beastcatcher had forgotten her name for the moment.

Zoe flashed a distracted smile as she lay down beside him. There was an aura of nervousness about her, and she half-heartedly returned Lycon's kiss. Now that he was sober enough to recall it, Lycon realized that Zoe had also been acting oddly last night when he arrived home after stopping over in Ostia to reminisce and forget recent events with Vulpes and a few cronies. He continued to smile, while his belly tightened at the suspicion that Zoe might have taken a lover during his constant absences. If she had, he could not blame her—but neither would he forgive her.

"I told the boys to play outside so they wouldn't disturb you," Zoe said, keeping her eyes on the baby. "But Perses came in saying he was hungry, and I thought I'd better feed them. It's midday."

Lycon yawned and caressed her generous hips. Zoe had put on more weight than he had during their fifteen years of marriage—but by Herakles, she still was the stuff of his dreams on nights when he slept in the mud of another continent, and if he had some rival here in Rome for her love, he would soon learn his name—and then there would be no rival.

"No, no," Lycon told her. "I could have got up any time. It just felt so good to lie in for a change. No responsibilities. No beasts stalking me in turn. It's good to be home."

Home was Zoe and their children. It pleased

Lycon that he could afford an apartment—quite a nice apartment, too: spacious and only one flight up. Vonones might have far more wealth, but Vonones had neither wife nor acknowledged children, and Lycon sensed that his friend envied him for this. As consciousness cut through Lycon's hangover, he decided he was a fool to suspect Zoe of infidelity. True, he might not be the best of husbands and fathers, but Zoe had known that before they were married.

Zoe rocked the baby back and forth as though the motion would settle the correct words onto her own tongue. "Perhaps you'd like something to eat now, also. Just a second and I'll bring some bread . . ."

Lycon's arm anchored her as effortlessly as he would have immobilized a gazelle while it was being trussed—though there was little enough of the gazelle in Zoe's figure these days. "Here, just sit by me a minute, Zoe," he said mildly. "I'll be going to the bath in a little while, I suppose, and I may get something to eat there."

He paused, thinking over what Zoe had said a moment before and correlating that with dimly remembered scraps of conversation he had overheard while he dozed. "Alexandros isn't at school, then, today?"

Zoe turned her body away from her husband, placing Glauce against her other breast. "Well, Alexandros hasn't been going to school for some time now—for twenty days." Zoe spoke into the infant's fluffy hair. "There was trouble. You know, the whippings they get if Sempronianus doesn't like their recitations?"

"Alexandros is going to need an education, if

we're going to get him into the Civil Service, Zoe," Lycon said—almost gladly. It was a relief to understand now the reason for his wife's unease. Nothing here a good belting couldn't solve.

"I know, Lycon, I . . ."

"Or maybe you'd like me to start taking him with me on hunting trips, is that it?" Lycon went on, knowing that Zoe loathed that idea. She had already lost too many children—and most of her life with her husband. "I'd thought that, hadn't I? But no, it would be too dangerous. We owed him something better."

The beastcatcher swung himself off the bed. Despite his words, he had not raised his voice. A long-cherished dream was now unexpectedly within his reach; Lycon was already envisioning Alexandros at his side, watching lions group about their watering hole.

He pressed home his next point, already only for rhetoric. "Do you think cadging a ticket for the dole and picking up what he can in the way of petty theft is a better way of life?"

"I said," Zoe continued firmly, "that when you got home we'd find him another schoolmaster. I . . ."

"And just what is wrong with Sempronianus?" Lycon demanded in triumph. "He's the best I could afford."

Lycon continued to fume in Zoe's silence. "All right, he caned the boys—but none of the masters are going to suffer fools gladly. It's a tough world out there, Zoe, just as tough in the offices on the Palatine as it is for some unlettered dolt like me— beating through the reeds on the Nile. We won't do the boy any favors to teach him that if he whines, he won't have to do anything he doesn't want to do. I wish you'd waited for me to get back."

Zoe swallowed and sat up to face him. "Do you remember Rachel—on the fourth floor? Their Moises goes to Sempronianus too. Rachel, she . . . Moises told her that sometimes there are boys who are being caned for mistakes every day, every time they recite, no matter how well they do. And then Sempronianus takes them alone into one of the massage cubicles—the class meets in the Baths of Naevius. Afterward . . . that boy doesn't have trouble with his recitations for a week or so."

Lycon's lips were dry. They would not form the words. He dampened them very carefully with the tip of his tongue. His tongue seemed dry as well. "Go on," he said without emotion, as he reached for his boots.

"Alexandros won't go to class anymore. And I won't make him go."

"Well, well," murmured Lycon, as he laced onto his feet the army-pattern footgear he had worn in from the field. Normally he switched to lighter sandals whenever he was going to spend any length of time in a civilized area. "Who's the slave you were sending to school with Alexandros? Geta? I'll want him along."

"Lycon," Zoe began, "I just thought it might be better if we found Alexandros another schoolmaster."

Lycon stamped his foot and enjoyed the sound. Hobnails were a detriment to a man walking on slimy pavement. The iron skidded instead of biting as it did in soil—or in flesh.

"Zoe," the beastcatcher said, in a voice as hard

as the iron he had just ground against the floor, "I've just decided that Alexandros will be better off with me in the field than he will be here in Rome learning to recite Homer. I think I'm going to discuss that with Master Sempronianus. I'm certain he will agree."

"Lycon!" Zoe pleaded, as she rose and stepped toward him with her free hand outstretched. "You mustn't do anything hasty!"

"I'm not going to do anything *hasty*," Lycon promised, his tone a confirmation of her worst fears.

Perses stared open-mouthed as his father strode out of the bedchamber. Lycon's household was small; the four slaves were barely the minimum staff that respectability demanded for a man at his level of success. The slaves had ducked out of sight in healthy fear of meeting their master in his present state of mind. Perses' nurse reached out toward the three-year-old boy, bleated when she saw Lycon coming from the bedroom, and bolted back into the kitchen without her charge.

Lycon's walking staff was iron-shod hickory, and as big around as the beastcatcher's own powerful wrists. He snatched it with one hand, while he jerked open the door to the stairwell with the other. The family's doorkeeper was cowering in his alcove.

Vonones stood on the landing with his hand raised to knock. He looked terrified. The two men blocking the stairs behind him were soldiers.

"Lycon, thank the Light I've caught you at home," the dealer gasped.

"Whatever it is, it can wait!" snapped Lycon as

he started to push past. Zoe and one of the female servants were in the main room, wailing like mourners.

"It can't wait," Vonones said.

CHAPTER SEVEN

The barge was drawn up in normal fashion in one of the stone slips beneath the Portico of Aemilius, headquarters for the city's grain supply.

"Had to tow it like that the last three miles," said the foreman of the teamsters glumly. "Me on the steering oar, too, because the boys said Master could crucify them before they'd get aboard that barge. And you couldn't tell how bad it was, not really, till the sun come up after we'd docked."

The foreman was an Egyptian, but he spoke a dialect of Common Greek that Lycon had no difficulty in understanding. The beastcatcher had no difficulty in understanding the teamsters' fears, either.

There were now almost a hundred men standing on the levee, looking down on the barge slips in the Tiber. The numbers were nothing unusual for what was ordinarily the busiest part of the city—the lifeline by which was imported virtually all the food for a populace of uncertain hundreds of thousands. Slave gangs paced up and down the ramps from the levee to the slips. Each man carried a narrow pottery jar of wheat up to the measuring stations in front of the portico, then returned to the barges for another load.

The difference at this particular station was that the men were motionless and almost silent. The stevedores who would normally have been working the slips squatted on their haunches instead—naked except for loin cloths and, in rare instances, chain hobbles that permitted them to walk but not run. The heavily-armed Germans who glowered at the slaves and the surroundings in general might have dampened the normal enthusiasm of men released unexpectedly from work, but perhaps more of the reason lay in the closed palanquin that the Germans guarded. Lady Fortune, the only deity to whom Lycon still sacrificed, knew that the palanquin and the man it contained inspired such fear with good reason. The life of any or everyone here balanced upon the uncertain whim of lord and god Domitian.

Nonetheless, the men watching on the levee were in no way as silent as those sprawled upon the barge below.

"Let's go on down," Lycon said. "Yes, you too, dammit!" he added to the foreman, who had tried to edge away.

The barge had loaded grain at Portus from a North African freighter far too large to navigate the Tiber itself. The freighter would be refitting for several weeks, so a dozen of its crewmen had hitched a ride into Rome on the barge.

A yoke of oxen under the foreman and two subordinates drew the barge along the fifteen-mile towpath, while a helmsman guided it from the stern. Night had already fallen, but the process of feeding the city could not be interrupted by the cycles of the sun. One of the teamsters walked ahead with a rushlight—another firefly in the continuous chain of barges plodding toward Rome to be unloaded and then to drift back to Portus on sweeps and the current.

"They were singing," the foreman said. "The sailors were. There'd been some wine in the manifest too, you know." He glanced from Lycon to Vonones as they walked down the ramp to either side of him. The beastcatcher's face was impassive, the merchant's screwed up in an expression between distaste and nausea. Neither offered much sympathy for what the teamster thought of as his personal ordeal.

"Well, that stopped, the singing did, after a while, but that didn't mean much," the foreman continued. They were approaching the barge itself, and he had to keep talking to remind himself that it was daylight and he was alive.

"It looks easy enough," the foreman babbled on, "but it's a damned long trip, as you'd know if you ever followed a team of oxen. Usually some of the folks we give a lift to, they'll walk along part of the way and talk to us. Well, this lot didn't, but we had the escaped tiger and that African lizard-ape to talk about, me and the boys."

"Where did you hear about *that*?" snapped Vonones, who now understood how the authorities had known whose door to come knocking on.

"Why, wasn't it all over the towpath?" the teamster foreman replied in injured amazement. "There was a caravan of beasts pulled up not a quarter mile from the river, and the drivers with nothing else to do but come talk to us on the path. And don't you know how slow an ox walks, especially when one of the yoke's got a sore on his shoulder for that lazy bastard Nearchos in the stables not doing his job?"

Vonones swore. So much for loyalty—and the sanctity of a bribe. When he found out who had talked. . . . But first Vonones knew he would have to survive this day. He didn't like to think about the odds.

Lycon jumped onto the barge, balancing for a moment on the thick gunwale that acted as a fender while the vessel was being towed.

The foreman turned away. "We'd been talking, me and the boys," he went on, in a voice an octave higher than that of a moment before, "about what might have happened if they hadn't killed that tiger, and if it had gone for our team, you know? And what the Master'd do to us, no matter it wasn't any fault of ours, dear gods."

"You say there were a dozen sailors aboard when you left Portus?" Lycon interrupted.

"Something like that," the foreman agreed. He faced around again slowly, but he kept his eyes on Lycon's face rather than on the interior of the barge. "Can't really swear to it, you know. And there was Ursus on the steering oar."

"Can't really swear to it now," said Lycon grimly, as he walked along the gunwale.

There was no question in his mind as to what had caused the carnage. Nothing else could possibly have been quick enough. There were approximately six bodies in the bow, forward of the upright ranks of jars. Lycon was not sure that he could have duplicated their wounds with two hours and an axe, but these men had been killed before any of them could shout and alert the teamsters on the towpath. One man's chest had been hollowed out like a milkweed pod at summer's end. Another torso was untouched except for splashes of blood, but the head and all four limbs had been excised from it. The skin of the chest was smooth and an even tan—that of a healthy boy, perhaps no older than Alexandros.

For an instant, the thought of his son drove immediate concerns from Lycon's mind. Then the hunter glanced up toward the levee and the closed palanquin and the glowering guards. No, this couldn't wait.

The remains of three sailors lay amidships, sprawled over the upright grain jars. The ten-gallon containers were made as cheaply as possible, meant to be opened after their single use by having their necks struck off. Blood had soaked deeply into their unglazed surfaces, giving accents of darker color to the pinkish clay. One of the men looked completely uninjured, even peaceful. The body had stiffened, but when Lycon lifted it to search for a wound, the sailor's back and thighs showed only the usual post mortem extravasation.

"His ear," called Vonones unexpectedly from the slip where he stood. "The right ear. Those long claws. . . ."

Impassively Lycon shifted the body back. There was a trail of blackened blood from the ear canal, matting the hair on the sailor's temple. "It must see better in the dark," Lycon said, as he laid the corpse onto the jars again. "Better than they did, certainly. It must have taken part of them at a time, caught its breath, and—got some more."

He walked toward the stern, stepping again from the stoppered jars to the gunwale. The barge shifted a little under his weight, first fetched up by the stern line, and then quivering against the slip under the sluggish impetus of the Tiber's current. Lycon did not notice the motion in his preoccupied state. He had crossed gorges bridged by vines, more concerned for the load of brilliant, valuable birds he carried than he was for his own safety. After all, the real danger in this situation waited on the levee in a guarded palanquin.

The melange in the stern-hollow looked even more like meat for the stewpot than that in the bow had done. One of the things ripped during the night had been a skin of wine. Its contents had thinned and kept liquid the blood that pooled beneath the corpses.

"You!" Lycon called as he squinted down at the carnage. The stern wales were curved upward sharply. The hunter touched the steering oar with his left hand to steady himself. "Teamster! Come over here and tell me all you know about this."

Vonones gripped the teamster foreman by the elbow and thrust him toward Lycon. "Go on," he urged ungently. "Do you want to get us all crucified?"

"I called to Ursus," the foreman said, as if only by talking could he bring himself to step closer to the barge again. "I said, 'Give us another squeeze of wine,' you know, because we were out and I figured they had some aboard. And he didn't answer, so I got pissed off. I mean, he was senior man, but he could still be out stumbling along with the torch if I said so, Dis take him."

Lycon and Vonones were watching the foreman

carefully. He kept his eyes fixed on the sternpost, as if oblivious both of his audience and of the present condition of the barge. "So I let the stern come abreast of me," the teamster continued, "and I shouted again. And I should've been able to see him at the tiller—there wasn't any moon what with the clouds, but still against the water beyond— and he wasn't there at the oar. Nobody was. And just then the barge ground hard against the bank— *hard*—and so I go and jump aboard . . ."

"Which one of these is Ursus?" Lycon interrupted. He gestured toward the heaped bodies.

The foreman did not lower his eyes. "He was about my height," he said to the sternpost. "He never wore sandals in the boat, said he couldn't get a grip with . . ."

"Look at them, damn you, and tell me which one is the helmsman!" Lycon shouted.

"He had a beard!" the teamster shouted back. Tears were dripping from the man's eyes, and the veins on his neck stood out. "He wore a beard because of the scars on his chin from when a cable parted and slapped him when he was a lad!"

Lycon stepped into the barge, ignoring the sound his boots made. He began picking through the tumbled corpses. He'd seen worse. He'd *done* worse—across the Rhine, driving a village of Boii in panic through the woods at dawn. He didn't have enough troops to have surrounded the Germans or even to have beaten them had they stood and fought. But he could frighten them like deer into a pit trap, a covered trench filled with sharpened stakes, because the cohort commander wanted to show results without risking too many men in hostile territory.

Results that time had meant wagonloads of right hands. And the results had pleased the Governor and won praise for the cohort commander.

"I don't see anybody here with a beard," Lycon said, as he straightened and turned again to the teamster.

It didn't mean he enjoyed it, Lycon told himself; it meant that he did what he had to do. No matter what. "Are you sure," Lycon continued impassively, "that the barge was proceeding normally until just before you boarded her yourself?"

"It was," the foreman agreed quickly, bobbing his chin upward in a gesture of assent. "And I had to bring it in to dock then myself, even with all this here, because we couldn't block the towpath." He turned his back. The teamster had thrown away his sandals and washed his feet compulsively when dawn emphasized what the rushlight had only suggested. Seeing the state of Lycon's boots when the hunter stepped out of the barge recalled to the foreman what he prayed to forget.

"Then," Lycon said wearily, "I think we're ready to report. I suppose that's what he wants from us?" He raised an eyebrow, as much a gesture as he dared to indicate the Emperor's palanquin above.

"Yes," Vonones agreed without following the gesture even with his eyes. "He wants us to report directly to him. After that . . ."

The two men began walking down the slip toward the ramp. It took the teamster a moment to realize that he had been released from the nightmare. He ran after Lycon and Vonones. He was fleeing his memories more than the presence of the blood-spattered barge.

"It was reported to Domitian as soon as it was

discovered," Vonones whispered to his friend in a hasty, hidden voice. "The Prefect of the Watch has orders about such things—things that our lord and god wants to know. He came out in person to view it.

"I was unloading the shipment in my compound this morning, when Lacerta and the emperor's personal guard came riding in. Well, Domitian wanted to know about the animals that had escaped from my caravan. No, not the tiger, but the other beast—the lizard-ape thing he'd heard talked about. Where was it? Well, I offered to show them the skin of the tiger, and explained that you'd seen them fight to the death—seen the sauropithecus fall into the Tiber, where it doubtless died from its wounds or drowned, and was washed out to sea. Unfortunately, they had proof to the contrary . . ."

"I should have made certain it was dead," Lycon said bitterly. "I know better than to allow a wounded man-killer to slip off into the brush."

He more regretted his own loss of nerve that night than his mistake in ever allowing Vonones to involve him in this mess. Well, the merchant's neck was on the block more surely than his own, if that was any comfort.

The palanquin was of ebony inlaid with mother of pearl. In the sunlight it glowed without dazzling. Inlays—though the ebony was solid, not a veneer as Lycon had assumed at a distance—were sure to be knocked loose in the chaos of Rome's streets. However, in this case the way would be cleared for the palanquin not by staff-wielding slaves and retainers of lesser rank, but rather by men with long swords drawn and no reason to fear using them.

The palanquin had the least patina of wear, but no sign at all of abuse or battering.

The litter bearers were Syrians, solid men in scarlet tunics. They squatted at a little distance from the palanquin instead of sitting on the poles as most bearers would have done when the litter was at rest. Their voices and their shifting weight might have disturbed their owner within. The Emperor could have no greater control over his slaves than the power of life and death, granted by law to any slave master. The normal realities of human society took precedence over the law in all but the rarest circumstances.

The eight litter bearers, sitting apart and even then silent, suggested how rare the present circumstances were.

Two slaves stood at the far end of the palanquin. One of them held a set of wax tablets with his stylus ready. The other was reading aloud from a well-produced scroll. The edges had been sanded smooth and dressed up with saffron stain. The subject of the book seemed to be astronomy, so far as Lycon could tell from its hexameter verses in a Greek that seemed to him to be less pure than absurdly stilted.

The reader continued to chant the verse as Lycon and Vonones approached. The eyes of both the reader and the secretary waiting to take notes began to track the newcomers over the top of the palanquin. The palace servants were obviously afraid to indicate Lycon and Vonones to their master, but afraid as well of what would happen to them if they did not do so.

There were six guards in the immediate vicinity of the palanquin as well. Their officer, an Italian shorter by eight inches than any of his German troops—that would be Lacerta, Lycon guessed—solved the reader's problem by shouting: "Halt right there, you!" when Lycon had come within six feet of the litter. The curtained window of the palanquin quivered as the occupant turned from one side to the other. The curtains were of black silk in several layers, opaque from the outside. Nonetheless, Lycon felt himself become the object of cold appraisal. A similar impression in the darkness had once kept him from climbing into a hammock in which lamps later revealed the coils of a green mamba. This time there was no option of turning away. The reader fell silent with evident relief.

"You will be the beastcatcher Lycon," said a voice from within the palanquin. It was high-pitched to be a man's, and it spoke Latin with a casual elegance that must be inbred rather than learned.

"Yes, my lord and god," Lycon said, as he knelt and bowed his forehead to the dust. He was a free citizen of Arcadia, but a hungry lion would not be impressed by that fact, nor would Domitian be if he decided to send Lycon to that beast. Vonones, lagging a pace behind his comrade, threw himself down as well.

"Rise," the voice said languidly. The door of the palanquin opened.

Lycon straightened, keeping his gaze carefully downcast, as the Emperor stepped out in full view before him. Lycon concentrated on his first close-up view of Domitian, and while he realized that a personal audience with the Emperor was a rare honor, Lycon almost would have traded places with one of those on the barge. They, at least, were already dead and beyond even Domitian's power.

Domitian was of a height considerable in any company save that of his German guards. He wore the simple outer garment of a conservative aristocrat, a woolen toga with a broad stripe of dark russet—"purple"—along one border. The undertunic was of silk, however, and more in keeping with the titles of "lord and god" which the Emperor had assumed in the recent past.

Words and titles did not matter to Lycon. What mattered was that Lycon faced a man whose capricious sadism and uncertain moods would have made him dangerous, even if he were not Titus Flavius Domitianus, Emperor, Lord and God to every land washed by the Mediterranean and many other lands beyond.

"And you've seen the sauropithecus that escaped," Domitian said. "You've seen it kill a tiger."

The Emperor bent his head slightly toward Lycon. The beastcatcher had seen such an attitude of anticipation often enough, as spectators pressed forward on their benches to drink in the slaughter being played for them on the floor of the arena. There was nothing about the faces on the ivory chairs in the first circle to differentiate them from the common mob in the higher tiers. There was no difference in this face, either.

Domitian was not an unpleasant man to look at. He was bald and ruddy enough to pass for a jovial man, the best sort of dinner companion. The bulk of the toga could have counterfeited powerful shoulders, but the thick wrists suggested that the shoulder muscles were real as well. The upper torso's appearance of health and strength was belied by a bulging belly and calves that would have been spindly on a man three decades older than the Emperor's forty years. Part of Lycon's mind wondered about disease and the possibility that sickness, like the festering wounds that can turn an ordinary predator into a man-eater, had affected Domitian's personality as well.

But that, like a storm at sea, was a danger to be accepted, since it was beyond present cure. Aloud Lycon said, "Lord and god, I did see the lizard-ape fight a tiger. It was very quick, even quicker than the tiger, and strong enough to endure the tiger's battering until it succeeded in ripping apart the tiger's throat. If your divine excellency wishes, I will set off at once for Africa to trap another one for your divine excellency's personal pleasure."

"Yes—and I and my agents will accompany this greatest of all beastcatchers," Vonones declared. "We will provide the kind of support that will give Lycon's genius full play."

"No, hunter," said Domitian. He licked his heavy lips and smiled. "I don't need another one, not just yet. I want you to catch this one for me. The one that killed the tiger. And those others." He gestured with two fingers, down toward the barge, and he licked his lips again.

Lycon raised his eyes slowly to meet the Emperor's. He licked his own lips as he let his gaze fall again. "Lord and god," he said, "I will gladly recapture the sauropithecus for you if it still lives. But this beast has been injured. Surely your divine excellency would prefer that I journey to Africa and return with a score of such beasts, all in the peak of condition and capable of hours of entertainment in the arena."

"Do you think it used only its claws to kill them?" the Emperor interrupted. He was beginning to tremble, and Lycon could not tell whether the cause was emotion or physical strain. Those legs looked very weak.

"I don't recall it biting when it fought the tiger, lord and god," Lycon said, temporizing. "Its attack was very sudden. But the sauropithecus has strong jaws and savage fangs—imagine a huge serpent's jaw, all set with razor-edged needles. Its appetite is ravenous, and several of the bodies on the barge have obviously been partially devoured. The lizard-ape seems to favor the lungs and large organs such as the liver, my lord and god. But beyond sating its physical appetites, the lizard-ape seems to kill for the pure love of slaughter. One man—and this can only be true, my lord and god— one man it must have held helpless while it searched his brain by piercing one long talon into his ear and through his skull!"

Lycon cleared his throat, watching Domitian close his eyes—the better to envision Lycon's description. Lycon was used to queasy voyeurism and gloating conversations of this sort, but normally the payoff was a tip in gold or silver from a noble once his memories had been sated with imagined blood. The potential here was for much higher stakes than money, but it was also necessary to steer the conversation toward a direction that would permit long-term safety—such as flight to Africa and beyond the limits of the empire.

"I consider it highly significant," Lycon ventured, "that the helmsman was no longer aboard the barge when we inspected the evidence of the slaughter there."

"What does it matter that one of the dogs went overboard?" asked Domitian, coming out of his revery with some annoyance. The Emperor had fine prominent eyes. When he frowned, as he was doing now, the high forehead crumpled over them like a thunderhead with lightning at its core.

"Went overboard, yes, lord and god," Lycon spoke quickly. He restrained an impulse to kneel again. "Almost certainly with the sauropithecus clasped to him. It was badly wounded and in a killing rage. When it went overboard with the helmsman—well, the current is very strong there, where the Tiber channel has been narrowed by the north breakwater of Portus. And anyway, the sauropithecus looked as unlikely to swim as a frog would be to fly. I'm sure it's drowned and pickling in the sea already, excellency. Now, in Africa . . ."

"Don't be absurd," said the Emperor. The tone in his voice warned Lycon not to continue. "Of course it's alive. It killed a pack of Molossians, it killed a tiger, it killed that lot below—and you say, drowned in the Tiber! No more excuses. Catch it for me. But now, tell me more about the tiger again."

"Lord and god." Lycon's mouth was dry. Domitian's eyes glinted like those of a rutting boar.

"Yes, of course, it is as you say. Now then, the tiger. Never in my years on the frontiers of your divine excellency's domains have I ever seen such a battle! The lizard-ape lay in wait for the tiger—clearly eager to fight to the death with this, the most magnificent tiger I've ever had fortune to capture, and a proven man-killer as well. Vonones saved the pelt and will have it carefully tanned for you, my lord and god."

"And the sauropithecus!" Domitian demanded, only drooling eagerness now. "Describe it to me in full detail."

"The sauropithecus more closely resembles a small man than it does an ape, divine excellency." Lycon warmed to his task. "Instead of fur, it is covered entirely with fine blue scales. This skin must be as impenetrable as an armor linked from thousands upon thousands of sapphires, for the tiger's claws could scarcely rend it. Its talons draw back into its paws, just as a cat's do, only no cat ever grew claws so long and sharp as these."

"And it kills with those claws?" Domitian's ghoulish attention was unnerving.

"Indeed it does, lord and god. Consider that its forepaws are more properly hands than animal paws, and imagine razor-edged needles of diamond hardness that double the length of each finger when extended. Ten such deadly talons, divine excellency, coupled with the strength of a beast ten times the lizard-ape's size—tearing and slashing in murderous frenzy . . ."

"And thus it killed the tiger?"

"It hurled itself upon the tiger, divine excellency. Never have I seen any creature move so fast. Over and over they tumbled across the field—tearing at one another, the tiger foaming in rage. Blood seemed to spray everywhere, and most of it the tiger's. I thought that surely both beasts must die, but the sauropithecus proved too much for the tiger, and despite the terrible mauling it suffered, somehow it succeeded in virtually severing the tiger's head from its neck. After that, it retreated from my spear, fell into the Tiber—surely, I believed with every reason to do so, to die in its depths from the wounds it had suffered."

Domitian remained in revery, then sighed and shivered. "Fortunately for you, beastcatcher, it did not die. Now you must catch it for me. I have many tigers, and I shall not rest until I have witnessed such a battle for myself."

He smiled goodnaturedly at Lycon—much the same smile that a man bestows upon a whore who has just performed her arts well. "Lycon, you are called. I am told that you were a superb gladiator some years back, before you turned to hunting beasts for the arena. Now they say that you are a superb beastcatcher as well. I hope this is true. I like a man who shares my enthusiasm for arena sports, and I like you, Lycon."

The Emperor turned to his secretary. "Sosius!"

The secretary, still poised on the other side of the palanquin, twitched to full alertness. "Excellency?" he said.

"Give this man one thousand sesterces," Domitian commanded, then returned his smile upon Lycon.

"As you see, I am generous to those who are in my favor, Lycon. I am also swift to reward those who displease me. I am told that you have a family."

Lycon fought to hold his knees steady. "Lord and god, I thank you for your kindness. I shall recapture the sauropithecus and have it ready to perform in the arena with all possible haste."

"See that you don't waste time in doing so," Domitian warned. His manner was almost friendly. "And take care that the sauropithecus is in no way harmed. This merchant will assist you."

"At once, divine excellency!" Vonones almost

fainted to learn that his life, too, had been spared for the moment. "All my men and equipment are at Lycon's command."

"Don't be too long about your task, then," Domitian advised, dismissing them.

The Emperor took much of his weight on his powerful arms as he lifted himself into the palanquin. The door slapped closed behind him, and the bearers sprang to their posts.

"Excellency, I . . ." Lycon began. He continued after a pause to allow Domitian to settle himself comfortably. "I may need official support as well, authority to levy beaters and net-bearers. Maybe military units too. I don't know what we're getting into—we may have to cordon off entire estates and search every hedgerow."

"Take care of it, Sosius," ordered the bored voice behind the black curtains. There was a rapping sound on the frame of the palanquin—the Emperor's fingernail or a stylus giving coded directions to the bearers. The sharp noise could be understood through the bustle of city crowds, as voice commands might not be. The closed litter was lifted in two stages to the shoulders of the bearers. The Syrians gave simultaneous controlled gasps at each pause. Then they strode off in unison while the mounted guards fell in around the palanquin.

Vonones and Lycon backed away to avoid being trampled by the litter bearers. The merchant dusted his palms against one another, then began to wring them unconsciously. "Well, Lycon. We're both still alive, and you're a wealthy man. My advice is to spend it quickly."

"Idiot!" Lycon snorted. "Don't you realize that if we don't produce that damned lizard-ape and quickly, Domitian will have not only us but our households as well feeding tigers in the arena!"

"Lycon," said Vonones earnestly, "I'm honestly sorry I ever got you involved in this mess. I know you were doing me a favor, but if I'd had any idea what this would lead you into . . ."

"Forget it," Lycon answered roughly. "I didn't enter into this blindly. We'll just have to catch the damned thing. That's my profession, after all—catching beasts."

The merchant licked his lips. "That's what we'll have to do," he said. "After all, the Numidians managed to catch it."

"Yes, in open country," Lycon reminded him sourly. "Who knows where the thing is hiding now—or how we'll catch it."

Vonones had a sudden thought. "I wonder who's going to cover all these expenses? Probably me. You noticed that our lord and god made no mention of payment for the sauropithecus."

"He damn well indicated what sort of reward awaits us if we don't catch it!" Lycon reminded him, as they walked toward Vonones' tethered horse. "The trouble is, it may well be that all we can do is just go through the motions of hunting the damned beast, and hope the Emperor loses interest."

"Do you really think the sauropithecus might have drowned in the Tiber, then?" Vonones asked. "I almost hope it did, even though that's the worse for us. I'd rather not have to see any more massacres like that, that mess on the barge."

"There's a good chance it went over the side in a struggle with the helmsman," Lycon said. "After all, it didn't attack the teamsters when it was finished on the barge. That's one good thing about the lizard-ape's savagery: if it's still alive, we'll know about it as soon as it makes its next kill. We shouldn't have long to wait."

The mount Lycon had ridden was that of one of the German guards who had remained with the Emperor when he summoned the beastcatcher. He had ridden off with the remainder of the troop once the audience was concluded, but Lycon had never needed more than his own legs to get him around. Dockworkers, released by the absence of the guards, were streaming down to the slips to get their own view of the bloody carnage. It was much closer than men of their class would ever be able to get at the amphitheater.

"The problem that bothers me," said Vonones as he clucked to his horse, "is that the barge made it as far as it did—without a helmsman."

Lycon nodded. His face was tight. The thought had occurred to him also.

"I don't think that would have been possible," Vonones continued. "The barge would have grounded, just as it eventually did when the teamster foreman boarded her. The current and the thrust of the towline both would have driven the bow into the bank without a hand on the tiller."

"That's true enough," Lycon agreed.

"Let's go back to my house," Vonones suggested. "We'll need to get organized on this right away, and we'll use my men." He looked for landmarks. They might do better to hire one of the City Watchmen as a guide through the unfamiliar streets between the grain docks and his house on the Caelian. But the merchant did not especially want anyone else present during their conversation.

"The lizard-ape had a couple of days to recover from its fight with the tiger, probably holed up under the river bank along there. Either it had escaped serious injuries, or else it heals exceptionally fast—perhaps both. We know it couldn't have been crippled or badly hurt to have killed all those men without causing an uproar. It may well be that there was an hour or more between the separate attacks, while it caught its breath and . . . ate its fill. And that means it didn't go into the river at Portus."

"All right," Lycon said grimly. "What else do you think it means?"

"I don't . . ." Vonones began, not liking the conclusion he had reached. "I don't see any reason to assume the beast went into the river at all. Lycon, on the tiller—I saw that you noticed it too—there were fresh notches cut into the wood. I don't believe it was from the helmsman whittling at the tiller with a knife just before he was killed. And I don't think you believe that either."

Lycon spoke, but he spoke so softly that Vonones could not hear him. A great derrick lay halfway across the street ahead. Its axle squealed as men paced within the winding cage, providing power to raise a twenty-foot beam to the building crew awaiting it on the third floor of an apartment under construction.

Instead of trying to force his way around the obstruction, Vonones reined in and dismounted. He put his arm around Lycon's shoulders and bent his ear to the other's voice.

"I said," repeated the hunter with finality, "that if the sauropithecus is still alive, we've got to get it, and quickly. I've seen it kill, my friend. If it was smart enough to steer a barge up the Tiber, then it's too dangerous to be alive, that's all."

"Too dangerous to be loose, at any rate," said the merchant.

"I mean exactly what I said, Vonones," Lycon shouted, more loudly than Vonones thought prudent. "I hope we find it dead. I really do. Because no matter what, it's going to be dead the next time I leave it. I'm not turning it over alive to anybody." His voice dropped to a whisper that Vonones understood only because he knew what the words would be even before they were spoken: "Especially not to our lord and god, the Emperor."

Vonones pulled himself onto his mount again, lifting his weight with one hand on either of the pair of forward pommels on his saddle. Under normal circumstances, a slave would have given him a leg-up, but he would not ask a friend for that service.

"We'll see when the time comes," Vonones agreed cautiously. "We'll see when we've actually found the sauropithecus."

CHAPTER EIGHT

The imperial lodge east of Rome was not itself very large, but its grounds enclosed over a thousand acres of the Alban Hills. The Emperor was at his leisure in a clearing within sight of the main house. There were over a hundred men around him: guards, slaves, and a half dozen of his closest advisors.

"Loose!" the Emperor called.

A slave opened a basket and gave it an underarm swing that tossed the pigeon within airborne in the right direction. One of the bird's flight feathers on either wing had been clipped. That slowed its rise, but it also gave the bird a deceptive stagger through the air. Domitian drew his bow and tracked the pigeon's flight against the arrowhead. When he shot, the bird was almost twenty yards out. The release was part of the same smooth motion with which the Emperor had drawn the bow. The arrow's flat arc flicked it across the pigeon and past. The bird fell in two pieces, the head and the remainder.

Onlookers cheered wildly. The boy who was sprinting to pick up the arrow well down-range began to turn cartwheels. A microcephalic dwarf in a saffron tunic waddled up to Domitian and hugged his knee. The Emperor reached down and caressed the dwarf's head.

"What do you think of Glabrio for Upper Germany, Crispinus?" the Emperor asked, as he handed his bow to a slave to have another arrow nocked.

Crispinus, a greying man with a wizened face and eyes like a shark's, shrugged. "I think he's trustworthy, lord and god. I just don't think he's bright enough to tell dung from mincemeat."

"With four legions under him, I think we'll go with trustworthy," Domitian remarked languidly, as he reached for his bow.

A party of men, half a dozen of them, was coming from the lodge. That was unexpected. The six guards closest to the Emperor stood in an arc at his back, facing outward. They already held swords naked in their hands, but they stiffened to lift their armored heads a half-inch higher, like cats sighting prey. The outlying curtain of guards straightened also, but the newcomer, whoever he was, was being escorted by household staff members in normal fashion.

"Excellency, I'm so embarrassed," now whined a plump steward who had been conversing in a low voice with the slaves who were handling the pigeon baskets. "We haven't any more birds ready for your excellency. Some very nice deer, some panthers, or . . ."

The steward broke off and swallowed. Domitian had said nothing, but the Emperor's eyes were focused unblinkingly upon the steward. The unhappy servant forced his tongue to continue speaking, although he had very little consciousness of the words. "Or we could drive peacocks by, of course."

"Regular arrow," Domitian said, handing his bow to the loader without looking away from the steward.

Down the field, the slave boy was still cartwheeling expertly with bloody palms and sandals toward the distant arrow. There were scores of pigeons strewn between ten and forty yards of the imperial archer. Almost all of them had been lopped apart by arrows like the one now being exchanged for a normal point by the loader. The heads of the arrows that Domitian was using on the birds were double-pointed sickles a hand's breadth wide. The crescent blades were razor sharp across the whole inner curve. A few of the pigeons had fluttered to safety in the distant woods, but very few; the blood of the remainder had spattered the grass across a wide area as they fell. The slave had cartwheeled across the expanse of carnage, concerned only that he not slip in the blood and loose feathers. He had often seen worse.

The last six arrows had fallen at some distance one from another, depending on the angle at which panic had taken individual pigeons into the air. The slave stuck the shaft of each arrow into his mouth so that he could continue to cartwheel to the next. He had known before the steward had realized it that there were no more pigeons ready to be shot. The slave was determined to end his performance on a high note.

At Domitian's feet, the dwarf attempted a cartwheel of his own. Midway through, he shifted into a series of forward and backward somersaults, then stood on his hands giggling.

The slave boy caught up the sixth arrow and sprang into the air with his arms spread wide, a trio of arrows in either hand. Domitian moved, drawing the bow as if he and the bow and the boy down-range were all part of the same complex machine. The slave had a bright smile as his feet touched the ground again. His eyes did not have time to focus on what the Emperor was doing, much less on the arrow that was only a flicker in the air as it snapped toward him.

The boy yelped and fell over.

The house staff—a senior usher, two ushers, and a pair of armed Germans—had arrived with the newcomer, a richly tanned foreigner over six feet tall.

"You go stand against that beech tree there," the Emperor said to the steward responsible for the morning's recreation. He gestured with an eyebrow toward a tree ten yards away. Its size, four feet in diameter at head height above the ground, had caused it to be spared when lesser trees were cleared for the sports area. "Hold your hand above your head and spread your fingers."

"Master and god . . .?"

The boy who had been gathering arrows bounded upright with an amazed look upon his face. His right foot was now bare. He held not only the six crescent-headed bird arrows but the last shaft as well—spiked through his right sandal between where his first and second toes had rested.

The gathering—the freemen and the higher-ranked slaves—hummed with "Brilliant!" and "Magnificent!" The steward was particularly enthusiastic, until the Emperor's eyes turned back to him. The pudgy servant scampered toward the beech tree with a fixed smile on his face.

"Yes, it was rather good, wasn't it," the Emperor said with a pleased smile. He was already beginning to forget that only chance could have been that accurate, and that all he had been trying to do was to pin the slave's foot to the ground.

"And what are you, barbarian?" Domitian called from behind a hedge of armed guards. The Emperor's nose was wrinkling, although the newcomer had no odor discernible to the servants and counsellors closer to the man.

"I am N'Sumu, lord and god," said the tall man. He spoke Latin with a pronounced Iberian accent, though the words were intelligible enough. "I am an Egyptian from south of Elephantine Island in the Nile. In my native land I am renowned as a great hunter of the strange beasts that dwell beyond the cataracts of the Nile. Your Prefect of the Watch, Laurus, thought I might be of service to you because of my long experience in capturing sauropitheci. I understand from certain talk I have heard during my visit to Rome that you have one that needs to be recaptured."

"Yes, whatever did happen to that one?" the Emperor demanded of no one in particular. He did not care so long as he got an answer. If no one answered, then so much the worse for whoever and however many the Emperor decided should have answered him. The counsellors—one of them seventy and blind, all of them learned and powerful men—began to perspire.

The third secretary in a rank of six began to recite while his fingers danced through the tablets thonged to his belt. "The beastcatcher Lycon has been reporting lack of success at five-day intervals. The area of search has been focused in the region between Portus and the third milepost on the Via where the barge was first discovered to have been attacked. In the course of the past three reports, the beastcatcher has expressed doubts that the sauropithecus is still alive and has requested that the search be terminated in order that he may seek to obtain more of the beasts from the Numidians."

Domitian chuckled and whispered into the ear of his loader. That slave began to lay out a sheaf of arrows.

"I can help you capture the beast, lord and god," said the bronzed Egyptian with the incongruous accent.

Domitian wondered: Did the Tartessians have a trading base beyond the first cataract of the Nile?

"Moreover," N'Sumu continued, "I can help you breed as many more sauropitheci as you may want for the amphitheater. Can you imagine," N'Sumu bent forward—his torso lumped in unfamiliar ways beneath the formal toga, "a thousand of them, loosed all at once on a legion of armed convicts in the arena? Against war elephants? Battling to the death!"

Domitian took the bow his loader was proferring silently. He turned his body toward the steward whose hand, raised as high as the man could get it above his head, was spread palm outward against the beech trunk. The Emperor drew and loosed, nocked the arrow his loader offered fletching-forward, drew and loosed again ... and again ... and a fourth time.

"The hunter in charge of the business," said Crispinus to the bronzed man, "is convinced that the sauropithecus drowned in the Tiber. Given the way it made its presence known earlier, on the estate and on the barge as well, I'd say that lack of further occurrences was good reason to agree with the hunter."

The snap of the bowstring and slap of each arrowhead against the tree bole were so close together that they merged into a single sound repeated four times. The scream that almost all of the onlookers expected did not come. The steward's terrified grimace melted into something close to religious awe. He wriggled his fingers. The web between thumb and index finger had been nicked, but beyond that the steward's hand was untouched. The four arrows, driven far enough into the beech that none of the iron heads was visible, stood out against the flesh they did not harm.

"Bravo!" shouted the onlookers. "Magnificent!"

"Other hand," said the Emperor, as he returned to the discussion behind him. He was sweating and flushed with exertion and pride. His face, ruddy at all times, was a brighter hue, but there were mottled patches of red upon his bald scalp as well.

"It's hardly likely that it drowned," said N'Sumu. "The sauropithecus is a powerful swimmer in its native rivers."

He spoke to Crispinus, but with a nod toward the Emperor to indicate that he was simply continuing the discussion with no intended disrespect. "While a badly injured sauropithecus might have been pulled under by heavy currents—their bodies are too densely fleshed to allow the creatures to float—we know this one was quite fit enough to slaughter a boatload of men. Almost certainly it has made its lair in some secret place—such a place as only a hunter of my considerable experience with these beasts would suspect."

Domitian had caught his breath from the previous rapid-fire burst. He took the bow again without speaking.

"Then why haven't we heard more from the creature, Egyptian?" demanded Crispinus, as four more arrows slapped from the Emperor's bow. The microcephalic dwarf was staring at N'Sumu and was pulling his own lips outward as if to draw them into a ring-shaped sucker like that of a lamprey. "Why haven't there been reports of more farmhouses ravaged, travellers massacred—that sort of thing?"

"Masterful, lord and god! Incredible! Divine, truly divine!" twittered the crowd.

"It learns quickly," said N'Sumu. "And I have no doubt that the beast was indeed injured, as your Lycon says—though I doubt he can imagine just how much punishment a, a sauropithecus can withstand and live." The bronzed face twisted into a too-wide smile that was uncannily reminiscent of the dwarf's contortions a moment before. "Live and live to kill again, I should emphasize. They are very aggressive. But not so aggressive that this one could not find a cave to hide in, to limit itself to small game while it recovers its strength. They are very clever, for animals."

"How are you going to breed them?" asked Domitian suddenly. He was breathing heavily as he handed the bow again to his loader. "Unless you already have another, you'll need to return to Africa to capture a breeding pair." The pads of

Domitian's right thumb, index finger and middle finger were callused, but even so the long morning of archery had turned them an angry red. "Best to recapture this one for the arena, and if the sauropithecus provides as entertaining a spectacle as has been reported, then you and Lycon can journey to Africa and bring back a shipload of the beasts."

"Lord and god, such will be most difficult," the Egyptian said with an obsequious tilt of his head. The guards were still a bronze-breasted wall between him and the Emperor. "The sauropitheci come from beyond the upper reaches of the Nile, from the very heart of Africa—a long and uncertain journey to be sure. Moreover, these creatures are exceedingly rare—a severe drought in recent years has all but annihilated their natural hunting grounds."

"I'd understood the creature was from the Aures Mountains," Crispinus interjected, to show his determination to protect the Emperor from charlatans— and anyone else whom imperial whim might decide to add to the court circle along with the dwarf, various sorts of prostitutes—and Crispinus. "And as any educated man knows, the Nile flows across Africa and into the ocean on the other side. The Phoenicians found species of crocodiles there identical to those of Egypt. Are you sure you know what you're talking about, Egyptian?"

"Quite sure," N'Sumu said. His eyes focused on the courtier as if Crispinus were a slab of meat on a butcher's block. Still staring at Crispinus, the Egyptian went on. "If I may have your leave, lord and god, to proceed in informing you?"

"Granted," said Domitian softly. He was beginning to smile also, though no one around him could be certain of the reason Crispinus was beginning to perspire heavily, as if he too had been a participant in the archery.

"Doubtless this sauropithecus was driven far to the north by this same drought I have described," N'Sumu continued, smiling again and toward Domitian now. "There it was captured, almost certainly in a weakened state, by the Numidians. Now, the sauropitheci invariably travel in pairs, but no doubt the other one died from starvation, and just this one survived. From the description I've heard, there has been no mention of the striking red crest and the long curved horn in the center of the forehead that characterizes the male of the species. So it is the female which survived, and she is almost certainly gravid. They breed very actively, these sauropitheci, and the female continues to lay fertile eggs through several broods. All we have to do is capture this one, provide her with a secure place for parturition, then wait for her to produce chicks."

The Egyptian paused. With a smile whose humor only the Emperor himself seemed to appreciate, he added: "And we must provide her with food, of course. Considerable quantities of food. But the meat need not be slaughtered before we offer it to the creature—and your divine excellency will not find these feedings dull."

Domitian began to laugh—a high-pitched cackle that increased the fear of those about him. He nodded to his loader and took the bow again, but it was to N'Sumu that he said, "You've spoken to the hunter, then? This Lycon?"

"Not yet, lord and god," the tall man replied. "I did not wish to interfere in the present search without your divine approval. I questioned only those who had some knowledge of the sauropithecus."

"All right," said the Emperor, as his fingers toyed with the bow. The nocked arrow had an ordinary head with a sharp point and edges in the form of a narrow wedge. "You're in charge of the hunt. Sosius!" The first secretary was already jotting shorthand notes on the tablet he held ready. "Cut the orders on that. Lycon is to take orders from you, N'Sumu, and if the beastcatcher objects to being placed under your command, send word to Crispinus here. That Greek's had time enough to recapture the beast."

"I don't think there will be any difficulty, lord and god," N'Sumu responded smoothly, as the Emperor's attention returned to his arrow and to the frightened steward still with his arms back against the beech. "I gather that your man Lycon is competent enough in the ordinary way. He simply lacks experience with sauropitheci; but then I am certainly the only hunter on this shore of the Mediterranean who has such experience. Lycon and the support system he has developed will be very useful to me in my operations—so long as he cooperates."

Domitian shot and reloaded, shot and reloaded again. "As you wish, Egyptian," he said without concern. The crack of iron arrowheads striking hard wood had been damped somewhat this time, because the most recent pair of arrows had pinned the steward's wrists to the tree. The man's mouth opened and closed like that of an ornamental carp sucking air at the surface of a pond. Because of the shock, both physical and mental, the steward was not making a sound. He was pinned as neatly as if he were being crucified; the arrows, like the supporting nails on the crossbar, were driven beneath the wrist joint. The flesh of the victim's hands would not have enough strength to support the body's weight.

"Only I want you to remember," the Emperor went on as he drew the third arrow that the loader had handed him, "that I do expect success. I don't like it when people fail me. Remember that."

Domitian loosed. This time the steward screamed. The last arrow had been one of the sickle-headed missiles intended for birds.

"Oops," said Domitian, daintily covering his lips to hide the amused giggle.

As his giggle became a high-pitched cackle, the onlookers joined in on his jest. "Bravo! Magnificent! Exquisite!"

CHAPTER NINE

Formion was nodding his way from pleasant revery and into dream, when Dulicius shook him out of the warmth of the Gallic wench's body and back to the cold reality of the filthy alleyway in which the two lay in wait. The Greek boxer scowled for a moment into the darkness, wreathed with smoke and mist from the Tiber nearby. Formion did not utter a sound, despite relinquishing his dream. This was a familiar reality into which he returned, and if his partner's judgment proved sound as usual, there would be more visits to the blonde-haired whore whose favors defined pleasure to the full extent of the Greek's imaginings.

"Where?" It was more a sigh of breath than speech, as Formion unfolded to full height and alertness.

"There," Dulicius whispered, pointing toward the river. The full moon gave barely enough light to make out the moving silhouette. Once the figure glided into the shadow of surrounding buildings, it would be invisible.

"I've seen her before, I think," Dulicius confided. From its short stature, he had evidently decided the dimly seen figure was that of a woman—the tail of her mantle pulled over her head.

"Someone dressed like a Gaul with that hood," Formion advised. "We don't know who it is."

"Look again," sneered his partner. "Only a woman can move like that. I tell you, I've seen her here before. I ask you, why is she out at this hour of night?"

"Doesn't mean she has anything worth taking," Formion argued. He was cold from dozing against the wall, and his thick bunches of muscle seemed to grate together as he flexed them.

"Ass," Dulicius chided. "Any woman has *something* worth taking. Besides, it's growing late, and I'm near frozen."

"True enough," Formion acknowledged. Maybe it would be the blonde Gallic woman of his dream. He stretched his stiff muscles, glided outward into the fog behind Dulicius.

The two footpads had a simple routine, and it had always worked—at least, always worked when their mark was alone and more likely than not dull from drink and the late hour. Dulicius, a ferret of a man, approached directly—just another ragged beggar whining for a handout. Formion, moving quite silently for a man of his size, crept up from behind, choosing his moment to throw an armlock about the throat or to swing his weighted cudgel, as the situation required. If that situation required anything further, Dulicius could move very quickly with his knife he carried in one ragged sleeve, and that knife could pierce ribs or slit a throat with equal suddenness and finality.

"A cold night," Dulicius greeted the cloaked figure.

She had seemed to pause an instant before she could have been aware of his smiling approach, and that only confirmed his impression of tonight's victim. Coin or no, they would have a moment of pleasure, and then the Tiber awaited. In truth, she seemed hunched and thin within her cloak. Well, as was said . . .

Formion arose instantly from the darkness behind her—his strong right arm hinging across her throat, his left hand clamping over her face, doubly to stifle any outcry. Her feet lifted from the paving as the Greek drew back—she was smaller than her billowing cloak had indicated—and Dulicius glided in with his knife, to prove to her the sure outcome of any resistance.

The Greek's muscular forearm closed upon empty air and an emptier hood. His free hand only bunched her cloak together stupidly, as Formion's mouth opened impossibly wide and the big man stumbled backward. He sat abruptly down on the damp paving—damper now from the blood and fluids that spilled from his belly. He folded his hands over the tumble of intestines that rolled onto the paving. His eyes, as they focused dully upon his partner, were accusing.

He had never seen the backward kick of the spurred heel that had gutted him.

Dulicius had been expecting a short hopeless struggle, a leisurely rape, then all evidence into the Tiber. He and Formion had done it so often that any break from routine seemed unfair to him.

Whatever the cloak had enclosed—and he only had the briefest impression of blue-limbed nightmare leaping forth from the enveloping cloth—Dulicius would never see, for its talons closed upon his face in the same instant that the footpad knew something was dreadfully wrong. Needles dipped into his eyeballs, flipping out their lenses, as long talons expertly pierced his larynx and robbed from him the breath he needed to scream. A moment later the same probing talons searched the base of his spine, and then only consciousness—blind, mute, and helpless, but consciousness nonetheless—remained to Dulicius.

For a space he vaguely sensed that he was being carried.

He never knew how long it took Formion to die, but very shortly he would envy his partner that by far more merciful death.

CHAPTER TEN

It was raining again, and that only seemed to force the stench and the smoke of Rome downward onto the city. Still, Lycon gave thanks for a solid roof and a dry place to sit. After a week or more in the field, of chasing shadows and rumors along the banks of the Tiber, it was a welcome relief to rest here in Vonones' office. He had returned to the merchant's compound ostensibly for fresh supplies and additional men; in point of fact Lycon was more interested in seeing his family and enjoying one last night of good food, a soft bed, and Zoe's warm embrace.

The search for the lizard-ape had drawn a total blank—as Lycon had rather suspected and indeed hoped that it would. Vonones had gone to Crispinus with their latest report of failure, and Lycon no longer very much cared whether tomorrow would find him back in the field or hanging from a cross. Perhaps Domitian would order them to Africa; if there were no lizard-apes to be found there, Lycon knew of places where an exile might find a haven beyond the reach of the Emperor's wrath. For now the hunter only knew that he was tired, apathetic, and would cheerfully die tomorrow for one quiet night with his family.

Lycon grunted and massaged the old wound on his thigh. How many years had he carried that now? Too many.

He heard the din of Vonones' return. The entrance of the litter and its bearers inevitably set every animal in the compound into an uproar, but today the disturbance seemed more frenzied than usual. Lycon put it down to nerves. At least it wasn't Domitian's soldiers coming to arrest him.

He was expecting Vonones, but the merchant was the second person to enter the office. Pushing through in front of him was a tall bronzed man— towering easily over Vonones and his servants, and as self-possessed as an Eastern potentate entering his own palace.

"You are Lycon, son of Amphiction," the stranger said as he stepped toward the hunter. He bowed. His torso hinged higher than Lycon would have expected, and the bulges beneath the pair of linen tunics did not seem to be hip bones at all. "I am N'Sumu, an Egyptian hunter from Nubia. I will help you capture the sauropithecus."

"What?" Lycon glanced questioningly toward Vonones, then quickly back again to N'Sumu.

"His orders don't exactly say that, Lycon," said Vonones hurriedly. Lycon had to realize immediately what their relative positions had now become. Otherwise he might react in a fashion that would mean the cross—or the arena—for them both. "His orders say that our lord and god puts him in charge of the hunt, and that all subjects of the Empire, free and slave, will cooperate or face divine displeasure."

"What?" repeated Lycon. He must have fallen asleep.

"My only interest," said N'Sumu smoothly, "is to capture the sauropithecus. The credit, so far as I am concerned, will be yours."

He was speaking Greek. While Lycon had no trouble understanding the Egyptian, the effect was unnerving because N'Sumu's vocabulary and elocution were those of the classic stage. Even his elisions were those of metrical drama rather than of the sliding, careless Common Tongue that was the language of trade throughout even the Latin-speaking West of the Empire.

"Where in Hades did you learn that Greek?" Lycon wondered, dazed and focusing on the immediate puzzle before he moved on to greater ones.

"You prefer Latin?" N'Sumu said in that language. Even his voice was different, and his accent could not have been told from that of a Spaniard on the coast of Ocean.

"Yes, I think I do," Lycon said. "But that doesn't answer my question." He probably would awaken from this dream in another moment, find himself lying in the rain beneath a hedgerow.

"In Tipasa," N'Sumu said nonchalantly. He showed no sign of irritation at either the question or the dumbfounded tone in which it was asked.

His answer was true, as well. A touring company had been performing a series of the plays of Euripides in the theater in Tipasa when N'Sumu reached the city. The chorus master had provided the emissary with an expert if idiosyncratic knowledge of Greek during three hours in a private room.

The Greek had a very different memory of what had gone on during that time, but it explained in an acceptable fashion the way his head and muscles ached the next day.

A Spanish trader, met in the same North African port, had provided him with his Latin. It appeared that N'Sumu should refine that, refine both apparently, due to regional peculiarities. It pleased him, for all the additional effort, that he found it necessary to supplement the store of native languages provided him by the all-knowing Cora, who had programmed his communications nodes with North African tribal dialects. This evidence of their less-than-perfect intelligence of this planet's culture held promise for the emissary's personal intentions here.

"Gods," Lycon muttered. He rubbed the skin of his face with scarred, knobby fingers. "Where did Domitian ever find you?"

"I think we'd do best to get to a restaurant," suggested Vonones smoothly. "To determine how we best can support you, N'Sumu, and do the will of our god and master. Crispinus made it quite clear, Lycon, that the Emperor has complete confidence in N'Sumu's abilities."

N'Sumu smiled. "We can better discuss the things which are necessary in other surroundings, yes. You will lead us to what you think suitable."

His smile, thought Vonones, was *wrong*—but everything was horribly wrong, and if this N'Sumu were the creature of Ahriman, then Ahriman was clearly taking his turn on top as the Wheel turned and Ormadz the Light descended. "Yes," Vonones said aloud. "There's a nice place just down the street. Many a deal I've closed there."

It was only after the three men set out in company that Vonones remembered the deal he had most recently closed in that particular shop. It was for the shipment that had included the sauropithecus.

The restaurant's owner was tasting the soup in one of the stone urns set into the sales counter. He had a critical look on his face and was already beginning to shout: "Hieron! How many peppers did you . . .!"

At sight of Vonones and his companions approaching the counter, which was open to the street along its full length, the man broke off. "Service!" he called toward the back. "A table in the garden for Master Claudius Vonones and his friends? Master Lycon, is it not, sir? And your other companion? Or would you prefer the enclosed dining area, Master Vonones?".

"No, no—the arbor's fine," said the Armenian absently. "Unless N'Sumu would rather . . .?"

"By all means make whatever arrangements you prefer," said N'Sumu easily. "After all, I am a stranger here."

To get to the door that opened onto the back, they walked around the sales counter. Its top was covered with a mosaic of the beasts of the sea savaging one another. The centerpiece between two of the warming urns was a pair of octopuses dismembering a spiny lobster. It was balanced on the other side of the middle urn by sharks tearing a hapless sailor, while moray eels squirmed in for their share of the fragments.

"The fish stew here is excellent," said Lycon, tapping the countertop with the sharks as he passed.

The frescoes in the courtyard had, unlike the counter mosaics, been recently redone. Pride of place on the wall facing the door was a fresco of a chariot race—not in the Circus, built for the purpose with long straightaways, but in the Amphitheater itself. The nearly circular course meant that only the inside track had a prayer of winning. It also meant that when the gates opened and six four-horse chariots leaped for that inside track, there was an absolute certainty of a multiple collision.

The fresco artist had caught several of the high points of such novelty races in his panorama. In one, the driver for the Green Association was whipping his horses literally over the piled-up chariots, horses, and drivers of the other five associations. The painting showed the Green driver lashing at his Gold-tuniced opponent, who was trying to hold himself clear of the wheels by a grip on the frame of the Green chariot.

Further along the same wall, the artist focused on an individual rather than on a general collision. Philodamas, a Blue Association driver with an impressive series of wins, had been thrown forward when a wheel-bearing froze. Normally that would have meant that the driver was pulled along by the reins laced to his left forearm. In this case, however, the reins had gotten looped around the driver's neck. Philodamas had been decapitated spectacularly to the cheers of the crowd, and given such immortality as this fresco could provide.

The table toward which the waiter was leading them was in a grape arbor. A customer was already relaxing there, waiting for his food to be brought. He was moved out with scarcely more

ceremony than that with which an additional stool
was snatched from another table and set beneath
this one.

"How much do you pay these people?" Lycon
asked, as he took the seat farthest within the arbor
and against the back wall. He did not fear men,
particularly, but he had never been comfortable in
an arbor since the night a leopard clawed him
through a blind of woven brush. The four parallel
scars on his buttocks were still quite obvious, ten
years after the event. The scars on his mind showed
only in situations like this one, and then only to
those who, like Vonones, knew him very well.

"I don't expect the service my business requires
to come cheaply," Vonones said airily. "After all, I
pay enough for my animals so that the beastcatchers
who contract with me always see to it that I have
my pick of the healthiest ones." He sighed and let
his mind concentrate on dining—thank the gods,
civilized dining once again.

"And your pick of the exceptional ones as well,"
Lycon said pointedly. Vonones had told him of his
ill-advised purchase here.

"Your orders, gentlemen?" the owner of the shop
interjected from the mouth of the arbor. "Will we
have a meal today, or merely something from our
selection of fine wines?"

Vonones blinked. Lycon had almost ruined his
appetite. The merchant grimaced and returned to
his best professional mood. This was going to be
expensive—always worth the expense to create the
proper impression, of course—and he wasn't going
to let the bad business of the lizard-ape sour his
digestion.

Lycon was already ordering for himself. "Rhod-

ian," he said. "One to two with water." As much
to himself as to his companions, he added: "You
can get it anywhere, and with the resin and seawa-
ter blended to help it travel, it's always just the
same. Right now I don't need any surprises." He
rubbed a sore toe against the nearest of the three
table legs. They were cast bronze, shaggy, and had
feet like those of a goat or satyr.

"The Caecuban, I think—mulled," said Vonones.
He was no more a connoisseur of wines than the
beastcatcher was. Therefore he accepted as the
height of sophistication what the literary snobs
told him—despite the fact that the vineyards of
Southern Latium had decayed to a shadow of their
former quality during the century following Horace's
enthusiastic remarks. It didn't really matter since
Vonones—as with Lycon—would really have preferred the taste of resined wine with which he had
lived for decades in the field.

Now he turned with a smile, he hoped, of quiet
sophistication to the Egyptian and said: "Master
N'Sumu, may I recommend the Caecuban? Urbi-
cius, the owner here, lays in a stock for me
personally."

Lycon had relaxed enough that he had to smother
a snort. That was a laugh—still, let Vonones impress upon this Egyptian, the Emperor's chosen
sauropithecus stalker, that he and Lycon were themselves men of the world.

N'Sumu looked at the merchant without interest and said, "Water for me. Only water." The
filters implanted in his esophagus would keep most
of the local foodstuffs from playing hell with his
digestive processes, but that did not mean that he
intended to press his luck. Nourishment prepared

in private from local raw substances would sustain life for as long as he had to remain here. Certainly the notion of actually eating alongside these animals was more unpleasant than the food itself was likely to be.

The shopowner bowed and snapped his finger to a waiter who scampered off. Bowing again, the owner backed away also. Vonones, thought Lycon, probably spent more lavishly on his wine than he did on his animals. And that brought them back to the business at hand.

"All right," Lycon said bluntly before the merchant could waste more time with small talk. "You've hunted sauropitheci in your own homeland, so I can see you might do a better job catching the lizard-ape than we would. When I'm in the field, I always talk to the local hunters before I set up my own plans. Even when the quarry is an animal I'm familiar with, the local terrain may affect hunting conditions. Good enough—you know lizard-apes and I don't. But that isn't going to help either one of us capture something that's at the bottom of the Tiber by now."

N'Sumu shook his head in a gesture unfamiliar to Lycon and Vonones. It was sometimes difficult to fit particular gestures into the correct cultural setting on a world as fragmented as this one. The bronze-skinned man then bobbed his head downward in the proper sign of negation for the locals whom he now faced.

"There is a very good probability that the sauropithecus is not on the bottom of the river," he said confidently. "The beasts are quite at home in the water, being in some aspects related to fish. And I very much doubt that the beast would have died from its wounds. In my homeland we often find it necessary to chop them into their separate parts to make certain we have killed them, so quickly do they recover from seemingly mortal wounds. Besides, we know what it did on the grain barge. I suggest that you have simply been looking in the wrong place."

Lycon, his face blank and his voice emotionless, said, "We've been looking in a lot of wrong places, then, I guess. We've got a network of informants throughout every farm and hamlet between Rome and the coast, fifteen miles to either side of the Tiber. We've caught or killed maybe a dozen packs of feral dogs, so I wouldn't say the effort was wasted—but it didn't bring us any closer to the damned thing we were looking for."

"Because you weren't looking in Rome," N'Sumu said. This time he suited the correct gesture, a lift of his chin and eyebrows, to the words. "Because you were looking for a wild animal, Lycon, when in reality the creature is very cunning—and practically as human as you are."

N'Sumu was smiling when the waiters arrived with the order. There were five of them: one with a mixing bowl and three cups, one with two jugs of wine, and one with a larger jug of water—dark with the moisture that sweated through its unglazed surface to evaporate and cool the remaining contents. The last pair of waiters carried a freestanding stove of bronze by the handles on either side. They walked gingerly with their burden, because live coals had already been shoveled into the firepot.

The stove was of hollow construction. When the men carrying the piece set it down by the arbor, one of them lifted the lid from the container, which was cast integrally with the firepot. A servant with a wine jug tipped it to fill the stove container. The wine gurgled as it rushed through the passages cast into the walls of the firepot. The thin bronze popped and hissed as the fluid cooled metal which the charcoal had already expanded. The other wine bearer poured from his jug into a cup, while the man with the water filled a second cup for N'Sumu with a flourish.

"We can serve ourselves, boys," said Vonones. He did not offer to pay. That he would do discreetly at ten-day intervals, feeling that the show of credit was more impressive than an open display of silver would have been in a business setting. The waiters—one was the cook, Hieron; the owner must be alone in the front—bowed and backed away obsequiously.

The wine in Lycon's cup merged and blended in the swirls it cut through the previously poured water. Slowly the richer color smoothed itself to blanket the buff glaze of the cup's interior. "Where would you look for a lizard-ape, then?" he asked. "And no more jokes about looking for it in Rome."

The Egyptian hunched forward. "A grain of sand would hide on a beach, would it not? A wisp of straw in a hayfield. Where would something human hide, beastcatcher?"

"Well, now, we don't want to overestimate the lizard-ape's cunning," Vonones scoffed, wondering if they were meant to laugh. He held his cup beneath the spout of the mulling stove and opened the cock. Steaming wine gushed from a bronze faucet cast in the form of a lion's jaws. "The lizard-ape, it *isn't* human, not at all. It couldn't just walk around in the midst of Rome—no more than could an escaped lion, or any other large and dangerous beast."

"I remind you that it isn't like any other beast known to you," said N'Sumu with his dreadful smile. "The sauropithecus is right here. In Rome." He touched the faucet of the mulling stove, opening it just enough in curiosity to jet a thin line of Caecuban onto the brick paving.

"If you know that," said Lycon sarcastically, "then you can tell us how you know." He sipped his diluted wine and savored the bite of resin and alcohol, as he stared at the strange Egyptian.

N'Sumu paused with his fingers still on the lion's head. He met Lycon's eyes. "Simple logic, my friend. We know that it was on the barge. Now where could it have gone from there?"

As N'Sumu talked, he lifted the lid of the container portion of the hollow stove and peered inside. "It did not jump to the bank of the river between here and Ostia. Either bank. It would have been easy to track if it had done that."

Lycon was trying to hold his cup still, but the tension in his grip set the wine adance in the shallow vessel. "True enough. We've found no sign of tracks, and we've had our noses to the ground up and down both banks of the Tiber. That's why I'm convinced the beast must have drowned."

"It seems reasonable that the sauropithecus stayed with the barge even after it had finished with the sailors," said N'Sumu, as he let the lid fall with a rattle of hollow bronze. "If it had been watching other barges pass along the Tiber from its place of concealment, it is cunning enough to have understood their navigation. Whether the helmsman fell overboard in the course of the struggle or whether his body was deliberately let fall into the river by the lizard-ape is an interesting question for speculation. Since there was no report of a large splash being heard that night, I've drawn my own conclusion.

"Regardless of that though, the lizard-ape almost certainly manned the steering oar until it drew close to Rome. At that point it *may* have then left the barge, but more likely it clung to the hull for the remainder of the distance. In the darkness, it might well have even hidden within the hold—it sees very well in the dark, you understand, while the teamsters had only sputtering rushlights for illumination. Quite possibly it left the barge only at the docks. Now the sauropithecus has all of Rome to hide in—and to hunt in."

Lycon downed half his wine. "An interesting theory. But why hasn't the lizard-ape been seen? And even if it's managed to hide, why haven't we heard reports of wholesale slaughter?"

"I warned you that the lizard-ape is extremely cunning," said N'Sumu, as his eyes returned to the mulling stove. He began scraping with one square-cut nail at the soot that coated the interior of the open cylindrical firebox.

"I think it will have found a lair—a ruin, an abandoned building, perhaps the sewers. I can't say where. But if it hunted by night, and killed only for food instead of sport . . . Well, how many murdered corpses greet the dawn from Rome's alleyways, or vanish forever during the night? I tell you again, these lizard-apes are very cunning."

"Well," said Vonones, holding in both palms the cup of warm wine from which he had not drunk.

"Then we need to set up a reporting network in Rome like the one with which we've covered the countryside. That shouldn't be very difficult, Lycon, should it? We'll operate through the Watch commanders, offer rewards for any information that might be in point—mutilated bodies, or reports of disappearances that center upon one particular district. It won't cost us all that much—and if we do manage to learn something concrete about the lizard-ape's whereabouts, we can call in all our men from the countryside."

The hunter spat into the firebox of the mulling stove. The gobbet of saliva struck the bright metal where N'Sumu's finger had scraped away the soot. The spittle hissed in serpentine anger as it boiled away from the hot bronze. Lycon pointed the index and middle fingers of his right hand at N'Sumu's chest. "So you really think the lizard-ape's lurking about right here in Rome? I find that hard to accept, but it's a new tack, and maybe that will impress Domitian for a while at least. You know you're going to be standing there in the arena beside Vonones and me if this proves to be another waste of time."

"It's unlikely that *I* will end up in the arena," said N'Sumu, and the other two understood his threat. "I know I'm right. I'd capture the sauropithecus by myself, but I need good men, and that's why I chose to work through you. My authority from our lord and god is as great as may be required for my purposes. But you have the experience—" the smile spread across his face without showing any teeth beneath the broad lips "—of working in local conditions. And you will have the credit when we succeed."

Lycon swallowed the last of his wine without taking his eyes away from N'Sumu's face. "Then we'd better get started, hadn't we."

Lycon's tone gave Vonones the same feeling as would the sight of a lion in the grass—its body taut, its haunches raised slightly, and no part of it moving but the tip of its tail, quivering like the trigger that would shortly launch the beast upon its prey. But after blinking up at his friend, the merchant's gaze returned to the sizzling bronze that N'Sumu's bare finger had cleansed.

CHAPTER ELEVEN

Lycon was running—running a hopeless race, for he knew his pursuer could run faster by far than he could. He wanted to risk a backward glance to see how close behind it was, but he knew that with that glance he would die.

The problem was these hedgerows. It was impossible to run when he had to crawl through all these hedgerows, one after another. Their branches already were slippery with blood, and their thorns tore at his flesh as Lycon plunged through. He told them he couldn't run any faster, but Domitian danced easily ahead of him—leaping over the hedges on his scrawny legs—and N'Sumu raced alongside him, laughing at him past his deformed smile.

"Old man! Old man! Old man! Old man!"

He had to keep running. He was too slow, too old—and he desperately feared the thing that pursued him.

There sat Vonones. The Armenian's stout chest had been folded open like a broken loaf of wine-soaked bread, and his hands kept fumbling inside his chest cavity in search of his missing lungs.

"Why didn't you kill it?" Vonones asked in a tone of betrayal. He held out a dripping bag of coins. "Didn't I pay you well?"

"I have to get through this hedge!" Lycon explained, plunging forward into the next thorny barrier.

Pamphilus, the first man he had ever killed in the arena, wagged his head back and forth upon its broken neck, and said: "Here's the door." But Lycon had seen the retiarius' net swimming through the air, and he bolted headfirst through the hedgerow instead.

The lizard-ape was waiting for him this time, and Lycon cursed himself for having paused to talk with dead men while the lizard-ape had vaulted the hedgerow. The lizard-ape had Domitian's face, and N'Sumu and Lacerta were carrying his bright-blue palanquin back and forth about the grain barge.

"You should have killed me when you had your chance," said the blue-scaled Emperor. His long talons reached out for Lycon's face, and needles of agony drove into the hunter's skull.

"Lycon! Lycon! Wake up!" Zoe was shaking him. "You're having another bad dream! Wake up! Please!"

Lycon opened his eyes, gaping at her stupidly. The nightmare was still full in his mind. "What . . . ?"

"A bad dream, Lycon." Zoe's face was taut with concern. "You're having another bad dream."

Lycon blinked into the darkness, recognized the familiar surroundings of their bedroom. He was

sweaty and he was cold, and the familiar shaki-
ness was returning.

"Can I get you something?" Zoe begged. She
was slimmer than since they had married and
more lovely than Lycon had ever remembered.

"Wine!" he muttered thickly. "Yes, wine. Bring
me more wine."

Zoe slipped out of bed and opened the door. The
lizard-ape was waiting for her there, and it tore off
her face as casually as a man pulls off his hat.

"*Zoe!*" Lycon's scream pierced the night.

"Lycon! Wake up!" Zoe was shaking him. "You're
having another bad dream! Wake up now!" At her
breast, Glauce was wailing out her protest.

This time Lycon swung his feet to the floor and
sat up—rubbing his face as if to scrape the nightmare from his eyes. Zoe anxiously massaged his
shoulders and back, trying to ease the tension there.
Lycon considered the opaque greyness within the
apartment light shaft beyond his bedroom window,
decided it was close enough to dawn. Pulling away
from Zoe, he stood up and began to dress in the
darkness. He would not risk sleep again this night.

"Where are you going?" Probably there would
be no more sleep for Zoe, either. She was crooning
to their daughter, trying to soothe her as well.

"Over to the compound. Vonones will be there
soon, and maybe there'll be something to report
from the Watch. Maybe something from our men
who are still positioned between here and Portus.
It was N'Sumu's great idea that we concentrate
our search here in Rome."

He found her face in the dark for a quick kiss.
"At least I get home nights now."

"I'd almost rather have you away on some collecting expedition," Zoe murmured. "I keep thinking you'd be safer off in some far wilderness, stalking the beasts you know."

"There's always some new beast to be found, if you go looking," Lycon tried to reassure her. "And N'Sumu is in charge now—at least he thinks he is. He's hunted lizard-apes since he was old enough to crawl."

Lycon couldn't imagine N'Sumu as a child, although the fantasy of a crawling N'Sumu suddenly conjured forth an unpleasant image of the tall Egyptian—bronze-scaled and wriggling on his belly like a monstrous man-snake.

"Have Geta bring Alexandros to the compound, once he's had his breakfast," Lycon said, changing the direction of his thoughts.

"Lycon! Won't it be too dangerous?" Zoe protested. "Alexandros is just a boy!"

"Time he becomes a man, then," Lycon told her. "Besides, there's no danger. Vonones' people can show him around the compound—let him get a close look at the beasts his father hunts. No more faggot schoolmasters for my son!"

"But I'm not sure Alexandros will want to go!"

"I didn't ask about what he wants to do! See that he's there! Chances are I'll be sitting on my ass in the office with Vonones all day anyway. I'll keep an eye on Alexandros. Stop worrying about the boy."

Lycon didn't add that the actual danger arose from just this sort of inactivity. Domitian's patience—even with his imported lizard-ape specialist—was not going to last much longer. If they couldn't produce a sauropithecus for the Emperor soon . . .

Well, he and Vonones had discussed it often enough. The merchant had discreetly arranged to have a ship in readiness at Portus. They might be able to flee beyond Domitian's wrath, but Lycon didn't like to think about having to try it. In the field he had only his own life to consider—that was quite acceptable—but if he failed here, Domitian would spare not even the lowliest household slave.

CHAPTER TWELVE

Carretius the rent-taker climbed the stairs to the sixth level between his two assistants, Smiler and Ox. Carretius was wheezing. It was growing dark, this was the third and last building on the day's rounds, and each flight of stairs grew longer as the day dragged on.

Besides, he'd been a fool at one of the initial stops. A cobbler rented a nice ground floor location for his shop and workroom that should have guaranteed a decent living, had the fellow not insisted on drinking all his profits—and the rent money. In a voice thick with tears and redolent of the heavy, sweet wine lees to which poverty had reduced him, he had offered the services of his daughter in exchange for the rent money. Carretius had badgered him down to an extension—a minor misjudgement for which he would have to account next month when the craftsman inevitably missed another payment, and the bailiffs were sent to seize the fellow's chattels.

As her father had promised—saying that he

should know—the girl was quite accomplished. Too accomplished for a man of Carretius' flabbiness and years. He had only a hazy remembrance of that morning's dalliance, and now he was not only running behind schedule, but his back ached beyond endurance.

The close weather amplified the odor of the huge waste jar at the bottom of the stairwell. It held the contents of the chamber pots—at least those of the tenants sophisticated enough to understand what a chamber pot was for. The upper levels, not only of the units Carretius serviced but of all apartment blocks in Rome, primarily held displaced country folk of one sort or another. One lot of Numidians had been found keeping a live sheep on their balcony, planning to slaughter it for a wedding feast in a day or two. They had objected strongly when the animal was removed, but that sort of discussion was what Ox and Smiler were along for.

Smiler led on the stairs as he always did. Carretius himself, with the wooden-backed wax tablets of the account clattering on waist thongs, was in the middle. Ox closed the rear. He carried the collected rents in a leather pouch hung against his chest on a neck strap. The real advantage of Ox's size was that he literally blocked the staircases in the buildings Carretius serviced. It was impossible for a footpad or desperate tenant to reach the rent-taker from behind.

Nor was Carretius worried about a frontal attack. Smiler was a nondescript fellow, a Gaul by birth Carretius suspected. The rent-taker had never asked; questions about his assistant's background were at best impolitic. Smiler's nickname—and the only name by which he was known in the city—had nothing to do with his expression. He was a generally morose man but no stone-face, especially when he had downed enough wine to loosen up a little. But when his hand moved just so, the razor he carried could open a throat all the way around before the victim even felt the sting of the metal.

However, there was no potential for danger on the sixth floor here. The whole area, a loft whose ceiling was the tiled roof and the laths on which the tiles were laid, had been rented for over a decade by a white-bearded patriarch named Mephibaal. He and a woman who was either his wife or mother housed a troop of beggars, whom they directed with a rigid discipline of a sort from which the Jewish revolutionaries of twenty-five years earlier could have benefited.

Carretius dealt with no one but Mephibaal himself or sometimes the woman of whose name he was as innocent as he had been when the couple first rented the loft. The type and numbers of the subtenants would normally have been a matter of concern, even on the top floor. Rogues too poor to own a brazier had been known to cook over sand spilled on the bare floor boards, and the chance of saving a building if a fire took hold was no better than Carretius' personal chance of deification. Mephibaal would not permit any such nonsense, let alone allowing one of his charges to get out of hand to the point of trying to rob the rent-taker. In fact, a detail of the beggars on the sixth floor carried the chamber pots every morning to the shop of a nearby wool-finisher. The urine was used in the fulling process, and Mephibaal collected a modest commission for what would otherwise have been refuse. Carretius both admired and envied Mephibaal's industry.

The door at the stairhead was a solid one, set there by the tenant himself—more to restrain his charges than out of fear of burglars. Smiler knocked on it with his left hand. It was late in the evening. Even here at the top, very little light ever came through the slats of the cupola that covered and ventilated the staircase. They would have to light a torch on the way back.

"They don't answer," said Smiler puzzledly. He rubbed his knuckles against his cheek instead of the opposite palm. "I hear them inside, but they don't answer." He openly displayed the razor which was normally covered, with his hand, beneath a fold of his tunic.

"Do you suppose something happened to Mephibaal?" Carretius wondered aloud. He was too tired at the moment to respond with real enthusiasm to any unexpected difficulty, but he saw the dim crescent of the blade in Smiler's hand. "Pollux! He always seemed like he was older than Numa, but I never thought he'd die in bed. Do you suppose that lot have murdered him?"

Ox looked up stolidly at the two smaller men. "Should I?" he asked in a voice thick with his German accent. His short hair was so pale that it seemed to disappear in bright sun, but here on the stairs he seemed to be wearing a casque of fine gold. When he hunched, the points of his shoulders lifted but he still had no neck—only a triangle of muscle where lesser men had necks.

"Wait a minute," the rent-taker said. His mind had aroused itself from dull fatigue to a state of general concern. He took a tinder pump and a wax candle from his wallet. "Knock again," he ordered, as he rotated the thumb-sized pump to unlock it.

As Smiler, his face gone blank, obeyed, Carretius gave the bronze piston two quick strokes, then withdrew it. The shaved bay twigs in the chamber, heated by the sudden compression of the air, flared into open flame. The rent-taker ignited the wick of his candle—a poor light, but more practical to carry against the need than was a lamp with oil sloshing in the bowl. His fingers were trembling, and when he had a proper candleflame he dropped the pump onto the landing. The tube and piston were hot from use as well as the resulting tiny fire, and at the moment Carretius did not have the patience to put the pump carefully back in his wallet.

"All right," he said to Ox, glancing to see that the tinder was only a dying glow on the boards.

Both of the smaller men flattened against the lath and plaster partitions as the grinning German advanced. Smiler held his razor vertical beside his right ear. Its edge and its wielder's eyes were equally chill in the candlelight.

Ox tested the panel with his fingertips. It was meant to open inward. Smiler fretted impatiently, as uncomfortable with the big man's plodding deliberation as was Carretius himself. The door creaked beneath Ox's touch, and there was an expression of childish delight on Ox's innocent face.

"Open it, damn you!" Carretius demanded.

Ox slammed his palm against the point on the door at which he had felt the resistance of a bar. The staples that held the bar in place within ripped free at the impact. Ox shouldered the sagging panel inside, ahead of his rush. Carretius and Smiler lunged in at either heel—half expecting the on-slaught of up to a score of beggars, desperate from the murder of their master.

The smell was not expected.

The loft was crisscrossed by the studs that sup-ported the tile roof above, but it had no interior walls. The stench permeated the loft's entire expanse—a miasma that choked them despite their acquaintance with the filth commonplace in such dwellings.

The candle's circumscribed illumination hid the outstretched interior. There were windows—in fact, the outer walls were comprised of removable wicker screens in order to reduce the weight upon the exterior walls beneath—but none of them was open. There were rat-scuttling sounds, but not the antici-pated assault by beggars. What it looked like, hud-dled on the floor and even hanging from the rafters, could not possibly be. . . .

"Get some more light in here!" Carretius shouted to his henchmen. The dagger he always carried, but had never had to draw, was free in his left hand as he held the candle high in his right.

Ox threw down the door panel and started across the creaking floor toward the screens. He shouted and snatched at the back of his neck. Wood splin-tered as Ox's berserk rush carried him through a roof stud.

Smiler spun about, searching for an unseen threat. His razor flicked through something in mid-air that was neither a bat nor a pigeon. Something else that had clung to the tiles overhead dropped silently onto Smiler's face.

Carretius screamed in terror—an instant before he felt the pains that lanced through both ankles.

He bent and hacked with the point of his dagger at the agony, oblivious of the fact that the blade was cutting his own flesh as well.

A new rush of pain seemed to dip Carretius' right hand into molten lead. He flung away the candle, killing the light. The rent-taker's throat was already locked in a cry for which his lungs no longer held breath, but he straightened and slashed his weapon toward the unseen bulk that was savaging his right hand. The blow brought relief, even though the steel gouged along his wrist and the back of his hand—ripping *something* loose from his flesh.

For an instant, the only light in the loft was the dim rectangle of the doorway through which the men had entered. Then there was an explosion of laths and wicker as Ox plunged blindly through fragments of screen, out into the twilight and a fifty-foot drop to the street below. Carretius could not possibly have scrambled across the stretch of timbers and horror between him and that new opening, even if it held hopes of anything but a fatal drop. The doorway was only a few yards behind him, but as he turned both the rent-taker's ankles gave way. It was more than mere pain—the Achilles tendons were severed. Carretius crashed to the floor—still trying to crawl toward the door.

A figure appeared in silhouette against the open doorway. It was small and hunched—a woman with the tail of her mantle flipped over her head for propriety's sake, or a short man in a hooded Gallic cloak. The figure paused, just inside the loft and not quite close enough for Carretius' desperate hands to touch.

"Help me!" the rent-taker shouted, knowing the

other could not see him in the darkness. His calves prickled as tiny needles advanced, tearing into his flesh. The pain cut through the anesthesia of his fear. Dimly he was aware of other tiny assailants, dropping unseen onto his writhing body.

"Pull me out of here, and you'll never want for anything!"

The figure stepped past the rent-taker and disappeared as it moved out of the light. Carretius clutched toward the whisper of legs on heavy cloth—the only sound the figure made—but his bloody right hand touched nothing, or felt nothing it touched.

The figure reappeared. It was carrying the door panel that Ox had flung away as the three men had burst into the loft. The open doorway, the last hope in the blackness of Hades, disappeared as the figure carefully fitted the door back into place. There was a gentle tapping, as a scrap of timber was wedged between jamb and panel to hold the door in place until permanent repairs could be made. Carretius felt, rather than saw, the figure as it turned back to him.

The jagged touch of unseen climbing things had already shredded the rent-taker's garments across his back. His ragged breath was the only sound in the foetid loft—that and a scrambling, tearing sound, as of many crabs in a wooden trap.

He still had time to wonder what had become of Smiler, and in another moment he knew.

CHAPTER THIRTEEN

"He's going fast," said the Watch Centurion, as if Lycon needed help in judging serious wounds. "Maybe it's not what you're after, but I thought maybe—you know—that thousand sesterces reward you're offering for evidence of killings that don't look like your usual brawls and muggings and the like."

"You may have just earned it, Silvius," said Lycon, uncinching his belt so that his tunic could flap and cool him as he bent toward the victim. They had been held to the pace of Vonones' chairmen and the pair of lantern-carrying guides leading them all. In daylight and by a route with which he was familiar, Lycon would have run on ahead of them.

The big man was obviously near death—should be dead already from the injuries suffered in his fall. Perhaps with a body that huge it took time for the brain to know it was useless. Lycon remembered the giant German warriors he had seen in his youth—pierced by a dozen fatal wounds and still shambling forward to slay, froth on their lips and death frozen in their eyes.

The Watch station was converted from what had been a bakery on the corner of an apartment block—two rooms on the ground floor, and a connected upper room in which on-duty personnel could sleep until needed. Although public order was a concern, the fourteen battalions of the Watch were intended primarily for fire-fighting duties, despite their military organization and helmets. The front room in which the dying man now lay was steamy and odorous from the sausages that a few of the men on duty were grilling for supper. They watched and munched, more curious about Lycon than they were about what was, after all, just another corpse —or soon would be.

"All over me," the dying giant whispered. His eyes were open but unfocused, so he probably did not see Lycon bending over him. "They just kept coming. I hit them and it was like knives, like knives . . ."

"His name is Ox, and he and another bad one work with a rent-taker named Carretius," Silvius explained. "Don't know where they are, but it seems Ox fell off a roof or out of a window or something. Broke his fall somehow, and we found him crawling along the street out of his head from pain. Couldn't have happened too far from here—can't get too far with your arms and legs all busted up, no matter how strong a man you are. But it's these wounds he's got all over his back that puzzled me, so I thought maybe you'd want to see."

"Wine!" Lycon called. "We've got to get him to talk!"

N'Sumu's long-fingered hand reached past Lycon

and raised the dying man's right arm. The flayed palm and the obvious break in both bones of the forearm could have been results of the fall. The cuts on the upper side of the arm had been made by dozens of piercing claws that had sunk an inch or more into the powerful arm before they were dragged free. They were sharp enough to cut rather than simply tear. Lycon thought of a net tied with fishhooks—fishhooks with their inside curve sharpened to a razor edge. The wounds covered his arms and shoulders.

Silvius handed Lycon a scrap of wine-soaked cloth. It was a rag that had been used to polish brass, but at this point that mattered as little to the victim as it did to Lycon. The hunter swabbed at the dying man's mouth. The astringent wine rinsed blood momentarily from broken lips. Lycon wrung the cloth, trying to get the man to swallow a little wine.

"Mephibaal was never no trouble," the dying man whispered. "Why'd he want to do this? Like knives . . ."

The three of them—Vonones, Lycon, and N'-Sumu—had been dining together to discuss a week's accumulation of useless rumors and wasted searches, when the messenger from the Watch station had appeared at Vonones' ground-floor suite. The merchant had thrown a cloak over his tunic of pastel blue silk—Lycon would have permitted him no time to change, even had Vonones wanted to.

Now Vonones grasped the Centurion's shoulder—his grip firm with excitement. "Mephibaal," Vonones whispered urgently. "Find out who he is—and where he lives!"

"We went in when he didn't open the door," Ox

mumbled. A heavy leather strap was sewn over the shoulders of his tunic and down the front, and the rent purse nestled upon his chest like a well-fed tick.

Lycon indicated the purse. "Well, we know he wasn't mugged and robbed."

"Ox?" laughed one of the Watch members as he strolled closer. "Nobody'd go for Ox. Not Hercules. Even without Smiler there to change their faces with his razor."

"We're close," said N'Sumu, trying to examine the back of the dying man's neck. Ox resisted his efforts. "He must have discovered the lizard-ape's lair."

"Couldn't see," whispered Ox. "Couldn't see . . ." The big shattered man lunged upward from the bare couch as N'Sumu tried to lift him. Lycon tried instinctively to hold him back. Ox swept him aside unnoticed, flinging the beastcatcher across the room.

"Got to get *out!*" the dying man shouted, in a spray of blood and spittle. His eyes were open, but they saw nothing in this world or the next. Ox took two steps, and the sound of the bone ends grating in his right thigh was audible even over the cries of the startled men around him. He struck a wall, rebounded, and struck it again—as if the bright splash of pulmonary blood he had coughed onto the stucco at his first impact were a target for the second. The back of the big man's tunic had been shredded by sharp claws, and bright bone showed yellow beneath the bloody tatters.

When his knees buckled, Ox sagged like a half-filled wine skin. His head fell forward onto his chest, and he might have been praying for the first and last time in his life. A circular hole the size of a pigeon's egg gaped from the back of his neck. Blood oozed but did not spurt from reopened wounds.

Lycon swore as he got to his feet from where Ox had sent him sprawling. He was not so much concerned that the man had died without saying much, as he was that Ox apparently had had very little to say. The attack had been unseen and unexpected. Perhaps it had been the work of the lizard-ape—N'Sumu thought so—but the question remained: where had it taken place?

The Centurion had stepped to the inner door of the station. "Basileus!" he shouted. "Check the codices for someone named Mephibaal in this district. Hurry!"

The patrolman who had been standing near tapped Silvius on the shoulder. "Mithras, sir," he said. "Don't worry about that. Everybody knows where old Mephi lives: the whole top floor of the building Hieronymos the tax-farmer owns, across from the Baths of Pulcher."

Silvius' eyes narrowed. "Where the dice game meets?" he asked.

"Other direction," said another Watch member. "But Castor—that's where they brought Ox from. Could've jumped from the seventh floor as well as from a roof, like we figured."

"Sixth floor," said a short man with Hamitic features, who trotted from the inner room with a volume of square-cut papyrus sheets open in his hands. "Mephibaal, son of Jeroboam, freedman of . . ."

"Basileus," said Lycon, pointing a finger toward the clerk though his eyes were on the Centurion.

"Shut up for a minute. Silvius—can you locate the room we want?"

The Centurion nodded. "Yes, yes. But there were to be one thousand sesterces. . . ?"

"N'Sumu," said the beastcatcher, turning his gaze. "You're in charge. Tonight, or do we wait for daylight?"

"You'll get your money," Vonones murmured to Silvius. "Maybe a lot more—if you help us and be quick about it."

N'Sumu shrugged. "Daylight would be better," he said, "but if we wait—who knows? The sauropithecus might shift its lair. Certainly it *will* shift it if it thinks this one could have led others to it." He waved toward the huge, half-flayed corpse.

"I think it may have difficulty moving just now, but . . ." During the pause, the bronzed face was as still and false as a statue's profile. "Yes. Best we go after it at once."

Lycon rubbed his face with his hands. "Right," he said without looking up, his palms covering his eyes and mouth. He brushed his hands down sharply. "Vonones," he said in a crisp, emotionless voice. "We'll use your litter bearers for messengers. I've got people waiting at your compound with gear. We'll need nets with the men too.

"Yes, and we'll need your troop," he added in an aside to the Centurion of the Watch. "Don't worry. You'll be paid for it—and our lord and god will have your guts out if there's a moment's delay."

"I said, we'll go at once," said N'Sumu. "Ourselves." His expression was unreadable, but there was a clear note of command in the words.

"We'll go when I say we're ready," snapped Lycon. "I've seen this beast work, and you haven't.

And I don't mean to be gutted like a perch—or end up like this one." He toed Ox's corpse without looking down at it.

"You *have* been at close quarters with these lizard-apes before, of course—haven't you, N'-Sumu?"

N'Sumu seemed about to assert his authority, then backed down. "Make your plans, beastcatcher," he said. "Then *I* will deal with the situation in the way best suited."

He continued to stare at Lycon as the hunter scribbled orders onto pieces of papyrus supplied by the Watch Centurion. Vonones felt his dinner roil uneasily in his belly, but his fear was not only of the lizard-ape.

CHAPTER FOURTEEN

From the street where Lycon waited with the others, the preparations on the rooftops around them were invisible. An occasional wedge of broken tile pattered between outthrust balconies to smash on the pavement, and the fitful glow of lanterns overhead provided uncertain evidence of the men who moved into position above the streets.

There were laws regulating set-back from the street against building height—intended to guarantee sunlight for every stretch of pavement in order to burn away the noxious effluvia that would otherwise, according to the best medical opinion, propagate themselves in shadows. Save for a handful of major boulevards, however, the laws were an excuse for Watch commanders to extort bribes instead of being genuine subjects for enforcement. There had been nothing about this portion of the north slope of the Aventine Hill that precluded the builders from developing it as they pleased—and at a price.

So the close-shouldering apartment blocks hid

the direct sun from the streets except at noon on certain days. It also meant that a fire in one building involved potential disaster for the region or the city as a whole—as had already happened twice since a blaze had given Nero room enough for a sprawling palace and grounds in Rome's center. So far as Lycon was concerned at the moment, the interlocking balconies and eaves might prevent him from directing his men by sight, but this amounted to no more of a handicap than the scrub or high grass in which he normally worked. The narrow interstices made it possible to reach the roof of their objective without going through the top floor that Mephibaal leased.

Had leased until recently, at any rate. Lycon wiped his palms on his tunic, not for the first time.

A three-note call drifted down from above. It was from no certain direction by the time it bounced through the maze of walls and projections.

"That's Hippias," said Vonones, gripping the stock of his whip with his hands and firmly enough to flex it into a bow. "They're all in position."

N'Sumu waited with the placid arrogance of one of the huge stone dolphins at the horseraces, ready to tip and signal completion of a lap but utterly disdainful of all other matters of human endeavor. Lycon noticed that when the Egyptian turned his gaze upward toward darkness, his eyeballs frosted into dull opacity. The beastcatcher thought that it might be a trick of the light, until the same thing happened when N'Sumu looked directly down the street past him, and his eyeballs gleamed, dulled, and gleamed normally again without any change in external circumstances. N'Sumu grinned starkly when he noticed Lycon's attention, but he made no comment about what the Greek thought he had seen.

Lady Fortune, Lycon thought, we need you now and always. But especially now. "Right," he said aloud. "Time we made *our* move." His fingertips checked the net slung over his left shoulder, then the dense ivory baton he had slipped through the sash of his tunic in preference to a weapon with an edge. "Let's go."

There were seven in the party that Lycon led up the only staircase of the apartment block. Two of the men were Vonones' slaves, recent arrivals from Ethiopia who did not even speak Greek. They would be a deadly liability on the roof, where coordination was crucial and only shouted orders were possible in the darkness. They could, however, accompany Lycon on the direct assault, carrying large lanterns. One of the slaves was directly behind Lycon on the stairs, holding his light aloft and so close that the back of the hunter's neck quivered with the heat of the triple lampwicks flaming within their cage of lead and horn. The other Ethiopian brought up the rear.

Most of the Watch unit, with their Centurion, were on the roofs with the bulk of Vonones' crew and the additional specialists Lycon had hired from the Amphitheater for such need as this. Two patrolmen accompanied the beastcatcher up the stairs. Except for spears, they wore the full military equipment that was normally a matter for parades and riots only. Lycon was not certain how much use the men's laminated-linen body armor and shields of spruce plywood would be, since protection had to be offset against weight and the lizard-ape's awesome quickness. Still, it was worth trying tonight, since only N'Sumu professed to have any knowledge of the beast they stalked.

N'Sumu himself followed the first lantern-bearer. The Egyptian carried no weapon at all, and he walked with both hands outthrust before him as if in benediction. His palms were of the same richly tanned, almost bronze shade as the rest of his skin, and Lycon again shivered at the unbidden thought of some huge bronze serpent looping its way along the branches of a jungle forest. Lycon had heard of certain warriors who were skilled in some sort of open-hand combat technique, but he thought such men were said to live beyond the Empire's easternmost frontiers, not in the lands south of the Nile's first cataract. If N'Sumu chose to wrestle with the lizard-ape barehanded, that was fine by Lycon.

Vonones was directly behind N'Sumu. The Armenian merchant was so nervous that Lycon could hear his sandals catch and skip as he repeatedly missed his footing. Vonones need not have come at all, and certainly there was no reason for him to be one of the group that entered the loft. He had insisted, however. With so much at stake, Vonones was determined to see it through personally, whatever the risks. Lycon hoped he wouldn't get in the way.

They had not attempted to evacuate the lower floors of the building. The noise and confusion would have been colossal—and in the event their supposition about the creature's lair was incorrect, the probable riot caused by the affair might have led Domitian to indulge one of his whims. There were ragged men and women sleeping at each landing. Lycon and the boots of the patrolmen prodded them into the hallways where others of the very poorest already huddled. The presence of those folk was mildly troublesome—they would almost certainly drift back to block the stairs down which the assault party might need to retreat abruptly. Still, they proved that the creature had not made its escape in this direction when it heard the boots and murmured orders of the men taking up positions on the surrounding roofs. If the lizard-ape indeed had made its lair here, Lycon assumed it would normally reach its lair from the adjacent rooftops. By night it could easily leap across from roof to roof—silently, unseen . . .

The top flight of stairs was closer to being a ladder of rough poles than a proper staircase. There was no railing, but the wall was worn and slimed by the hands of a decade of beggars. The lantern-bearer following Lycon cursed and stumbled and cursed again: some of his obscenities, at any rate, were Greek. The remainder of the group, especially Vonones and the heavily-armed patrolmen, were also having difficulties. N'Sumu, though graceless, mounted the stairs without actually touching the wall over which his open hand glided in readiness to brace him.

Lycon moved up the steps on his tip-toes, only the faint creak of the wood beneath his hobnails betraying his ascent. The beastcatcher held his net in both hands, swinging it waist-high and ready for an underarm cast in an emergency. It wouldn't stop the lizard-ape for long, but anything that would slow the beast down was worth trying.

The door beyond the topmost landing was a solid one, out of keeping with the upper levels of this or any other apartment block. If the sauropithecus *had* chosen this particular place for its lair, the choice was either a very lucky one for it—or else luck had nothing to do with it.

It's nearly as human as you are, N'Sumu had said.

"We may have to cut this down," Lycon whispered toward the men behind him. "Didn't expect anything this sturdy, or I'd have brought axes."

There was scant room for three on the landing proper. Lycon had half expected N'Sumu to squeeze aside and let pass the Watch members with their swords. Instead the Egyptian himself stepped to the door and ran his palms over its framework. The gesture was not casual, but rather a precise survey of the edges of the panel where they butted against the jamb and where, presumably, the bar or bolts were engaged. So far as Lycon could tell, N'Sumu did not actually touch the heavy wood.

The slave with the lantern cowered aside with a look of rigid fear—directed at N'Sumu rather than what might be beyond the door. Neither of the Ethiopians had a good grasp of what was going on—they were present to carry lights, and nobody had bothered to explain the business further. It was reasonable enough that the slave would not regard their quarry with the taut anxiety of those who knew what they were seeking—but why the fear of N'Sumu? It was almost as if the slave, who might well know the Egyptian peoples of the Nile south of Elephantine Island as familiarly as Lycon did Thracians, nonetheless found N'Sumu both unique and unpleasant.

"It's wedged in place," N'Sumu decided. "Not firmly at all. If you want, I think that I can . . ."

Lycon shook his head in negation. A drop of

sweat from the climb stung his eye and made him blink. Vonones panted two steps down from the landing. Behind and below him on the stairs, the backlighted bronze helmets of the Watch patrolmen gleamed like halos. One of the men had drawn his sword and was trying to brace himself upright against the wall with his elbow.

"You," said Lycon, pointing over the rolled and ready net at the lantern-bearer. He spoke a sort of bush dialect that worked well enough in the field and which the Ethiopian understood as much through Lycon's tone as his words. "Jump in and put your back to the wall to the left side of the doorway, while I go to the right. Any delay, any foul-up, and I'll feed you to a hyena. Believe me. One bite at a time."

The slave nodded with his lower lip sucked between his teeth. It would be worth any unknown danger to get away from N'Sumu.

"All right, then," said Lycon. He kicked in the door and it fell with a crash like that of a catapult firing.

The lantern-bearer followed orders with an alacrity that impressed Lycon himself. N'Sumu was inside as abruptly, his eyes blank as marble, and his palms again outstretched.

Lycon spun within to the right, because he was right-handed and his direction of movement would aid a cross-body cast of his net. The shadows cast by the lantern slid across walls and beams in a counterfeit of activity, but for a moment only the newcomers themselves moved in the low-ceilinged attic.

The man who was already sprawled just inside the doorway certainly did not move. He had worn the usual two tunics, the inner one of a fine close weave of linen, before it was stripped away in threads and tendrils. Now he lay in a semicircle of fluff. His face was upturned and frozen in a startled expression. His arms and torso were naked, and from his hips on down all that remained were bare bones that gleamed yellow beneath the dried blood and thin patches of adherent flesh. Blood still oozed from the exposed tangle of guts and organs laid bare above his pelvis.

Most of the other corpses humped against the floor of the loft had not been stripped with anything like the same playful enthusiasm. In general, the clothing—rags to begin with mostly—had been slashed apart crudely, and the flesh beneath treated in a similar fashion. Lycon could not guess how many corpses—most of them no more than picked and scattered bones—were strewn about the loft. The number itself, a hundred or so perhaps, would not be particularly startling to one who had seen a thousand bodies dragged from the Amphitheater on a long afternoon. Those had been fresh, though— and most of these ... such flesh that remained had heated to dripping liquescence under the roof tiles.

Always before, Lycon would have said that a smell was something you got used to. He did not want to believe that now. Not even the accustomed stench of Rome's slums could have continued to mask the presence of this charnel house much longer.

Vonones and the two patrolmen burst into the loft behind N'Sumu. The second lantern-bearer stopped in the doorway, his nerve failing. Vonones snarled a command, and the slave entered—increasing the amount of light available without in the least improving the scene it displayed.

"They're," said Vonones, "they're all . . ." He slashed out with his whip, not aiming at anything in particular.

"Is it here?" one patrolman demanded as he twisted—fearful that the sideguards of his helmet were keeping him from seeing the taloned demon that approached him.

Recovering from the sight, Lycon jerked his own head to the side. Nothing seemed to move—only N'Sumu, who was walking cautiously toward the man who hung from a roof truss, held there by a swath of something that seemed more like spun metal than any fabric, even silk, N'Sumu's hands were raised and his eyes, when Lycon stepped alongside, were dull.

"By Isis, that's Smiler," muttered the other patrolman. "Ox's partner, and—why that's Carretius!" He pointed toward the half-consumed body whose torso lay before the entrance—only now was the man's memory grasping some sort of awareness out of this nightmarish scene.

"What . . . ?" Lycon said to N'Sumu, and something leaped at them from the hollowed ribcage of one of the corpses.

The shadow thrown by the lanterns distorted and exaggerated both the creature and the motion. It was that exaggeration that called Lycon's attention to the movement while it was within the capacity of his reflexes to respond to it. The creature that launched itself toward his eyes was not the lizard-ape he feared, nor yet was it anything that he had ever seen before.

It was cat-sized and perhaps quicker than a cat,

but its leap was a long one—long enough for Lycon
to react. Lycon's net, cast by reflex, opened like a
spider's web catching the sun. The bronze weights,
as delicate as the silken cords themselves, held the
net in a momentary orb that collapsed around the
leaping thing in midair. The motion with which
the beastcatcher had cast his net, still gripped by
the cord that pursed shut the outer edge against
the weight it held, carried the furious creature
safely past Lycon's left shoulder.

The net had been intended to tangle the lizard-
ape for the minimal instant Lycon might need to
press his attack or to escape. This creature—whatever it was—was well within the size of the prey
for which the net had been designed. His unexpected success gave Lycon a momentary thrill of
triumph—one that stuck in his throat as he saw
the floor and walls of the loft seeth with sudden
movement like bubbles rising in a cesspool.

Something the size of the first creature twisted
in the air toward N'Sumu. An instant before touching him, its blue-scaled body exploded in a burst
of light as green as spring hay. In the fluff that
remained of Carretius' linen garment crawled a
dozen bright blue things no larger than baby rab-
bits and fully as blind, but with the bloody determination of so many gadflies. One of them clamped
to the ankle of the leading lantern-bearer, and his
shriek was louder than that of the two patrolmen—
who knew from experience what the hurtling lantern meant in a place like this.

Smiler hung with his mouth and muscles slack.
Lycon had assumed the man was as dead as those
he had accompanied here, Ox and the halved corpse
facing the doorway. Now Smiler's eyelids opened

and his head rocked back, trying to tear loose from the shimmering band of stuff that clamped and supported him. One of the dangling arms lifted and pointed toward the beastcatcher. There was a touch on Lycon's sandal, something crawling, and his hobnails ground it against the flooring as he started for the hanging man.

Smiler's throat convulsed. Then his lips moved and spewed not words but blue-shimmering larvae the size of men's fingers—dozens of them, gouting up to flop onto the wood and writhe on vestigial legs toward the man who had just approached. Blood sprayed from Smiler's lips and throat together as the entire substance of his body seemed to convulse and give way to pass more of the things that had just hatched within his living flesh.

There was a second green flash—something incomprehensible that N'Sumu seemed to conjure forth. Lycon had no time to think about it, as Vonones' whip popped close enough to draw blood from the hunter's ear—ripping a cat-sized horror that had just dropped down from a roof tile and onto Lycon's head. The thing in Lycon's net was squirming; he swung it against a pillar to quiet it, as he jumped back toward the door and safety.

The clot of men blocking the opening was to be expected, but the effect two men carrying shields would have on the tight doorway was a shock even to Lycon, as he caromed off the back of one of the patrolmen.

"The mother isn't here!" shouted N'Sumu. His right hand moved as if to fend something away. Although there was no visible motion beyond that, things curled off a truss ten feet away like spiders

swung through a flame. A nimbus the color of
copper burning danced over the timber and nearby
tiles, but it was pale in comparison to the yellow
flame of the olive oil that spread from the shattered lantern. Oblivious of the crackling flames,
N'Sumu was raging: "Wait! She must have left
by the roof! She'll be back! We've got to wait here
for the mother to return! I order you to wait!"

The wicker screens closing the outer walls shuddered as the fire began to suck in its breath. The
panel directly across the loft from the doorway
had been smashed out and replaced by a tunic—
neatly opened and hung to conceal the interior of
the large room from eyes in adjacent buildings.
The cloth flapped inward, drawn by the breeze,
and drew with it the edge of the boar net that had
been hung around the entire top floor of the
building. Men on the roof shouted at what they
thought was success—the sauropithecus slashing
its way through a wall panel to escape the powerful party by now blocking the stairwell exit.

Of course, it had also been possible that the
lizard-ape would burst through the roof instead.
For that, there was no help but to trust to the
expertise of men with hand nets like the one Lycon
himself carried. The operation might or might not
have succeeded if the sauropithecus—if the mother—
had been in its lair. Lycon had not, at any rate,
sprung his trap on empty air.

Only now it was they who were trapped—or soon
would be—in this rapidly spreading conflagration.
N'Sumu seemed to ignore the danger. Either the
man was possessed—or else the danger of being
trapped inside a blazing building was something beyond the Egyptian's Experience. Assuming N'Sumu
was an Egyptian.

Assuming—there was another green flash, a very brilliant one; an arm that might have been a small child's, only blue-scaled and with claws already longer than a leopard's, was blown past N'Sumu from where its owner had crouched twenty feet away—assuming that N'Sumu was even human.

The two patrolmen and their shields were crossed like X-shaped barricades in the doorway. Both men were screaming unintelligibly. Because their oval shields were strapped on, it would have taken greater coordination than either man was showing to drop them. Even so, they could have got out easily had they simply backed up and tried the opening again, with their shields and bodies parallel—the way they had entered the loft. Panic, whether from the fire or the charnel house itself, did not permit that.

Vonones and one of the Ethiopians were tugging at the outer Watch member—their efforts hampered by their own fear and the need to watch for what might be creeping toward them. There seemed to be no more of the larger creatures, though quick motion at the shadowy edges of the loft suggested what might happen if N'Sumu relaxed his blank-eyed vigilance.

"Don't let the one you've caught be harmed," N'Sumu shouted to Lycon in piercing Greek that filled the loft. "Domitian is certain to want it if the mother escapes us."

The second lantern had been set on the floor with the caution it deserved, but the horn lenses of the first now burned as well and added a bitter stench identifiable even through the general foetor of the loft. Lycon snatched up the shortsword a patrolman had dropped. The wooden hilt was greasy with something from the floor, but the hunter's hysterical grip would have held the trotter of a pig in a mud wallow.

The Ethiopian who had flung down the shattered lantern sat with his knees slightly raised and his expression frozen as he appeared to stare at the creature on his ankle. It was small, really not much larger than the tarantulas of the coastal regions of Italy and Provence. No one would confuse it with a spider, however, because its four blue-glinting limbs were patently wrong in number and in excessive strength. They wrapped around the slave's instep and leg, while the creature buried its tiny head into the ankle joint. As Lycon slapped down at it with the flat of his sword, the head withdrew from the red-rimmed hole it had dug, and its eyes winked in black fury at the steel that crushed it.

The slave toppled over. A similar creature, on the side of his face that had been hidden from Lycon, had its two arms dug the full four inches of their length down into the Ethiopian's eye-socket. The claws of one hind leg were anchored under the base of the jaw, while the others drew up the corner of the slave's mouth in a false snarl into which the humors from the eye had begun to drip.

Lycon struck this time with the edge. He fervently hoped that the lantern-bearer was already dead.

He had grasped the sword not as a weapon but as a tool. Now he struck the wall behind him on the follow-through of the tug that had cleared the blade from the cleft skull. The wall over the stairwell was of the same construction as the panels that enclosed the exterior, though here at least, the wickerwork had been plastered over to give it the look of solidity. Though the paneling was light and provided no vertical support, the woven twigs—even desiccated as they now were—comprised a resilient surface of considerable strength. A man like Ox could tear through them by main force, but there were few men like Ox and one fewer now.

Lycon had many times relied upon his quickness in moments of danger, but just now he thought he would prefer to carry a good bit more heavy muscle. He drew back and followed his first blow with a second—this time putting behind it the full strength of his right arm. Plaster exploded away from the sword in a choking cloud that gleamed saffron in the light of the conflagration behind it. Roof tiles were beginning to shatter as the flames licked upward. Upon the roof above, men had noticed the flames and were shouting out warnings as they scrambled to leap to adjacent buildings.

"Vonones! Help me!" Lycon shouted, as he smashed shoulder-first against the ragged opening his blade had torn. The wicker rebounded, but then the merchant's weight struck Lycon's back and sent both men head-first in a tangle of dust and broken twigs out onto the rickety staircase.

Lycon tucked himself under—head, knees, and elbows—and saved his neck through the same reflexes that had responded once when a treelimb sheared as he crawled along it to reach the cerval cat at the tip of the branch. Vonones might have come out less well without his friend to break their mutual fall. As it was, they caromed together from the stairs—which flexed but did not shatter, to the outer wall which had a brick core and ig-

nored their impact—and at last came to rest on
the landing at the next level down.

The two Watch patrolmen in the doorway had
finally sorted themselves out to the extent of tumbling through in turn. Vonones, wheezing like an
angry bear, caught the first man, used him as a
shield against the second, and hurled both of them
over his head and the huddled body of Lycon between his feet. The men pitched on down the farther flight of stairs—helmets dancing loose and
shields buffeting their owners and the walls.

"Idiots!" Vonones screamed after them.

Lycon twisted smoothly to his feet, ignoring pain.
That he was battered and bruised was inevitable;
the awareness of that could wait for the morning,
for the next few days, if he lived that long. Nothing had been damaged that would keep him from
functioning—and by all the gods, nothing short of
death would stop him this time.

Lycon had flung the sword ahead of him as he
broke through the wall. The blade still rang and
clattered somewhere on down the staircase, in the
general direction in which the two patrolmen had
gone tumbling.

The surviving Ethiopian slave now leaped down
the stairs, screaming mindlessly as he fell. There
was a look of horror on his face, and something
blue was squatting on his scalp. As the slave
plunged by him, Lycon reached out with his right
hand and peeled the creature from its hold.

It resisted like a tick imbedded firmly into flesh.
The Ethiopian's head snapped back, as if Lycon
had snatched a handful of hair instead of something so alien and malevolent. Momentum carried
the victim on, and the beastcatcher's hand and

arm held as if worked from iron. The four clawed limbs of the creature, itself no larger than the hand that caught it, pulled loose with bits of the Ethiopian's scalp and hair still dangling. Blood washed across exposed skull where the creature had gnawed into the bone.

A lance of pain touched Lycon's palm just at the instant that he drove his open hand against the brick wall. The impact left a blotch of glaucous ichor on the wall, framed by the red of his own human blood. The hatchling burst apart between brick and a hand as unyielding as brick, dropped twitching onto the floor.

Something stabbed at Lycon's left calf. He had let his net dangle too closely to his leg. The lizard-ape chick within had managed to hook one arm through the mesh; its claws gashed into Lycon's calf, only momentarily foiled by leather straps. Lycon backhanded the creature twice against the wall to quell its murderous activity once again.

"Come on!" he shouted up the staircase. "We've got to get out of here!"

The two Watch patrolmen were rousing the lower floors of the building. It was either a triumph of training over panic, or else they hoped to drive the madness of the loft above from their thoughts by concentrating on familiar duties. Out in the street, others were shouting now as well, while the orange flames winked with a hellish intensity through the interstices of the paneling. There was no part of Rome in which fire and disease were not the constant companions of the residents; of the two, the brutal suddenness of fire made it the more feared. The apartment dwellers beneath would block the stairs in their attempts to save their goods as well as themselves—bedsteads and braziers, clothing or even a cracked bowl made important by the fact that it was the owner's sole chattel.

"It will come back to save its brood!" N'Sumu called over his shoulder. He had backed into the doorway now that the rest of the party had escaped the loft, but he remained poised there instead of descending. The firelight threw his shadow, more lumped and awkward than the man himself, onto the wall of the staircase behind him. The ragged hole Lycon and Vonones had torn in the inner wall glowed now as well with the sooty yellow flames. "We have to wait here until it . . ."

The last of whatever N'Sumu might have said was drowned in the crash as the central section of the roof collapsed. That crash was echoed when the weight of tiles struck the fire-weakened floor of the loft and precipitated it and N'Sumu down onto the fifth level. Residents gabbling in a dozen languages had already crowded the hallway and begun to force their way past the two men on the landing. Now flames and debris showered down onto the hall and those within it. Air pistoned through the hall, then sucked itself back upward through the new opening with a roar and a column of sparks.

N'Sumu twisted as he fell, landed on his feet, struggled toward them. At last the Egyptian seemed to recognize the danger of their position.

Lycon was willing to use his elbows or the ivory baton he still carried, if that could have broken a pathway down the stairs. The press of terrified humanity was too solid for such tactics to be of any help.

A woman from a fifth-floor apartment hurled herself against Vonones, as if the screams of those buried under blazing coals were scourges to drive her away. Vonones struck her twice with the stock of his whip, pulling the blows. She continued to scream and claw at him. Vonones smashed at her a third time, with the terror of a trapped animal bursting through his civilized restraint. The woman fell backward, nose broken and a vertical welt along her forehead from nose to hairline. The infant slung at her breast bawled as the rest of the crowd in the hallway surged forward.

N'Sumu reached past his two shorter companions and touched the head of the nearest of those who blocked the four flights of stairs remaining.

Lycon was dizzy with pain and the heat, barely able to focus on one clear idea at a time now. He turned his head and shouted to the Egyptian who leaned over him: "We're going to have to cut through the outer wall and take our chances we can find handholds to climb down!"

The man N'Sumu had touched slumped to the side like melting wax. The hunter could have beaten in the back of the fellow's head by brute force without achieving such an instantaneous effect.

N'Sumu slid between Lycon and Vonones without their objection. A bald man with a short club raised stood on top of the mother Vonones had bludgeoned down. The snarl on his face transformed itself into a look of amazement as the second body slumped toward him without a struggle. Lycon punched the man in the solar plexus, just in case the wonder wore off and his thoughts returned to the cudgel.

N'Sumu swept down the narrow staircase like

fire through dry grass. Men and women sprawled at his touch, either clearing the way as they fell or at least proving easier to maneuver past. They did not appear to be seriously injured; their hearts beat and sometimes their mouths moaned soft nonsense, but their limbs remained flaccid.

There was an odor like that of hot bronze. It grew stronger as they forced their way downward, clinging to Lycon's nostrils despite the choking smoke. N'Sumu began to flutter his hands in the air as if to cool them; then he would reach out again, and another body would sag like a deflated bladder. Occasionally there was a green nimbus, and a pattern of blisters marked the victim's skin at the point of contact. Lycon sweated and tried to ignore what he could not change, as he slung humans and their possessions behind him and out of the way. He worked with his right hand only, despite the fact that his palm was swelling badly. The tiny creature had bitten him there in the moment that he crushed it, and for all Lycon knew its bite could have been venomous.

It was too dark to examine the lizard-ape chick trapped in Lycon's net, even had there been time for that. After being slammed against the wall, it moved only as it jiggled within its silken wrappings. That might mean the cat-sized killer was dead, and thus useless to the beastcatcher's half-formed plan—but it had come this far, and it was going the rest of the way.

The full complement of the Watch for the district had been present before the fire broke out, so matters were in surprisingly good order at street level. One squad had wrenched the stairwell door off its pivot pins, and patrolmen were tossing peo-

ple and possessions into the street with scant
ceremony. Half the value of chattels rescued from
a fire went to the State purse, but it was necessary
to get the humans out of the way before the more
important work of salvage could proceed. Ladders
were raised to windows as high as the third floor,
and there the shutters had been beaten in and
furnishings were being passed into hands of teams
ready to secure them. If the building itself could
be saved, so much the better, because the value of
the structure would also be applied to the Emper-
or's share. But such was unlikely here, since the
upper floors were already fully involved. By the
time the fire was low enough for bucket brigades to
reach it, collapsing masonry would have cleared
the area of even the boldest.

Hands seized N'Sumu as he reached the street
door. The Egyptian was stumbling now with
fatigue—or some more doubtful reason. Nonetheless N'Sumu was enraged at being manhandled.
He snarled something in a language Lycon had
never heard, and pointed his finger in a motion
quite different from the casual touching movements with which he had cleared a path down the
stairs. Lycon, staggering himself, caught N'Sumu's
wrist from behind—certain that the lethal flash he
had glimpsed in the loft was sure to follow. Whether
N'Sumu was an Egyptian wizard or a god who
might hurl lightning bolts, Lycon judged that the
fewer witnesses to his strange powers, the better.
Roughly he steered N'Sumu clear of the melee.

Vonones tumbled out after them. The merchant
had been facing backward against the press that
would have overwhelmed them despite N'Sumu's
best efforts, had Vonones not threatened its lead-

ers with the sword he had picked up from the stairs. There was blood on the sword-tip now, besides the plaster grit the blade had been covered with when Lycon hacked through the wall. The dealer's bare skin was scratched and sweaty and spattered with blood not solely his own. His whip was in his left hand, his palm gripping the tip against the base of the stock—a leather-wrapped staff whose core was the penis bone of a lion. Vonones looked wild and deadly, and he was both those things at the moment. The men of the Watch lurched back to let the three pass through their ranks.

"Come on, we've got to get back from this!" Lycon called out. He had no idea in the world where they needed to go—nor did it matter, so long as it was out of the chaos and congestion caused by the fire.

Refugees, spectators, and those trying to limit the damage of the blaze clogged the streets. Many of those who had made their initial escape were now trying to return to the building in hope of saving some of their belongings. Of the spectators, some watched with the greedy wonder brought out by any major disaster—an expression that Lycon had seen multiplied by tens of thousands in the seats surrounding the arena. Others, though, wore something closer to the look of victims waiting for the lions. The orange claw that dripped cascading sparks might not be satisfied with a single kill. If a breeze sprang up, if the hinted rain chose not to fall, fire would maul the whole quarter— dozens of buildings, perhaps hundreds. Those watching from their windows or from the street outside their shops saw sooty victims weep for the dead and the lost, in full realization that in another hour they themselves might join the parade of mourners.

Lycon put his right palm on N'Sumu's shoulder. The Egyptian felt hot, even through the pain throbbing across Lycon's injured hand. "We'll gather up a light and some of my men, then lock this thing away in the compound."

He hefted the net with the lizard-ape chick—now fighting once more to escape the mesh. The column of fire roaring from the stricken building was reflected from low clouds in a yellow-orange glare. It was the first time Lycon had both light and leisure adequate to inspect what he had captured.

In general, the immediate victims of the fire shuffled along too absorbed in their own concerns to pay any attention to the creature Lycon now viewed at arm's length. Even those who did look up let their eyes dully drift away without the curiosity they might have displayed under other circumstances.

Not that there was anything particularly terrifying about the little beast—not so long as it was safely ensnared. It was about the size of a cat, as Lycon had thought from the initial glimpse, although this thing was tailless and had fangs like broken glass. It was snapping crookedly at the net, unable to close its jaws properly—Lycon guessed he likely had broken its jaw when he slammed it against the wall. One of the chick's eyes was open and glaring murder; the other had swollen shut. Its rib cage seemed almost skeletally thin due to its coating of scales where fur would have given it a greater appearance of bulk. Its sides quivered at a rate too rapid for lungs, even driven by fever and injury; perhaps it was the thing's heart beating.

One of its arms reached through the meshes of the net—slashing at whatever came near. The claws were extended and dark with the blood they had earlier snatched from Lycon's calf. The head of a human baby looks large because it is nearer to its adult size than is its body. The claws of this month-old chick could not have really been as long as those of its mother, but they gave that impression—and they were surely as sharp.

"Let me have that," N'Sumu demanded unexpectedly. "If you've harmed it, you fool, you'll . . ."

"Don't be an ass!" Lycon snapped. "It's bait to bring in its mother! How would you bait your traps back home in Nubia, N'Sumu?"

"Save your quarrel for afterward!" Vonones broke in. "We've got worse trouble than the lizard-ape to deal with now. Look!"

Beyond the barrier of the milling crowd, a double file of troops was riding toward them from the north. The troops must have made good progress to have covered the distance between here and the palace in the time since the first sparks had cascaded into the sky. There could be little question of where they came from—hulking Germans in bright armor and the tribune, Lacerta, one of the pair in the front rank.

There could be little doubt about who had sent them to investigate, either.

CHAPTER FIFTEEN

N'Sumu, who had been glowering at Lycon, turned his attention toward the direction Vonones indicated. His uncanny gaze seemed to glance at the oncoming troops without recognition, as his pupils suddenly went opaque. N'Sumu jerked upright, facing the distant roofs—his hands raised palms-outward as if in an exaggerated gesture of surprise. "It's up there!" he hissed. "It's come back!"

Passersby eddied around the men as all three paused to stare skyward. The troop of guards had been halted by a barrier that they could not lash out of the way: a builder's wagon loaded with bricks, overturned in the street when its driver tried to back his team away from the commotion and danger of the fire. Shouts and curses in German and Latin scattered even those refugees numbed by the conflagration, but the heaped bricks were not affected in the least.

"Between the buildings," N'Sumu said, pointing overhead. The cloud glow made a dim, jagged ribbon of the sky, interrupted completely at some points by the degree of overhang and cross-building. Lycon could see nothing, nothing exceptional at any rate—but remembering the way N'Sumu had swatted away dangers hidden in the loft, the beastcatcher was willing enough to believe the other's warning.

As Lycon opened his mouth to ask where the creature was now, N'Sumu forestalled him by saying: "It's gone, just the one flash. But it's stalking us."

For the first time, Lycon and Vonones felt what they were sure was fear in the Egyptian's manner. N'Sumu had been coolly arrogant in his dealings with them, and he had showed a clear willingness to enter the lizard-ape's lair with no support or very little. Evidently this hunter had very little stomach for becoming the hunted instead.

The beastcatcher looked at his friend. Vonones voiced their mutual puzzlement, saying: "You wanted it to come to you, didn't you? Wanted to wait for it even after the building was starting to collapse?"

Lycon lifted the netted creature in his left hand and added, "I'd planned to use this for bait—back at the compound, where we'd be able to determine the direction the lizard-ape would have to approach from. Listen, N'Sumu—you *can* deal with it here, can't you? Do whatever it was that you did to its brood back there in the loft?"

N'Sumu whispered something inaudible and possibly in an unfamiliar language. His face continued to be emotionless, but there was evident nervousness in the way the tall Egyptian twisted and jerked his head in an attempt to look everywhere at once. More intelligibly, he went on, "It didn't know *I* was here looking for it. It would have attacked just as if I were one of you. Now it's sensed me. It *knows* . . ."

The words were spilling out in N'Sumu's accented Latin, but Vonones had the feeling N'Sumu was unconsciously begging their companionship in danger, without fully considering the import of his words.

"It knows I'm its only real threat! It knows it has to kill me first!" N'Sumu burst out in something between a shout and a scream. "And it can come from *anywhere*!"

He whirled about, bumping Vonones away and extending his index finger toward the shutters of the fabric shop beside them. Lycon felt the air seethe as it had when the bronzed man struck down threats in the loft, but there was no green flash on this occasion. Neither, of course, was there anything alive in the direction N'Sumu had pointed—unless someone within the shop had made the mistake of listening with an ear to the shutter.

What in the names of all the gods was N'Sumu? Or was the correct question: what *god* was N'Sumu? Lycon had never believed the tales of mortals coupling with deities—of stories like that of Memmon the son of Zeus, who had ruled Ethiopia in the times that were now a myth and a memory. But, who or what was N'Sumu?

"Then we need more space about us," Lycon decided. First things first, and unless they survived this night, N'Sumu's parentage and provenance were of no matter at all. "There—by the fountain! It's the best place we'll find in a hurry."

Twenty yards away, half the distance to the oncoming imperial guards, the street met two others in the Y-intersection normal for all cities, save those laid out on bare ground by military surveyors. The pavement widened there and held the fountain that supplied water from the Appian Aqueduct to all the buildings within a one-block radius on the intersecting streets. The intersection was crowded, especially since the arms and curses of the cavalrymen had diverted those who might otherwise have scrambled over the load of bricks—easy enough to do on foot, but a perfect barricade against men who refused to lower themselves by dismounting in the midst of a mob.

"Come on!" Lycon thrust his way through the crowd, holding the struggling lizard-ape chick ahead of him—let it vent its rage on those who moved aside too slowly. Vonones and N'Sumu surged through behind him. The beastcatcher was too busy with the press of bodies to keep an eye on the rooftops and overhanging balconies. He didn't like to trust to luck, but tonight he had to. N'Sumu was obviously quite correct—the lizard-ape could leap upon them from any direction, and in the narrow confines of the street they would have no effective warning no matter how carefully they attempted to watch. Their best hope was to reach the cleared area around the fountain, and after that they could make a stand. First things first. . . .

The tribune, Lacerta, caught sight of them over the ruined wagon—probably recognizing the tall Egyptian first, but choosing to call out: "You! Merchant! Beastcatcher! Come here at once!"

Lycon heard but ignored the tribune. He continued to barge forward with the others behind him. Vonones threw a backward glance, then followed Lycon's example.

The fountain itself consisted of a square basin six feet to a side and approximately eighteen inches from its upper lip to the pavement. The basin was of tufa, a porous volcanic stone whose light weight and abundance made it the city's single most common building material. The corner blocks were decorated beneath the slime of algae with neat rosettes, freehand reminders by some stonemason, almost certainly a slave, that craftsmanship does not depend upon the craftsman's status.

There was a column in the center of the fountain. Water entered the basin through the cup from which a nymph, carved in low relief upon that column, poured continuously. The overflow dribbled through cuts in the basin rim and along grooves in the pavement, then off into the nearest sewer. Even in the hot, rainless days of the summer, overflow from fountains fed by the aqueducts went some way toward flushing the sewers and limiting the occurrence of fevers and agues. There was no effort just yet to organize a bucket brigade from here, but many of those whom the fire had routed out were bathing their heads and arms directly—and illegally—in the fountain.

"Are you ready, N'Sumu?" Lycon asked. If the Egyptian's magic would not serve them now, they were all dead men. Lycon had made the decision that looked best in terms of survival—and if those terms still weren't very good, then there was all the more reason to act promptly before fear made impossible that which was necessary. The hunter's eyes were bright with a mixture of joy and madness. It was unfortunate that the conflagration had scattered his men, burned their nets—but Lycon would have been dead years ago if he had had to rely upon anyone but himself in times of danger.

"You're going to draw it here?" Vonones demanded. Even as he spoke, he turned his body away from Lycon to scan the roofs and facades in the vicinity—none of them farther than twenty feet of horizontal distance. His words were barely audible above the din.

"Yes," said N'Sumu. He seemed to have regained his composure. "It's just that I've lost the element of surprise. I'm certain that the phile—the sauropithecus—caught my scent . . . We are old enemies, my people and these lizard-apes. It knows I am here—and it will certainly single me out when it attacks."

"You people! Better move away!" Lycon warned the nearest refugees. His tone was so emotionless that he would have been ignored even had he spoken loudly enough to be understood in the uproar. The hunter grinned at N'Sumu. "The lizard-ape won't ignore *me*," he said. "Watch."

Lycon braced his right foot on the coping of the basin. It was slick with algae, but he had forded streams where a slip meant half a mile of battering along granite boulders. He would not slip now. The nails in his boots gouged into the tufa, as the hunter jumped to the top of the pillar. From this position he now stood two feet above the surface of the basin. Lycon's arms hunched back to balance himself. Vonones thought he looked rather like a bird of prey balancing on its perch. The net, closely bunched, swung in one hand; in the other, the ivory wand shone a smooth orange in the glow of the flames.

The column was rectangular and only a foot

across at the top, but that was adequate for Lycon's purposes. He held up the burden in his left hand at just enough of an angle so that the netted chick, squirming angrily, could not tear his forearm.

"Come get it!" he shouted to the rooftops. "Do you want it? Here it is!" The ivory baton flexed no more than a hair's breadth as Lycon slapped it against the net with all his strength. There was a crack of impact, and something too shrill to be a sound raised hairs on the neck of all those clustered about the fountain.

Lycon had attracted little attention when he forced his way to the basin, and little more even when he leaped atop the central column. His shout and the eerie shriek that followed the blow of the ivory baton drew the crowd's eyes, and then drove back the nearest of those around him.

Lycon had worn only a simple, light tunic tonight—wanting freedom of movement. Thus far the tension and activity had counteracted the effect of the night chill in this, the month Germanicus—September, until the Emperor had renamed it following his triumph over the Germans. Lycon had sweated in the loft and during their escape from it. Now he shivered. His garment was torn loose from one shoulder and shredded on one side where the chick had clawed at him. The trembling in his limbs was both emotional as well as physical, but that would not prevent his muscles from reacting when needed.

It was questionable whether his reactions could save him this time, but a failed hope is nonetheless hope for a time.

"There!" cried Vonones. Lycon turned, but there

was nothing in the direction his friend pointed, not even hinted motion.

Because the light was diffused from above, the nearby facades looked as if they were veiled by cobwebs that thinned as they hung closer to the street. Cornices and eaves of red tile, whose true color was only hinted by the light that washed them, dripped long shadows downward. Something could have leaped across a roofline, have clung like a shadow-drenched bat beneath a projecting beam, but it would be invisible.

"Here it is!" Lycon shouted. He struck again with the baton, letting rage drive his arm. He heard a dull crunch of bones; blood spurted from the tiny body broken within the net. Vonones shouted. The adult sauropithecus launched itself toward Lycon, forty feet beneath the ledge upon which it had hung.

The lizard-ape was no more than a blur, an impression too sudden and ill-lit to be seen in detail. Another man would have frozen there, gaped stupidly, and died an instant later. Lycon knew well the blinding speed, the razor-edged deadly claws—and at the first shimmer of movement from above, the hunter was already in motion himself.

Lycon raised his ivory baton—the lizard-ape's scales might turn tiger claws, but in another instant he would know how hard its skull was.

N'Sumu had already reacted to Vonones' shout. A split second after the lizard-ape leaped, midway between the ledge and its quarry, its hurtling form was caught up in a sudden glow of verdant light. Lycon had hoped for the eye-searing emerald flare that had shattered blue-scaled bodies apart earlier in the loft. Instead, the hurtling lizard-ape seemed to stagger in midair—to lose full control of its muscles—but its leap carried it full onto Lycon.

Stunned or not, the lizard-ape struck Lycon and knocked him backward—carrying the hunter from his precarious footing atop the column. Lycon cushioned its impact as best he could—there was no room to duck, nor time to try. The lizard-ape was heavier than he had expected—its flesh must all be of iron-hard muscle—and the force of its fall would have broken half his bones had Lycon not twisted aside, merging with the creature in midair, falling with it into the fountain. The belly-ripping stroke of its claws had no strength, brushed him with only a shadow of their lethal intent—shredding his tunic even so.

Lycon hit the water backward, half-way into a somersault, and the tufa coping grazed his scalp an instant before his back struck the floor of the basin. Water sprayed across the screams of everyone around the fountain. Lycon's arms flailed, but he struck instinctively with his baton, felt it strike hard. The net was slung to one side, balancing the thrust of his right arm in the opposite direction—arm, ivory baton, and the blood-mad creature locked by its teeth to the ivory, as water exploded in all directions.

Lycon was screaming, "Kill it! Kill it, N'Sumu!" The fear and fury in his voice would have made the words unintelligible even without the surrounding chaos.

The wand struck the lip of the tufa as Lycon and the blue killer crashed down again. Ivory was denser than the porous stone, but the stone provided a fulcrum against which Lycon's hysterical grip and the teeth of the lizard-ape could lever with all their strength. The ivory baton shattered at the point of stress—fragments spalling away in layers of concentric rings.

Lycon sprang upright as the baton shattered, narrowly averting the claws of the lizard-ape's hind legs—a kick that would certainly have gutted him had the creature not been stunned by N'Sumu's magic. N'Sumu himself was shielding his eyes with one hand—the other hand pointing threateningly toward the falling spray. A green nimbus burst over the stone nymph.

Whatever magic the Egyptian commanded, the lizard-ape indeed recognized the danger. Abandoning its attack on Lycon, it darted amongst the panicked onlookers. Either the fall or N'Sumu's magic had weakened the sauropithecus, for Lycon was almost able to follow the lightning-quick movements of its claws as it ripped apart anyone too frozen with fear to leap out of its path.

A green lambency snaked through the heart of the crowd, twice, again and again—toppling people as they fled. Weaving through a cover of human bodies, the sauropithecus had already disappeared. Twenty feet from the fountain, the slab covering a sewer catchbasin rocked back onto its seat. The lizard-ape *could not* have sprung so far, so quickly after N'Sumu had stunned it and it had absorbed the shock of its fall. But the lizard-ape was gone, and the slab clacked as it settled, still ajar, over what had just used the sewers for a bolt-hole.

"You heard me, Armenian!" said a voice in easy Latin, high pitched and angry. "I ordered you to stop!"

Lycon turned. The Emperor's bodyguards had

dismounted at last and by now had advanced in a wedge about their tribune. Civilians scattering from the brief, nightmarish struggle at the fountain rebounded in turn from armored chests and bare swords held forward by flat and hilt as fenders and threats. Panic can overload nervous systems, but even those in that dazed condition retained some urge for self-preservation. Cringing citizens curled back from the Germans like clods from the mold-board of a plow.

As the merchant turned to face Lacerta, one of the bearded guards used his own blade to swat the loosely held sword from Vonones' right hand. Vonones shook himself and drew stiffly upright, expecting the worst.

Lycon would have vaulted out of the basin, but the water and his weakness trapped him so that he stumbled. He no longer had normal control over his body. It was a puppet whose strings he could play, but every motion was unexpectedly delayed. He bent to brace himself on the fountain coping. The water still bubbling from the pillar washed blood from his thighs. He was aware of it for the first time.

Lacerta stared at the beastcatcher and swore. The order he barked to the nearest men of his troop was a curse in itself. Two of the big Germans paused long enough to sheath their swords. Lycon had started to clamber out of the basin, embarrassed by his lack of agility but too exhausted to care much. The net still hung from his left hand. Gripped in his right was the lower half of the baton. The lizard-ape's teeth had scarred the smooth ivory as they slid along it before finding purchase. The parallel gouges stood out down to the shattered end of the stump. Those same teeth would have cut far deeper into the bones of Lycon's forearm, and the muscles of that arm would have been no more to them than grass to a scythe blade.

The armored guards caught Lycon, one to either wrist and armpit, and hoisted him unceremoniously from the fountain. His laced boots squelched as the Germans thumped him down in front of the Tribune. Another man shoved Vonones forward.

"Caught one of the lizard-apes," said Lycon drunkenly. "Got it right here. It's a little beat up." He held out his net.

The net was badly torn, far more so than Lycon had expected would be the case. The lizard-ape chick had chewed away all the cords within reach of its teeth. Because the chick had been enwrapped and not merely entangled in the net, that had not even freed its head. Similarly, the claws had been sharp enough to make ragged tears in the immensely strong silken cords, but even so the fibers had reknotted into new patterns in the violent struggle. Lacerta took the net from Lycon, but he found it impossible to unwrap the tangled fabric because of the damage.

The damage to the creature within the net had quite clearly been fatal. In death, the thing seemed even smaller than Lycon had supposed. It probably weighed little more than ten pounds, granted the unnatural density of its flesh, and it reminded Lycon of a drowned cat. The last blow of the wand had crunched the chick's skull, but the eye that remained open still glared with unslaked hatred. Even in death, it projected the feeling of a scorpion caught under a boot, not only lethal but strong—a mistake the universe had spawned in some black pit or poisonous desert.

Lacerta paused in unwrapping it, as he began to get a better look at what he held. There was something on his hands, colorless but slimy, like the track of a slug. His aristocratic face worked in disgust, and he thrust the burden toward one of the German troopers with a curt order.

"You *killed* it, beastcatcher," the tribune accused, in anger that swelled to burn away the disgust and fear that soiled his emotions. His hands wiped themselves compulsively on the studded leather apron that hung to protect his thighs. "You were to capture the animal, but you killed it. I saw you."

Lacerta's eyes flicked reflexively toward the netted thing that one of the stolid Germans was trying to untangle as directed. Seeing the creature again made the tribune's face draw up in a flinch, and he quickly looked away.

"Had to draw the mother in," Lycon mumbled. "That's just one of her brood. The rest are cooked by now." Not even he could have understood his own words. Two of the guards still held him, and that was probably fortunate. Otherwise he would have fallen. Louder and more clearly, the hunter said: "N'Sumu—tell them that we had to get the adult where you could ... you could catch her. That was the one we were after—the adult sauropithecus."

The bronzed Egyptian squatted at the edge of the catch basin. There were spectators about him, but none of them had moved closer when he ordered them to lift the stone plate for him. Now N'Sumu balanced the slab on edge with one hand, while the index finger of his free hand seemed to point into the opening. After a moment, he waved his palm slowly over the gaping hole.

Men and women knocked down moments ago by the flashing bolts of power that had missed the escaping sauropithecus were now beginning to stir upon the cobblestones. A few of those who had escaped the swathe were kneeling beside victims, weeping and chafing wrists to raise a pulse. Those who had been too slow to get out of the lizard-ape's path lay about where they had fallen, blood seeping in widening pools beneath them. What the crowd had made of it all was beyond conjecture.

Nothing burst out of the sewer. The gurgle of water and the waste it bore toward the Tiber was loud and alone in the pause before N'Sumu dropped the slab back into place.

He stared at Lacerta with an arrogance that made the tribune seethe. "I believe my authority has precedence here, Tribune. See to this rabble, while I give orders to my staff concerning the Emperor's sauropithecus. I'm sure that any problems arising from tonight are entirely within my capacity to deal with."

Down the street behind them, one wall of the burning building collapsed inward, closely followed by the remaining walls. Sparks gushed and dripped back as if the dying apartment block clawed at its neighbors. The sky-reaching inferno did not spread beyond its pyre, however, only cooled and fell away upon its dead.

Rome was fortunate, this time. That danger had contained itself.

But from beneath the lid of a catch basin hundreds of feet from where the phile had last been seen, eyes watched the mounted guards begin to clear the streets of the frightened mob. Its eyes focused upon one man out of all the crowd there, and the stone slab quivered as the clawed hand holding it ajar began to tremble with fury.

CHAPTER SIXTEEN

"The only reason you two are not lion-bait in the Amphitheater right now," said N'Sumu firmly, "is because *I* said I needed you. Lacerta wanted all three of us thrown into the arena. He was not pleased when he was made to recognize that my authority from Domitian was greater than his."

N'Sumu resettled himself in Vonones' chair, then added: "The next time there's a screw-up, I'll feed you both to Lacerta. Understood?"

"I'm certain there will be no further difficulties," said Vonones with practiced urbanity. Inwardly the merchant was furious with the Egyptian's casual assumption of his office. "I'm sure Lycon and I have the situation well in hand." He hoped that was so.

"Just hold it!" snapped Lycon, reacting as Vonones had feared he would. "What's this about a screw-up!"

It had been past dawn by the time they had made their way back to Vonones' compound to regroup from the debacle at Mephibaal's loft.

181

N'Sumu had ridden with Lacerta to the palace to settle matters with Domitian. Vonones had paid out the thousand sesterces to Silvius, indicating to the Watch Centurion that discretion regarding the night's events might earn a bonus. Lycon had pitched himself onto a couch and slept as if dead, too exhausted to see to his injuries. When Vonones had awakened the hunter upon N'Sumu's return from the palace, Lycon was in too much pain to care particularly whether the Egyptian had managed to placate the Emperor or not.

Now Lycon was a scorched and tattered spectre smeared with filth and dried blood. His mood was considerably worse than was his physical appearance.

"*We* didn't screw things up!" Lycon snarled. "*You* were the one who gave the order to go after the lizard-ape by night. *You* are supposed to be the master sauropithecus hunter—*you* should have known that the damned thing would likely be away from its lair and hunting at night."

"Of course I was fully aware of all that," N'Sumu responded. "But my decision was to capture the sauropithecus before it changed its lair. I had no idea that the creature had already begun to produce a brood."

"Then don't forget that we did a damn good night's work in wiping out all traces of that brood," Lycon persisted. "Our lord and god may wish to have a lizard-ape or two for his entertainment in the Amphitheater, but not even Domitian would long be amused by the spectacle of a hundred of the murderous killers on the loose here in Rome."

Vonones chose this moment to interrupt. Any distraction might help to forestall a fight between the other two. While Lycon might be reckless of the fact that N'Sumu held their lives in his hand, Vonones had not forgotten.

"There in the loft," Vonones broke in. "Just what was that we saw . . . with Smiler?"

N'Sumu regarded him blankly for a moment, then chose his words. "The sauropithecus is somewhat akin to a species of wasp, in that the female lays her eggs within the living body of a helpless host. You understand, the region of Africa in which the sauropitheci dwell is so abounding with other dangerous predators that any normal sort of nest would surely be destroyed. Often I have seen elephants whose bodies have been infested with the larvae of the sauropithecus."

"Certainly, there are always new wonders to come forth from Africa," temporized Vonones, praying that the beastcatcher had mastered his anger. "Is it true, as has been written, that in a certain region of the interior there lives a race of men whose heads are in the center of their bodies?"

"This is certainly true," said N'Sumu. "Many times have I hunted in their lands."

"And is there also a race of men who can hurl lightning bolts from their hands?" demanded Lycon. No sooner had he spoken than he began to regret his audacity.

N'Sumu considered the two men impassively, and Lycon had faced death too often not to recognize that he again faced death in this moment.

"There are many secrets known to the priests of Egypt," said N'Sumu finally. "It may be even that some of the secrets of the gods are known to certain ones among us. It would be well for you if such powers remain a secret. I suggest that you both forget whatever you think you might have seen last night."

"And are you priest now as well as hunter, *Egyptian*?" wondered Lycon boldly. Vonones shot him a pleading glance.

"And who are you to inquire of me, *man*!" sneered N'Sumu. It was time to put an end to dangerous lines of thought. "*I* am master here! At my whim, you and your household are fodder for the arena! Remember that! I won't remind you again."

Vonones laid a firm hand on Lycon's arm, urging the hunter to let matters rest. Lycon subsided, but the merchant had the sensation of standing upon the slope of a volcano whose next unexpected rumbling would bring annihilation.

"The simple fact remains that *your* man dropped the lantern that destroyed the sauropithecus' lair, thereby ruining our chances of lying in wait there for the mother's return to the loft." N'Sumu was unconcerned over the consequent human casualties and suffering, just as he chose to ignore his own panic that night. "Thanks to your blundering, we don't even have a live chick to offer to the Emperor. Well, then—I'll not dwell upon past mistakes. What matters is the present, and I want to hear your suggestions regarding our next move."

N'Sumu paused and smiled his ghastly smile. Lycon found the expression as reassuring as a shark's gaping grin. "After all," the bronzed Egyptian said, "you are my field experts. I rely upon your advice."

"We can continue our reward offer for information on the lizard-ape's kills," Vonones suggested quickly, avoiding the stark look on Lycon's face. "And we can offer a reward for sightings. We know

now for certain that the lizard-ape is here in Rome—you were perfectly correct about that, N'Sumu. We'll search for its new lair, now that we know what to look for."

"The sauropithecus may not seek another lair immediately," N'Sumu argued. "She had implanted her eggs within the one called Smiler only yesterday. She won't be able to produce another clutch for about ten of your days, and if conditions are not favorable she can refrain from doing so for an interval of many days. It seems most probable that the beast will remain in hiding for now, moving about by night in search of another secure lair.

"While we could play a waiting game again, I don't think we can count upon the Emperor's patience much longer. Domitian seems ready enough to accept slaughter in the streets and even on his own estates—although it may be just as well that no evidence remains of what we found in the loft. However, your lord and god expects results, and if we don't produce the sauropithecus very soon now. . . ."

"*Our* lord and god won't limit his attentions to just Lycon and me," Vonones warned. "You may be a stranger here, but that won't spare you from Domitian's displeasure. Maybe you'd better get a head start back to Nubia now, and leave this lizard-ape to professionals."

"We don't need to play a waiting game," broke in Lycon—not so much in an unfamiliar role of peacemaker as due to the fact he had been only half listening to the other two. "We know where the lizard-ape bolted for cover. We'll track it from there."

"Track it?" Vonones considered the idea. "Through

the sewers, you mean? But there's miles and miles of them. And there's water."

"Easier than tracking it in open country," the hunter went on, "where it could just as easily hide its trail by swimming a stream or taking to the trees. We'll need some dogs—several packs of dogs—and we'll need enough men to break up into groups as needed. You know how the other animals hate the lizard-ape's scent—trailing it through the sewers will be easy with dogs. We'll corner the damn thing and . . . capture it with nets."

N'Sumu might have missed Lycon's hesitation, but he nevertheless reminded the beastcatcher: "Just make certain that the sauropithecus is not harmed in any way. As you have pointed out, *I* have a personal stake in our success as well. How quickly can you be ready to move?"

"Vonones?"

The Armenian considered for a moment. "I'll send word to Galerius—although he'll be expensive after that mess on the Emperor's estates. And we can call in some of our trackers from along the Tiber—that will take time, but we may as well bring them all in from the field now that we know the lizard-ape is in Rome."

"Take too much time," Lycon protested. "By the time Galerius gets here from Ostia and we've pulled in all our men from the countryside, the trail will be cold. We need to be after the thing right now, and I can't see waiting much past noon."

"The men are exhausted after last night."

"Show me any man of them who hurts worse than I do, and I'll buy him a day in the baths to rest up." Lycon's sooty grin was as horrid as N'Sumu's smile. "Come on, Vonones. We're running out of time. I can get us dogs from the Amphitheater right now."

Vonones shrugged. "Then we'll regroup here with all the men we can bring in and whatever dogs we can find—say, an hour after midday—and see what we've got. Is that to your satisfaction, N'Sumu?"

"The plan might work," said the Egyptian. "Let us hope that it does. Make certain that no time is wasted in assembling the tracking parties. I shall rejoin you at midday."

N'Sumu uncurled from Vonones' chair. He reached down and picked up the broken corpse of the sauropithecus chick, still enwrapped in Lycon's net. The Egyptian had managed to recover the creature from Lacerta—in itself a testament as to his authority over the Tribune.

"What are you going to do with that?" Lycon demanded.

N'Sumu stared at him impassively. "Why, take it back to my apartments and eat it."

"*Eat* it!" Vonones gasped.

"Of course. Why else would my people hunt sauropitheci? They are delicious when prepared with a sauce of pepper, lovage, carraway, laser, honey, pine nuts . . ."

"But the thing has fed on human flesh!" Vonones protested.

N'Sumu favored them with his widest smile, and left them standing uneasily in Vonones' office.

After a moment Lycon swore and lowered himself painfully onto a bench. "The Superintendant of Sewers," he said in a tired voice, "once told me they'd been working on the lines ever since there was a city here—six hundred years, eight hundred, depends on who you talk to. He thought I ought to go hunting for some of the rats his crews found. Said they'd do just fine in the arena, fighting leopards and the like. I finally decided he wasn't joking."

"Look," said Vonones. "I can see to getting the men and the dogs and whatever nets and weapons we'll need. It's going to be several hours at best before we can move. Why don't you get cleaned up and catch a few hours of sleep? You aren't in any shape to net peacocks, let alone go following hounds through miles of sewers after a creature that ... well, things aren't going to get better if we do manage to corner it."

"Things will sure as hell get worse if we don't," Lycon pointed out. "And anyway, when did you last get some sleep?"

"I haven't been wrestling with lizard-apes in public fountains," Vonones told him. "And you really should get those wounds looked after—that hand looks like a lump of raw liver. Come on, Lycon—if you're too exhausted to chase this thing down, you know none of the rest of us are up to the job. And if we fail, then we are all of us ..."

"All right," Lycon yawned, too fatigued to argue further. "I'll go to the baths, get cleaned up and have a good rubdown, maybe sleep a few hours until we're ready to move."

"And take my litter," Vonones urged. "No, don't argue. It will save time all around, and you can nap on the way. I'll be busy here, and I'll send a messenger for you as soon as you're going to be needed. Might even stretch out for a short nap myself." The last was a lie, but the dealer wanted Lycon to get some rest at any cost.

"All right," decided Lycon. "I said I'd go." A

memory stirred in his tired consciousness. "I'll be at the Baths of Naevius—that's not far from here, is it?"

He paused, not wanting to voice his thoughts. "Vonones, what do *you* think of N'Sumu?"

"I've known," said Vonones, and hesitated. Then: "I've known of people who claimed to be magicians."

"I've known of people who *were* magicians," Lycon stated in what was not precise agreement. "Still, I never knew a magician who did what N'Sumu did with his hands—not just by touching people, but at a distance."

Vonones bit his lip. "I don't believe in the gods, Lycon," he said, with his face twisted in a frown of concern. "Not like that, but . . ."

"Let's just pray that N'Sumu is a friendly god—or magician," Lycon said. "At least, friendlier toward us than toward the lizard-ape."

CHAPTER SEVENTEEN

N'Sumu rented a suite of rooms on the second floor of an apartment block in rather a better neighborhood than that of last night's conflagration. The block included another thirty or so similar apartment suites, most of them broken up and sublet to other tenants. That the strange Egyptian was wealthy enough to occupy an entire suite of rooms by himself did not excite half as much curiosity as did the scandal that N'Sumu lived there without a single slave to serve him—at least, none had ever been observed to enter or depart, although at times questionable sounds were to be heard from within the Egyptian's chambers.

There was a window overlooking the courtyard, but it seemed to be masked with some sort of curtain, and no one could catch any glimpse of what was within even when the shutters were open. This was not surprising, since the screen that blocked out this sun's dangerous ultraviolet radiation also insured complete privacy from any human range of vision. Another field had been calibrated to trigger sensations of fear and unease in any human who approached too closely. If this would not discourage a potential intruder, there were other measures inside the apartment that would terminate any unwelcome visit. N'Sumu had returned one night to find the corpse of a thief, obviously one who had been too drunken to react to artificially induced fear but not so drunken that he could not reach the window. The body lay broken upon the stones of the courtyard, and when the other tenants assumed that the thief had slipped and fallen, N'Sumu did not disabuse them.

N'Sumu unlocked the door of his apartment with the cumbersome key he had been given—after first disarming his own security system by means of one of the devices from the belt he wore beneath his tunics. Once inside, he reactivated all systems. Heretofore his concerns were limited to the chance intrusions and prying curiosity of this world's aboriginal populace; since the night past he now harbored a very real dread in the form of a blue-scaled killer that now had sensed the presence here of its original captor. The situation on this assignment was definitely deteriorating.

RyRelee—or N'Sumu, as he was known to the natives of this world—dropped the corpse of the phile hatchling onto the floor of the barely furnished room and began to pull off the stifling folds of his native clothing. That accomplished, the emissary stripped off the most accessible portions of the bronze-colored protective sheathing he wore over his natural scales—sheathing both a disguise and a protection from the deadly ultraviolet radiation of this scalding hot planet. Carefully he removed the major segments of the mask that enclosed his head. He dared not attempt to make himself any less uncomfortable, as it would take too long to reassemble all of his cosmetic features, and RyRelee had too much to do before he rejoined his native helpers.

The emissary considered them. Their cooperation seemed to be as necessary as it was frustrating. It wasn't that they blundered badly, the two of them. On the contrary, their competence and the way they chose to apply it were dangerous to RyRelee's plans. That was the problem, after all: they made choices instead of doing as they were told, the way Class 6 natives ought to do when given orders by a civilized life form. The plump one, Vonones—he seemed to be soft and safe enough to deal with, but RyRelee had witnessed the aborigine's courage, and he now recognized the shrewd cunning behind the merchant's overt attempts to be conciliatory at all times. The other, Lycon, too often reminded the emissary of a phile; this native was competent, ruthless—and too dangerous for RyRelee's comfort.

No matter. The emissary had already decided that the two of them would not outlive their usefulness to him. If they survived the phile, RyRelee meant to finish them himself—or better yet, leave them to a slower death at the hands of their enemies among the other natives.

RyRelee examined the molds that had matured in his crudely improvised incubator. They were unpalatable, as were the bricks of refined native foodstuffs, but at least they had begun the process of breaking down the complex structures that otherwise would have made even the refined residues as digestible to the emissary as a mouthful of straw to one of this world's aborigines. He managed to ingest enough to help assimilate the fortified concentrates of his stores, then washed it all down with osmotically filtered water. Again he cursed the Cora for allowing him only minimal field equipment: no artifacts must be discovered by the autochthones.

His hunger less painful, the emissary decided to maintain a heightened level of consciousness for the present and adjusted the external metabolism controls of his support system accordingly. He was pushing himself too hard, but there would be time for rest once the current crisis was resolved. And that resolution, RyRelee knew, must be accomplished soon. The Cora awaited results with the same impatience as did the deranged chieftain who ruled this region of the planet.

It galled RyRelee that his own efficiency was in part to blame. He should have foreseen that the phile would already have begun to produce a brood—either she had mated earlier than his agents had reported, or her gestation period was a shorter interval in lighter gravity than anticipated. If he had not interfered in his zeal to see the phile safely housed in the Emperor's menagerie, another few days would have seen Rome infested with immature philes, capable of hunting on their own.

Still, the Cora might have observed this as well, and then would come the cleansing. For all their fine talk of protecting the natural development of intelligent life-forms, the Cora would be willing to obliterate this failure of their policy with thermonuclear destruction. Of course, the philes' savage homeworld had given the creatures the capacity for sudden intracellular changes which made them immune to toxins and even to genetically-tailored viruses.

But there was in any case a hard edge to the Cora, an arrogance perhaps necessary in a race able to rule the galaxy. The emissary had no idea as to exactly what had provoked the wrath of the Cora and brought about the destruction of another native civilization on an island close to here some fifteen hundred of this world's years earlier—Creta, he believed they called what remained of the place today—but he supposed someone had been supplying the aborigines with illegal advanced technology. The Cora might believe that such demonstrations would serve as warning to others who might be tempted to violate their policies of galactic peace, but RyRelee could almost feel sorry for the natives whose civilization had been thus sacrificed for the example.

RyRelee spread the corpse of the phile chick onto a table and laid out the instruments required for his examination. He had to work with only edged metal cutting tools—more obsessive caution on the part of the Cora—but he was nonetheless able to lay bare the concealed genital cleft in the creature's abdomen. But at this stage of its development, it was morphologically impossible to distinguish the immature ovipositor from the male organ, and RyRelee gave it up in favor of conclusive cytological examination. Cellular tissues introduced into the more sophisticated instruments provided by the Cora established that the chromosomal pattern of the dead chick was male.

RyRelee hissed in exultation—was brought back to reality as the normal pleased-laughter sounds were horribly distorted by the surgical modifications of the Cora. Still, that couldn't rob him of his triumph, for within another few days his mission on this primitive world would be accomplished —and to RyRelee's satisfaction.

The situation was rapidly deteriorating, and every hour the emissary remained here increased his danger. Despite his contempt for these primitives, if their Emperor lost patience and demanded his arrest, a thousand natives with crude weapons would inevitably win out over one intelligent being with superior firepower. And now that the phile was aware of RyRelee's presence here, the creature would certainly attempt to seek him out—and RyRelee knew that a phile was not easily deterred from its intended kill.

But the emissary's success in this deadly game was all but assured. RyRelee now knew that the phile could indeed produce multiple broods on this world—and that the natives here could mount no real defense to a widespread infestation of the creatures. Earth was truly the perfect breeding ground for philes, as RyRelee had originally supposed. All that remained was to make certain that his dangerously competent native hunters did not kill the phile through their blundering—and to assure the Cora that this phile had indeed been destroyed as ordered. After that, this region and soon this world would be overrun with philes— worth an untold fortune to those who would pay for healthy specimens—and RyRelee would be secretly reaping his profits in the comfort of his palace. Even if the Cora eventually discovered the presence of philes on Earth and reacted with characteristic finality, this dead phile hatchling would preserve RyRelee from their justice. Clearly the emissary had destroyed a male phile as instructed by his masters, and if a gravid female had also escaped the crash of the starship, RyRelee had been informed of only *one* phile to seek out and destroy.

RyRelee activated his communicator. It was a compact device—both for portability and to disguise it as no more than an incomprehensible *objet d'art* to an aboriginal mind—but its range was sufficient to reach the orbiting Coran starship.

"I have destroyed the phile," the emissary reported. "Fortunately, it was male. Stand by to receive transmission of chromosomal data."

After an unpleasant interval, the artificial voice of the Cora—presumably—sounded from the communicator: "You have done splendidly, RyRelee. Are you now prepared to reach the nearest rendezvous point for recovery?"

"There remain a few matters to pursue," RyRelee stated. "I wish to make certain that neither the phile's appearance nor my intrusion here has resulted in any cultural contamination. It will be necessary to make subtle inquiries, perhaps blank out memories in certain instances, in order to establish to these primitives that any unnatural phenomena they may have witnessed were merely the actions of their gods."

"How much time do you require?"

"Ten planetary days should be sufficient."

"How is your personal situation at present?"

"I am in some danger. These primitives are inclined to unexpected violence. Also the ultraviolet radiation here is of greater intensity than my suit can safely screen out. Ten more days is the maximum."

"If there is danger, we can recover you in much less time."

"I accept the risks."

"Your courage has been noted, emissary. Good luck."

RyRelee deactivated the communicator, then hissed with pleasure—however grotesque the sound was to his ears. In ten days the phile would either be safely cared for in the Emperor's animal pens, or else securely laired in some undiscovered sector of the primitives' city. Either way, the only two natives who posed any real threat to the emissary's project would be long dead by the time RyRelee boarded the Coran shuttlecraft for home.

CHAPTER EIGHTEEN

The phile killed the rat without conscious awareness—a simple lethal reflex that struck out at a living creature within its power to kill. It had already devoured most of the rat before its hunger was appeased sufficiently to permit the phile to consider its tiny prey. Not a kill worth noting by any means, but food should never be taken for granted, even on this world where prey was so abundant and so easily taken.

That might be the explanation. *They* expected the phile to become complacent; *they* intended to lull the phile into a false sense of security because the creatures of this world were so pitifully easy to kill. No matter. *They* had shown their hand—the masters who had devised this game—and the phile would not be fooled so easily now.

Its instincts had been correct. The thin, quick biped—the one that had been presented to the phile before its escape from the wheeled cage—that one was its primary adversary. The phile had sensed their kinship even then, and it knew now that the other killer had recognized this as well. It resembled the other bipeds superficially, but plainly this one was a breed apart—like the phile, a creature bred for the art of killing.

The sudden appearance of their common master was the final proof. His physical disguise had confused the phile only for a moment, for there was no mistaking his scent—nor his terror at their mutual recognition when the phile touched his aura.

This had been a surprise to the phile, but as it considered the matter now, the gamemaster's presence should have been anticipated. The phile had erred in assuming that it had escaped, when in reality all that had happened here on this world had been the prelude to a complicated game designed to be played without the confines of a physical arena. No matter. The phile had been well trained. Unlike its wild counterparts, this phile had been bred for blood sports. Clearly its opponent, who resembled the native bipeds of this world, had been similarly bred and trained.

The destruction of its brood infuriated the phile, but now it realized that this atrocity had only been intended to goad it out of hiding and back into the blood game. Nonetheless, there must be vengeance for this—payment in kind for the slaughter of its offspring. And the gamemaster—he had chosen to enter the game as a participant; this was a bold move and deserved respect, but the master above all others must be killed. He was armed with concealed energy weapons, so his death must be carefully arranged.

But the phile was patient, and it knew it must succeed. No cages or force barriers contained it on this world, and once the game was over, the reward for victory would be an entire world.

CHAPTER NINETEEN

Despite his dislike of being carried on other men's shoulders, Lycon was asleep by the time Vonones' litter had been lifted clear of the pavement. From his youth the hunter had learned to catch sleep when and wherever possible, but his total exhaustion from the night before would have demanded rest even had he been astride a horse. The bearers shook him awake once they had reached the Baths of Naevius, but Lycon stumbled into the baths as if it were all still a dream.

The gardens were subdued by the chill of autumn, but they might have been at the peak of bloom for all that Lycon noticed. The doorkeeper goggled at the spectre of Lycon emerging from the sumptuous litter—then shrewdly decided that it was better to be needlessly obsequious than the reverse. Walking through the door of the changing room, Lycon handed his cloak to an attendant and clumsily began to unlace his boots. His deeply bruised back did not want to bend, but the hunter grunted with the pain and forced his muscles to work.

"Would you like these cleaned while you bathe, master?" an attendant asked, as Lycon stripped off his torn and filthy tunic.

"Yes, and see what you can do about mending this," Lycon told him. He should have sent a runner to his home for fresh garments, but he was too exhausted to care. "Just be quick about it, and don't worry about doing a careful job. These will look even worse by tonight."

The attendant was curious but exercised discretion. Any man who looked as terrible as Lycon might not react mildly to inquiries.

"Is Dolon still here?" Lycon asked. The Baths of Naevius were not his customary baths, although he visited here on occasion. Alexandros' class met here, after all, and . . . no, push that thought away, for the time being. "I'll be in the laconicum for as long as I can stand the heat," he said when the attendant advised him that the masseur was on duty. "Tell Dolon I'll need him there as soon as I've had a dip in the calidarium pool."

The beastcatcher stepped into the steamy warmth of the calidarium, let his aching body slip gingerly into the heated water. From his days in the arena Lycon knew that better than a full day's sleep was this restorative course: a warm bath, then a massage and scrape-down with the strigils in the scalding heat of the laconicum, followed by a plunge into the cold waters of the frigidarium. It might not undo all the damage from last night, but it would be the best possible means of preparing for today's ordeal.

Dolon was waiting for him when Lycon entered the laconicum. The muscular Greek gleamed with oil and sweat, his shaven scalp for an instant reminding Lycon unpleasantly of N'Sumu. Lycon wondered how the masseur was able to maintain such a sleekness about his generous stature, when working in this heat must melt away pounds of flesh every day. Dolon motioned him to a bench. Through the steam Lycon could see another man stretched out under the ministrations of a masseur— perhaps a personal slave—and he heard the rhythmic slap of hands on flesh, a sound made falsely distant through the steam.

Lycon steadied himself with a hand on the door jamb to keep from slipping on the slick tile. Condensation from the steam covered the walls, making a dreamland vista of the grey tiles and the horizontal bands of mosaic. A craftsman of Naisso who had never been to the coast had inset octopuses and dolphins sporting upon a bright green sea. Lycon stepped carefully to where Dolon awaited. Even so his foot brushed one of the perforated tiles through which boilers in the basement forced steam into the room. Beneath the floor, slaves stoked a fierce fire with great quantities of wood. Lycon swore and stumbled for the bench. The only light, once the door closed behind him, seeped through the skylight, a tracery of mica plaquets now virtually made opaque by layers of steam and soot. Even the minatory red glaze of the heating ducts blurred to grey in the damp darkness.

Lycon stretched his battered body along the bench. "Why don't they light this place?" he growled.

"There's a lamp on the wall, but it's always out of oil," Dolon explained. "Just lie down and relax; your eyes will adjust. Do you want your usual? I have an exquisite new perfume I can apply with the oils. I know that's really the job for a perfumer, but enough patrons have asked, and I got this really good price that I can pass along to my . . ."

"Just the usual," Lycon interrupted. "Where I'm headed from here, no one would notice if you dumped a bucket of perfume over me."

"Dis, you've done enough to yourself already!" Dolon exclaimed, his fingers almost flinching from the bruised and abraded flesh. "Say, are you back in the arena? Is that it? You know, I was just a boy, but I still remember when you . . ."

"I'm not back in the arena," Lycon cut in. "Not yet, anyway. Just do your work and let me try to rest. If I fall asleep, throw me in the cold pool before I start to roast."

Lycon was too fatigued to waste the energy to wince as Dolon practiced his art. The curved metal strigils scraped away at his scorched and discolored skin, removing the soot and oily filth that in an age without soap were otherwise locked into his flesh. The big Greek tried to be gentle, but the bodily damage was appalling to a masseur not used to working on survivors from the arena. Once the skin was scraped clean, he began to work soothing oils into the taut muscles.

The slap and pull of Dolon's hands merged with the sounds of a handball game in progress on the other side of the laconicum's back wall. Words came through the masonry as little more than high-pitched squeals, but the unfaltering *slap-slap-slap* of the ball wove a fabric for contemplation. Either one man was practicing alone or two perfectly matched experts were having a bout as precise as a dance of Oreads.

Lycon dozed, barely awakening when Dolon

needed him to turn over. He dreamed that he was at the restaurant again with Vonones and N'Sumu, but that he was trapped inside the thermospodium in which they were mulling Vonones' wine. It was unbearably hot, and they couldn't seem to hear him slapping on the sides of the thermospodium to be let out. At last N'Sumu raised the lid and peered inside at him. He grinned horribly and reclosed the lid. "I'll have a cup of this," Lycon heard him say.

"Master Lycon?" It was Dolon's voice he heard now. "You said to awaken you when I was finished. So you could move to the frigidarium for a cold bath. Master Lycon?"

"Yes, thanks," Lycon muttered, shaking his head to clear the nightmare. "Get me a towel, would you? How long have I been in here, anyway?"

"About an hour, Master Lycon," said Dolon, producing a towel. "Will you want me after your cold bath? A brisk rubdown after a cold plunge is most efficacious."

"I'll see if I have the time." Lycon counted out coins from the purse he had carried with him. Although it wasn't likely to happen to him today, by leaving his clothes and sandals in the changing room he ran a fair risk of having some thief exchange them for his own poorer garments. "I'll pay you for now, but look in on me shortly. It must be close to midday, is it not?"

"I believe so, Master Lycon. Thank you very much, Master Lycon."

I can afford to tip generously, the hunter mused, *when the odds are I'll be dead by the end of the day.* He said: "I'll be expecting a messenger from Gaius Claudius Vonones. Direct him to the frigidarium.

If I still have time for a rubdown, I'll wait for you in one of the massage cubicles. I'll probably be asleep."

The artificially cooled air of the frigidarium was a welcome change from the oven-like interior of the laconicum, but the plunge into the cold water there forced a gasp of agony from Lycon's lungs. Almost losing consciousness, the hunter made his limbs slash through the water in brisk strokes. He was an excellent swimmer—of necessity, else he would have drowned a hundred times over. The shock of cold water dulled the pain of his body as he swam. At this hour the frigidarium had not yet become overly crowded, and he was able to exercise without blundering into the usual hordes of bathers.

His legs were shaky when he pulled himself out of the pool, but Lycon felt reasonably refreshed and vaguely hungry. He would have some wine and dates, perhaps a little honey, when he rejoined Vonones—a light meal that had often provided energy for a day's exertions in the field.

Much of his earlier depression had lifted now, even as the gnawing ache of fatigue slipped from his body. Lycon's mood was strangely exhilarated, and his flesh tingled as he rubbed himself dry with the towel. He flexed the fingers of his right hand; although the hand was still somewhat swollen and horribly discolored, everything seemed to work. There might be some chipped knuckles, but the hatchling's bite had not festered, and his grip was functional, albeit painful.

Lycon entered an empty cubicle and let fall the doorway curtain—more to shut out some of the human uproar than from any need for privacy.

Everyone seemed to be shouting to his friends, and a youthful chorus—probably some of the students who made use of the library and reading rooms here—had begun to sing loudly and discordantly. The hunter stretched out upon the cubicle's bench. If Dolon got here in time for a final rubdown, fine; if not, Lycon meant to nap until Vonones' man called for him.

He had already fallen asleep when the curtain was opened, and a slim body slipped into the cubicle.

"I'm ready now," a young voice whispered hesitantly. "Is that you. . . ?" The naked youth was blinking in the darkness of the cubicle.

"Yes, it's me, Alexandros," Lycon greeted him, starting to sit up before he was fully awake. "Come on in, son. Did Vonones send you to fetch me? Just give me a moment to gather my wits. Go on and take a last quick dip, if you like. Hurry it up, though."

The hunter painfully stretched and fumbled for his purse and towel. Lady Fortune, how Alexandros had grown! Was the lad really going to be twelve soon? No, he was going to be thirteen. He was growing tall—would be taller than Lycon—and his boyish body was beginning to fill out into a man's. He'd soon be after the girls, if he wasn't already. He had his father's lean muscles and his mother's lovely features—those would harden as he grew older and knew the sun and winds of wild lands beyond Rome's frontiers.

It occurred to Lycon that Alexandros was still frozen in the doorway, gaping at him like a carp gasping for a floating crumb.

"Well, what is it, boy? You've seen your father

in worse shape than this. Hurry on, now! We've got to get dressed and back to the compound."

Alexandros would not meet his eyes. "Yes sir," he managed to stammer, and backed away through the curtain. Lycon sniffed. The boy must have taken his time in finding him; someone had already rubbed his young body with scented oils. Must have a girl already; maybe Zoe knew who she was.

Lycon encountered Dolon as the hunter made for the changing room. "I was just coming for you," said the masseur. "A runner has just come for you from Gaius Vonones."

"Yes, I know about that," Lycon said. "My son has already informed me."

Dolon looked puzzled, but he kept his own counsel.

CHAPTER TWENTY

Alexandros had little to say while Lycon urged him to hurry getting dressed and pushed him into Vonones' litter. That suited the hunter, as he was glad to catch a short nap on the way back to the compound. Despite his excitement over the coming chase, Lycon knew he would need all the strength he could muster, and a veteran's needs overcame the anxieties a novice would have suffered. Alexandros, he sensed, had nervously sat bolt upright throughout the journey.

Vonones was red-faced and bleary-eyed when he greeted Lycon, but the bustle of men and the raucous barking and baying of dogs were proof that the Armenian had put his morning hours to good use. "Well, you look hale and hearty again," he lied to Lycon.

"And you look like you've had a restful night yourself," Lycon agreed. "What have you got?"

"Look it over, but I think I've done all we can for now. Galerius should be here by nightfall, and there will be more men trickling in from along the

209

Tiber between here and Ostia, but this is the best I could find on short notice. Got you five packs—maybe fifty dogs in all—from one place or another. They're nothing much to look at, but they're arena dogs and they'll kill."

"Where's N'Sumu?" asked Lycon, glancing around.

"Not back yet. He doesn't need to know about the dogs. Want to start without him?"

Lycon considered it. "No, better wait. We're both dead men if he says so. My hope is to manage to kill the lizard-ape and make it look as if it couldn't be helped. If N'Sumu is along with us, he won't dare say different and face Domitian's displeasure. Could be we can all of us bluff it through, or if not we can let N'Sumu show us those people with their heads in their middles. Like that idea?"

"Lycon, don't joke," Vonones frowned. "We're likely to be dead—unpleasantly dead—no matter what happens."

"Then a joke is all that's left to us," the hunter laughed harshly. "But you're right, and I'd better send Alexandros home. This is no hunt for him to earn first blood."

"Alexandros? Is he here?"

"Yes. You sent him to tell me things were ready, remember? I brought him back with me from the baths. Should have let him stay there and have fun with his friends, but I'm sure the boy wanted to see the hunt."

"Well, I never sent him to you. I haven't even seen him today."

"You were probably too busy to notice Alexandros

hanging about," Lycon said. "He must have come on along with your runner when you sent him after me."

"That must be it," Vonones agreed uneasily. "Want to take a look at the dogs? Like I said . . ."

"They don't have to be hunters," Lycon assured him. "All animals seem to hate its scent—even the tiger went after its spoor. I just want enough dogs to make up a series of large packs—large enough that the lizard-ape can't just turn and kill a few hounds and then disappear again. We'll split into groups if we lose its trail, but we'll keep the groups big enough to deal with the thing once it's run to earth.

"We'll need plenty of lights for each potential group—five packs, did you say? Then we'll need nets and ropes—too close quarters for lassos, more's the pity. Archers won't be much use for the same reason, but short swords and boar spears—anything for close work will do. If we can track it, we can catch it, and once we manage to ensnare the lizard-ape, we can finish it."

"*Capture* it," Vonones warned. "Here comes N'Sumu."

"Let's get busy then," Lycon said. "These dogs. . . ?"

. . . Were nothing to brag about, Lycon decided, but they would do. They would have to do. He was gambling on the likelihood that the lizard-ape would wait for nightfall to quit the sewers—it needed the darkness to cloak its movements, after all. With enough dogs and men he could track it down below—no matter how fast it fled, no matter how many side tunnels it tried to hide within. The lizard-ape was fast, but once cornered by the dogs, a dozen men with nets and weapons would prove more than its match at close quarters. Or so Lycon hoped.

"Was that your boy?" N'Sumu joined them. He seemed to be in high good spirits, which did little but grate on the overstretched nerves of Lycon and Vonones. "What a lovely lad. You must be very proud, Lycon."

Was there a threat behind the kind words? Lycon said: "Alexandros isn't coming along with us on this. I'm sending him home."

"No need. He was on his way out as I arrived." N'Sumu smiled. If the Egyptian was trying to be pleasant after this morning's show of force, Lycon decided he preferred him angry.

"Well," said Lycon, "we're all here. Let's get on with it."

"Got wagons to haul everything," Vonones told him, justifiably proud of the degree of organization he had managed. "Be lucky if we don't have a dead dog or two by the time we pick up the trail. I've tried to keep these packs separated as best I could, but most of the dogs have never worked together—they're still busy sniffing asses and sorting one another out. You know, I think my people may have just rounded up alley curs half the time and charged me for trained hounds. When I think . . ."

"Never mind, Vonones," Lycon reassured him. "They're good enough to go after the lizard-ape's scent. You know damn well that most of them will be dead meat once they find the thing."

He thought, but did not say: *As will be most of the men—and maybe both of us.*

CHAPTER TWENTY-ONE

It was dark and damp and stank, but the dogs had no problem in picking up the lizard-ape's scent. The major difficulty had been in holding the first group in check while the rest of the dogs were lowered into the sewer from the street above. It quickly became apparent to Lycon that the sheer number of men and hounds were going to pose a problem at the onset of the chase. He reluctantly gave the order for one group to remain at the entrance to the catch basin. They would only get in the way, and Lycon had a better use for their pack.

"Release these." The beastcatcher pointed to one mass of straining hounds.

"We'll never be able to keep up," N'Sumu protested, not unreasonably. The Egyptian was studying the brick arches of the sewer, seemingly oblivious of the stench of the filthy water that coursed sluggishly along its channel. He seemed also oblivious of the fact that he was out of reach of decent lantern light. Lycon thought about N'-

Sumu's strange eyes, then pushed that thought aside.

"We can track the unleashed dogs with the rest of the pack," the hunter explained. "Just now we're too many, too noisy, too slow. The lizard-ape could keep its distance and lead us on a chase for a hundred miles of sewer, and we'd never catch a glimpse of it."

"But the dogs might kill the sauropithecus if no one is there to pull them off!"

"Come on, N'Sumu! You're our lizard-ape expert! You know damn well we'll be lucky to catch up with the dogs before your little pet turns and kills the lot of them!"

"*My pet?* What do you mean, *man!*"

"The Emperor's pet, then," Lycon retorted, too busy to note N'Sumu's sudden anger. "And let's be after it."

N'Sumu checked his panic. Just a chance expression, not a guess. Absurd to think that the Cora might have planted another agent here on this world. Or was it absurd? In any event this Lycon would be dead very shortly, one way or another.

The phile resubmerged. It had heard enough sounds of pursuit to be certain that its precautions—instinctive though they were—had not been needless. The bipeds had returned with their loud quadruped stalkers. It seemed absurd that these creatures would place such reliance upon inferior material for this game, until the phile reconsidered the obvious shortcomings of the soft-fleshed bipeds on this world. Their pathetic slowness was plainly evident; their perceptual acuity seemed no better, in that they seemed to rely upon other life-forms to extend the range of their senses. The phile, which understood non-phile life only as potential prey, felt contempt for such weakness as this reliance expressed. No wonder the game-master had brought in a more worthy opponent for the phile to destroy. The others were obviously intended to serve as no more than a distraction. And time they were removed.

The phile knew the sewers well. It had come here first when it had entered this city many days ago. For a time the phile considered these underground tunnels as a possible lair, but their sudden flooding with heavy, unpredictable rains drove it to seek a more secure refuge. Secure, until *they* had destroyed it.

The phile waited in the darkness as the pursuit loudly vanished into the tunnels, following a trail it had left hours before. It had discovered long before that the four-legged stalkers could not follow a trail through deep water. It was quite safe here in the main channel, rising from its depths only to take in a breath of air.

Very soon it would be night outside.

A runner had managed to find Lycon at last, so the beastcatcher had in some measure been warned—although still he was not prepared for the sight that greeted him.

The street seemed to be filled with dead men.

"Came up out the catch basin long about dark," Rebilus was able to mutter. Lycon had left him in charge of the group of men stationed behind at the entrance to the sewers. Now Rebilus was the sole survivor, and from the bubbling gashes in his belly, he wasn't likely to see another dawn.

"We'd all been sitting around," Rebilus continued, too much in shock to realize the extent of his wounds. "You know, waiting to hear how things were going down below. Every now and then someone would climb back up and fill us in. Nothing much happening. Even the crowd that had been here at first had pretty well given it up."

He shuddered and stared at his hands. There was so much blood staining the pavement that he might have been telling himself that it was not really *his* life-blood that seeped through his fingers.

"I'd gone over to the fountain for a drink of water," Rebilus said dully. "That's all I did." He seemed to be using his last strength to establish that the guilt for this massacre was not to be laid on his shoulders.

"I bent down, and everything was fine. I looked back up, and that blue thing was already out of the hole. Piso and Ligarius were closest, and they were already dead. It just shot up out of there, and its hands were moving too fast to see. It took their heads off just like you'd swat at a fly.

"Then it was on us. I tried to get to my net, but it just came straight at me. I heard the others screaming as I went down, and I guess I must have passed out for a while."

He grunted as one of Vonones' men tightened the sodden bandages that attempted to hold the man's middle together. "It just was too fast," Rebilus muttered peevishly, and he seemed to fall asleep.

Lycon sighed and straightened—none too steady himself after hours of slogging through a confusion of tunnels. This was worse than the scene on the grain barge. The lizard-ape had worked in haste, but in a span of only a few minutes it had killed or maimed more than twenty people here—many of them onlookers drawn by fatal curiosity to see what so many armed men were doing down in the sewers. The worst was that no one here had any clear idea as to where the lizard-ape had gone after its outburst of slaughter.

And night had fallen.

"*I* told you the sauropithecus was clever," N'-Sumu said. There almost seemed to be a note of gloating to his attitude.

"Damn thing doubled back, let us chase after these worthless dogs across half of Rome." Vonones sounded too worried to snap back at N'Sumu, and Lycon was too exhausted.

"We'll pick up its trail again from here," the hunter said wearily.

"And chase it down into the sewers again," gibed N'Sumu. He seemed to be deliberately baiting Lycon.

"You're in charge!" Lycon snarled, turning on the Egyptian. "You tell me what to do!"

"I did warn you," N'Sumu smiled. "Lacerta! Your men! Here!"

The tribune had already stood scowling at the three men, trying to decide on a course of action that would not make him lose face again to the Egyptian. The Imperial guard had seemed to materialize upon the scene of carnage an instant after the sauropithecus had disappeared.

N'Sumu pointed a long finger at the hunter's chest. "Arrest Lycon, the beastcatcher! His incompetence has again resulted in the murder of innocent citizens! Our lord and god does not tolerate bungling fools, and I will not tolerate insubordination."

Lycon lunged for the Egyptian, but the hulking German guards were already reaching for him. Something—a rock or a fist, its hardness was the same—crashed against the back of Lycon's skull, and he pitched headlong onto the bloodied pavement. An instant later he was jerked back onto his feet, to dangle like an unstrung puppet between a pair of giant guards.

"I've waited for this, Greek!" sneered Lacerta. The tribune stepped close to drive a fist into the beastcatcher's belly. Lycon vomited on the gilded leather of the tribune's boots.

Lacerta stood in open-mouthed amazement, looking from the beastcatcher to the thin bile etching his own footgear. The guards jerked Lycon back roughly. His belly spasmed again, but there was nothing further in it to be spewed out.

"Tie him behind your horse!" the tribune shouted to the pair of men holding Lycon.

The Germans looked at one another, uncertain as to the precise intention of the order, but unwilling to become overly concerned about what some little Italian said—even an Italian with putative control over their lives. One guard shrugged; then both began to stride away toward the horse-holders beyond the circle of bodies. Lacerta stamped his feet, either in a vain attempt to clean them or out of sheer frustration.

"Wait a minute!" said Vonones, stepping toward the tribune swiftly enough that another of the guards pinioned him from behind. Caught like a cricket in a spiderweb, the Armenian continued to shout: "That's not going to help anything! Without Lycon, we'll never catch the lizard-ape! Master N'Sumu, please tell them we need Lycon!"

"Shall we take the merchant as well?" Lacerta asked eagerly.

"Not just yet," said N'Sumu in fluting, silvery Greek. "This one may yet prove useful to me—now that he knows the penalty for insubordination. Do with the beastcatcher as you please."

Lacerta nodded, and the guards who had paused with Lycon between them now proceeded toward the horses again. "We'll take him to the Amphitheater," the tribune decided aloud. "The Greek won't be lonely there, because we'll soon find a nice cell for his family as well. They can all discuss what our lord and god is going to choose to do with them when he hears about this latest slaughter the beastcatcher has caused."

The breath caught in Vonones' throat. The German holding him spun the animal dealer around and pushed him, hard, in the opposite direction from the retreating guard troop. The crowd had thinned enough that Vonones had no one to grip to prevent him from falling over one of the corpses lying ten feet away.

Vonones staggered back to his feet, blinking away tears of panic. He had to remain calm if he were to save himself, much less Lycon.

N'Sumu smiled at him like a hungry shark.

CHAPTER TWENTY-TWO

It was probably mid-morning, but light in the cellars of the Flavian Amphitheater depended on lamps, not the sun.

They had talked a little after Lycon's family was brought in, dragged in, and locked two cells away so that eight feet and a double set of bars separated the beastcatcher from them. Zoe quieted the children almost immediately, however. She had long experience of her husband in his present state: the utter torpor that followed total immersion, mental as well as physical, in a project until he had nothing left to give. Every night after he had played for the blood-mad crowds in the arena, he had collapsed this way . . . and Zoe knew he had done the same more recently in the field after the days he survived but only just. She could forget about that, however, because she had not seen him as she saw him now . . . .

Lycon rolled abruptly, bringing himself to full alertness though he still lay on the floor of the cell where he had been dropped. The concrete surface was slimy with various grades of filth, but the beastcatcher had been in worse places—and he had more important things on his mind, now, anyway.

A single-wick lamp sat beside Zoe, lighting the left half of her face which was suffused with enough concern for the whole. Lycon smiled mechanically, falsely—but the wish to reassure her was not false, and that counted for much at this juncture. "I—" he tried to say, but he croaked instead with the phlegm clogging his mouth.

"Daddy's awake!" Perses squealed. "He's *awake*, Alexandros!"

"We almost had that bastard, love," Lycon said in a normal voice and with a normal expression on his face—the face itself normal, because it was normal enough for it to be scratched and bruised in any of the lines of work Lycon had followed during his life. "Despite everything, right up to the end. We could have tracked it from there—and then that bastard N'Sumu screwed it up or . . . something."

Zoe heard the words, but she could not fathom her husband's meaning. There was no need for her to understand the story, of course: the real point of it was that something had gone wrong but that he was all right, lucid now and healthy enough to discuss events without screaming in pain. The way he lay, ostensibly relaxed now but at full length on the concrete, his torso lifted by his left elbow and flat palm, belied the impression he was trying to give of being in reasonable condition.

Though no doubt it was reasonable for someone who had been through whatever her husband had been put through, this time as in former times.

Aloud, Zoe said, "Alexandros has been reciting the *Iliad* to me, darling. It was so *very* clever of him to bring the volumes with him. Would—" the plump woman reached beside her without looking; her hand caught that of her older son and the two stepped together, side to side, as they both kept their eyes on Lycon "—would you like him to read to you, too? Because he does it *so* well."

"Are we going to leave now, Daddy?" Perses demanded.

"Not quite yet," the beastcatcher said with the touch of wry humor that made the truth speakable, "unless things are even worse than I think they are." He reached out with the hand that had braced him on the floor and caught one of the bars. "*Up* we go," he coaxed himself in an undertone, and it wasn't too bad. Herakles, he'd be fit for another try tonight just like the last one, if they could only find the lizard-ape again.

And if they let him out on his own feet instead of being dragged from the arena through the Gate of Death by his heels.

"Yeah, right," Lycon said as he let his face shape itself into normal human lines from the mask into which it had drawn itself to hide the pain that might have accompanied movement. It hadn't been too bad, though it might be a while before he wanted to eat again, especially the sort of food he could expect to be offered here. He wondered how the old friendships he had made in the arena were going to stand up now that he himself was in a cell.

If Zoe and the kids were offered slops this time around, there were a lot of people who'd better pray Lycon *did* leave the Amphitheater by his heels.

"Right, ah," the beastcatcher repeated, remembering to smile at his family. The baby was still asleep, thank the gods, and Perses was clutching the side of his mother opposite his elder brother. Lycon did not reach toward them. Eight feet was too far for the gesture to be other than pathetic or absurd, and they didn't need either of those things. "I'd like to hear you recite, Alexandros. Good way to pass the time, and good for you too."

He licked his lips as he paused. They were dry and hot; he wondered if he'd picked up a fever, *gods*, Rome was worse than the fetid swamps of the Nile Delta, for things to send you to Hades in screaming delirium. "Look, I don't know how bad things are, the situation I mean," he went on, because it was better to speak the truth than have them afraid of bogies which were worse—and this *was* the truth, there *was* a fair chance of it working out. The door at the head of the corridor clanked, promise of a meal of sorts . . . or perhaps a visitor, Vonones with a diploma releasing at least Lycon himself. . . .

Speaking very quickly, the beastcatcher went on, "I'm here now because things went wrong last night, but the decision was at a pretty low level. I'm pretty sure Vonones can square things—he *knows* how bad they need me if any of this is going to work."

Zoe nodded understanding with her lips sucked tightly together in hope that this would, by sympathetic magic, prevent the tears from slipping from her eyes. By looking down she managed without that disaster to say, "Then you aren't condemned to the, to . . . above, I mean." She lifted her head in a gesture and the tears did burst out, not single droplets but runnels that wavered as Zoe twisted her face away again and wiped it on the shoulder of her shawl.

"Oh, Pollux, nothing like that," the beastcatcher said with a brusqueness and near-anger that cloaked his own reactions—all but the catch in his voice, just a brief catch. There was only one set of footsteps rasping down the corridor, so it was the slave with food after all. Who knows, maybe he could eat something now that he'd stood erect for a while, a chunk of bread at least to scrub the tastes of bile and exhaustion from his mouth. "Look, I don't say it won't happen, but I've been in worse places. I won't kid you about this mess, but things have been a lot worse."

The slave was not carrying a lamp. In fact, he did not appear to have a tray of food.

"Father," Alexandros was saying, "I'm sorry about the way I, I ran away from you yesterday. And—before." The boy was looking at the floor of the intervening cell, but he had the courage to keep his face turned in the direction of Lycon as he spoke. "I won't make you ashamed of me again."

"You there!" Lycon called as he shifted his body and his full attention to the front grating of his cell. He was no longer conscious of his body, of the aches and nausea against which he had been struggling in the time since he had awakened. The slave who shuffled down the corridor past Lycon and toward the cell holding his family wore a Gallic cape with the hood pulled close over his face. "Come here, damn you, or I'll have you flayed this afternoon when they let me out of here!"

"Who is it?" Perses called as he ran to the corridor side of his own cell.

The man in the cape, maybe a woman, of course, the figure was so short, did not look aside despite the beastcatcher's shout. Lycon made a desperate snatch through the bars, but the figure was too far away as it passed.

"Father?" said Alexandros, his voice rising an octave in the course of the two syllables.

"Perses, come h—" cried Zoe, grabbing for the child as he started to repeat, "Who—?" to the figure in the corridor.

"*No!*" screamed Lycon, and the arm came out from beneath the cape, one arm only but quite sufficient for its purpose. It was quick, cat-quick or even more so, and its claws caught Perses not by his tunic but under the breastbone, punching their multiple paths through the boy's diaphragm and then curling back around the lowest ribs to penetrate the skin again. They held Perses like a fish hooked around the jawbone.

The arm snatched back into the corridor and the boy followed it to the narrow gap between the bars, jerked off his feet. Then the breastbone with associated muscles and cartilage ripped free and the remainder of Perses flopped back onto the floor of the cell. He was still alive, but he could not scream because his chest could no longer force air through his throat. One of the four-year-old's lungs, hooked by the tip of the claw, flopped outside his ruined chest.

"Zoe, Alexandros," Lycon ordered in a calm, clear voice, "get to the back of the cell. Leave Perses, we'll take care of that when it's safe. *Move!*"

Though they were safe where they stood, you could never tell. They might lunge forward to caress Perses or grapple with the thing in the corridor—equally suicidal, equally pointless. You couldn't change death, not even the gods could change that if there were gods; and there would be a time to kill the blue thing, the lizard-ape, and it would be a very long time in dying.

The beastcatcher no longer felt his body, though he knew it would respond as he thought, perhaps even quickly enough to grip the thing's arm if it were extended into Lycon's own cell. He bunched his tunic with his left fist, balling it out from his chest so that the claws would not snatch away his heart and life until his own hands had a throat to grip.

The sounds and everything Lycon saw within the cellblock were preternaturally clear, but they were distanced by the fact that he could not change any of them. He had been afraid when the figure shuffled down the corridor, but there was no longer any fear, any emotion whatever, only the taste of blood in his mouth as Alexandros shouted and stepped toward the thrashing remnants of his brother.

Zoe caught the older boy by the wrist and jerked him back, as she had done when he was an infant crawling toward the scorpion which had ridden Lycon's clothing back from the docks. As she held her remaining son, Zoe turned her back to the corridor so that the thickness of her body was between the infant at her breast and the sauropithecus. She was silent, and she held Alexandros in safety against the far wall, though he flailed and screamed to get at the thing which had murdered Perses.

The sauropithecus turned its hand, the only part of its body not still covered by the cape. The gobbet of the boy's flesh and bone dropped to the floor of the cell. One of Perses' feet kicked at it blindly as his back arched and lifted his gaping chest toward the ceiling.

The creature's long claws slid into their sheaths, clearing them of the clinging gore. The paw—*hand*—twisted back toward the cowl, and a slender tongue lapped at the congealing stickiness which smeared the delicate scales. The claws re-extended.

Lycon ran to the front of his own cell. He gripped the bars with both hands, all his icy planning forgotten. "Guards!" he shouted. The grating was solidly welded so that the bars did not rattle among themselves, but the whole clashed loudly against the locking bar. *"Guards! Somebody!"*

The click of the sauropithecus' claws working the wards of the lock down the corridor were inaudible under the present conditions, but they rang as clearly in Lycon's mind as the drooling whisper of the blood filling Perses' chest cavity.

"Somebody dear gods! N'Sumu!"

The creature dropped its cape as it swung open the door. The tiger's claws had left long scars of leprous white against the scales. It had been very badly hurt, and it could surely be killed, would be killed, but for now it stepped with the balance of a rope-dancer into the cell with Zoe and the children, two of them still alive. Had he thought it was an animal? The look in the eyes the lizard-ape turned on Lycon now was quite human, as human as the eyes of N'Sumu himself when he ordered the arrest of the beastcatcher's family. . . .

"*Gods!*" Lycon screamed.

But no god came; and hammer the bars as he

might, Lycon could neither tear them loose nor drown the noises in the adjoining cell. The noises went on for a very long time. He did not notice when they finally stopped.

The beastcatcher was open-eyed, his hands and arms as rigid as the iron which they clutched, when the figure left the cell. It donned the cape and shook the hood again over its features. Lycon did not see it leaving, nor did the creature appear to have any further interest in the man responsible for destroying its brood. As it moved off down the corridor, it could easily have been a shuffling beggar-woman, bent and wasted by age.

But there was nothing human about the footprints it left on the stone behind it, except for the blood of which they were made.

CHAPTER TWENTY-THREE

"Where—" muttered Lycon, aware for the moment only that there was sunlight on his face and that there shouldn't be, though he did not recall why. He recalled nothing, but he lay on a soft bed with the odor of food and light perfume nearby and that was all wrong. . . .

And then he did remember.

"Herakles!" Lycon shouted. His eyes opened and he tried to leap from the bed, but three days in and out of coma made his legs nerveless, and he fell back onto the feather mattress. He tried to focus his eyes, blinking dizzily. There were a half dozen men around him in the richly-appointed chamber, all of them slaves except for Vonones.

"Well, hold it to his mouth!" Vonones urged the boy who had just dunked a wedge of bread into a cup of undiluted wine. A warming rack over a brazier held a simmering pot of beef broth, and there were dainties of fish and vegetables waiting on a separate tray against the beastcatcher's possible whim when he awakened.

"Lycon," Vonones said, peering earnestly at him, "lie back and eat this bread."

"Can't do both, can I?" Lycon whispered. His voice did not sound like one he had ever heard before. He shifted himself upon the couch so that he faced the side where the slave knelt with the bread and wine. He did not attempt to take the morsel from the boy. Simply resting on one side was enough to overtax his reawakening muscles at the moment. He chewed slowly and carefully.

"You're all right, then?" said Vonones, looking away from his friend's face as he spoke the question. Only the slaves thought that the words had anything to do with Lycon's physical state.

The beastcatcher swallowed his mouthful of bread. He nodded away the boy's attempt to feed him more at the moment. A doctor in the background shifted from one foot to the other, waiting to offer the potion he held in his hands. "I'm all right," said Lycon. "Why am I here?"

"I arranged for it," Vonones said. He took the dripping bread from the slave and offered it with his own fingers. "Here, try a little more and then we'll help you sit up. I—offered Crispinus an arrangement which he found satisfactory. He explained to our lord and god that you were quite necessary for the hunt to succeed and that Lacerta had badly misinterpreted the events of that night. A party arrived with the documents for your release somewhat—" he swallowed and looked away "—a great deal later than I would have wished."

Lycon mumbled around his bread. Deliberately the beastcatcher lifted himself into a sitting position, swallowed as a pair of slaves stacked pillows behind him unbidden, and said, "It wouldn't have made any difference. Don't. . . ."

"Lycon, I—" the merchant began in the pause without any real notion of where he was going to take the sentence.

"I said it didn't matter," Lycon said. He swung his legs over the side of the bed and let the motion stir the blood throughout his body. "It was going to happen the same way, in the apartment or wherever, because I wouldn't have believed it could happen until it did."

"Don't stand up yet," the doctor blurted from behind the other slaves.

Lycon stared at him for a moment. "Right," he said at last. "And don't you open your mouth again."

No one moved until Vonones reached for the bread again.

"The soup smells good," said Lycon mildly. "I think I'd like the soup."

As the slave hovering over it handed him a steaming cup, Lycon continued, "What are we expected to do now, you and I?"

Vonones sat down on the bed beside him and said, "Catch the creature, the same as before. I understand that our lord and god has become increasingly interested since the. . . ." Vonones had not been looking at Lycon. Now he turned so that he could do so. "The whole staff in the guardroom was killed. I'm not sure Domitian knows about what we found in Mephibaal's loft, all the details, but he knows about the Amphitheater."

Vonones reached over and touched his friend's arm, pretending not to notice the tears. "Lycon," he said, "it's been three days. I've taken care of all the arrangements. There's a memorial plaque on the side of the monument I built for myself, and we can go there any time you like." He fumbled again for words. "I had over a hundred witnesses to the cremation. It was a nice one."

"We're going to kill it," Lycon said. He stood up, looking into the cup of broth, and took a deep drink from it before he tried to walk unassisted to the far wall. "I thought we should from the start, and now I think that would be a nice memorial. Better than stone."

He, too, was pretending there were no tears on his lined, weathered face. Keeping his back to Vonones made it easy for both of them. There was no one else in the bed chamber, only slaves, property with voices but no place in a computation of human beings.

"N'Sumu is still in charge," Vonones said carefully. "I don't know how he feels about your release, but I'm quite sure that he still intends to capture the sauropithecus alive."

"He could have killed it," Lycon said, staring in the direction of the wall. It was a fresco of a scene from the *Odyssey*—the Laestrygonians wrecking the fleet with huge blocks of stone hurled from their clifftops—but to Lycon it was simply a monochrome blue bounding his memories. "When it leaped at me that night at the fountain. He must have stunned it, and that saved me ... but it didn't save Zoe and. . . ."

That was not a direction in which his thoughts should have turned. He slammed his cup into the wall, denting the thick plaster and shattering the delicate vessel—a cup fashioned of porcelain ten thousand miles away, by the same folk who wove worm cocoons into silk garments.

"Pollux, I'm sorry," Lycon blurted, shocked into full consciousness by the splash and the prickling in his hands of shards of porcelain. A lifetime ago, he had killed a lizard-ape chick thus. "That was a good one, wasn't it? Probably worth more than I'd fetch on the block myself." He faced the Armenian with a crooked smile, holding a sliver of the cup between his thumb and forefinger.

"I think it's one you brought me yourself one year when you were trading on the coast of the Red Sea," Vonones said calmly. He recognized Lycon's mood and repressed a shiver. "I've got a really valuable one—a cup of hollowed out agate. If you like, I'll smash that one myself to show you how little I care about any of that now." He paused.

"Of course," he went on in the same tone, "that won't help us with what we need to do. To kill the lizard-ape ourselves."

Lycon flicked his eyebrows upward in assent. He walked to the tray of food—he was moving almost normally by now—and, ignoring the efforts of a slave to serve him, took a handful of crab paste and a wedge of bread to use for a napkin.

"All right," Lycon said, filling his mouth, "what do *you* think of N'Sumu?"

"I don't know what to think," confessed Vonones.

"We'd best go talk to him," Lycon said quietly. "After I've eaten. And after—" he ran his knuckles down the skin of his thigh, wrinkled and clammy with the days he had spent unconscious and un-moving "—I've had a long steaming at the bath."

He smiled at Vonones, dismissing the worry etched on the merchant's features. "You always try to get me to sit in the sedan chair with you. Well, today I won't argue."

Lycon hesitated. The brave efforts at sociability evaporated. His face had all the reassurance of a bleached skull. "Don't worry about me, Vonones," the hunter said. "I'm going to finish this one. Whatever it costs."

CHAPTER TWENTY-FOUR

"Gaius Cornelius Sempronianus?" asked the centurion wearing the scarlet tunic and sandals of the Praetorian Guard.

The doorkeeper who had opened the panel to an authoritative knock now blinked in amazement to see the third-floor hallway filled with troops and their servants. The Praetorians did not carry spears or shields for this assignment, but their helmets and belted swords left no doubt of what they were.

"But sirs, he's only a schoolmaster!" the slave in the doorway blurted.

The centurion grinned and knocked the doorkeeper aside as he strode within. Some of the servants behind him were carrying lamps, others held lengths of rope. The first three of the soldiers following the centurion simply trampled over the doorkeeper, but the next pair paused long enough to pinion the fellow's arms behind him. A servant trussed the doorkeeper wrist to wrist with one of the cords he carried already cut to length.

There were no proper doors within the small

suite. The Praetorians ripped down the curtains hung over internal doorways for privacy. The lamplight and the slam of hobnails on the floor brought the inhabitants off their couches, wearing tunics and frightened expressions. In one alcove a man and a woman, the latter with an infant in her arms, babbled in Greek, "But we just rented the bed today! Please!" as the soldiers dragged them into the center of the main room. More of the Praetorians' servants moved in for the menial task of binding the captives.

Lycon caught the nearest servant by the arm, halting him, and said to the soldiers with the couple, "Let them go. They aren't covered in the order . . . and anyway, the baby."

There was a curtained bed in one corner of the main room. The centurion himself tore away the orange-dyed linen. The gray-bearded man on the bed was holding an embroidered coverlet over himself with one hand as if the cloth were some protection. He wore a tunic. The boy cowering beside him was of a smoothly-olive cast with only a hint of pubic hair visible when the Praetorian jerked the bedclothes down. His mouth was covered by the older man's other hand. "Cornelius Sempronianus, I'd judge," the centurion said in a tone of grim satisfaction.

"I'm a Roman citizen," Sempronianus said, his voice cracking in the middle of the clause. He clamped his thin arms across his chest in a pitiful attempt to deny purchase to the soldiers reaching toward the bed. "What are you doing to me?"

Soldiers lifted the naked, squealing boy, one by each arm, while the centurion stood grinning, arms akimbo. One of the Praetorians pinched the boy's

buttocks with his free hand. "Hey," he said cheerfully, "save this one out. Be a crime to send him to
the arena."

"Quintus," said the soldier holding the little
gunsel's other arm, "this is the wrong outfit to talk
about seeing how boys lasso the ram. Unless you
want to see the Amphitheater from the inside
yourself." He gave a meaningful nod toward their
commanding officer.

Together, the Praetorians handed their slight burden to a servant to be tied. "A-arena?" whispered
the schoolmaster.

"Get up, Greekling," ordered the centurion in
the silky voice of a man who would just as soon
meet resistance.

Lycon stepped into view around the centurion's
blocky torso. "Good evening, Gaius Sempronianus,"
the beastcatcher said. "I heard you'd gone to spend
some time with a brother in Akragas, folks in the
apartment thought. I'm glad it was a short visit."

"You were condemned," Sempronianus said in a
voice choking with awe and dawning awareness.
"To the arena."

The centurion kicked away one leg of the bed.
The frame scrunched down, tipping the schoolmaster onto the floor. "I thought I said get up," the
centurion grated.

"You know," Lycon said, "for a while there, I
really wanted to talk to you about the education
you were giving my son ... but one thing and
other came up, and now there isn't much point in
that after all. It made me think you might be the
perfect man to serve our god and lord in a special
way, though."

"Oh Zeus, Father Omnipotent!" shrieked Sempronianus as he squirmed on his belly to clutch the beastcatcher's ankles. "Oh dear master Lycon, you mustn't send me to the arena, I swear by the bones of my mother I never touched your Alex—"

The centurion, to whom Lycon had talked about Sempronianus while the section formed up in barracks, kicked the schoolmaster hard enough in the ribs to lift him off the floor. The soldier rubbed the toe of his foot against the calf of the leg on which he balanced. Looking over to the beast-catcher, he said, "It doesn't really dirty your hands to touch his like, you know? But there isn't any need, either. I mean, why *not* use your foot?"

The centurion had mentioned that he had three sons of his own, the eldest just turned twelve.

"It wasn't so much what he *did* to Alexandros," Lycon said. "It was when I figured out that he'd made the boy *like* it. I wouldn't dare touch him." His voice was trembling, just as were the big muscles in his arms and legs. He was not tight but rather janglingly loose like the links of an iron chain. The beastcatcher turned away and slapped at a wall, not particularly hard. He was trying to burn off the nervous energy that surged through him and made it hard for him to stand, much less talk.

"Keep that one separate," the centurion said to the servants bending over Sempronianus with their lengths of cord. "That one comes with us to the compound of Claudius Vonones. The rest of the household is transferred to the arena for tomorrow's games." He smiled down at the schoolmaster, twisting like a salted slug. "Slave and free alike, Greekling," he said in a voice as harsh as the hobnails which had lifted Sempronianus. "To convince you of just how serious the Emperor is that you do everything master Lycon here tells you to do."

"Because if I touched him," Lycon said as he struck the wall again, with both hands this time, and the heels of them, hard enough to make a bronze lamp jounce on its bracket, "then I'd kill him myself for sure. And I need him alive.

"I really need him alive. . . ."

CHAPTER TWENTY-FIVE

The guards hired by the owner of the property watched Vonones and his crew—crews—with the universal interest of idlers for workmen. The guards—off-duty members of the Watch, in this case—had been placed to keep looters and tenants out of the smoldering rubble of the apartment block until the owner settled with a contractor for rebuilding. The Armenian merchant would have been willing to treat with the owner for access, but that was likely to cause delay and curiosity—besides which, the guards themselves could be squared for ten obols, the price of a quick lay for all five members of the contingent. Saving money was not a primary purpose; but saving money was never wholly apart from Vonones' purpose either.

The slave gang he had hired from a building contractor was doing the heavy work of moving stones and charred timbers. Trusted members of the Armenian's own staff watched as each lifted structural element exposed lesser rubble and a cloud of ash. Even four days after the event, there were still hot spots in the wreckage. Once when a beam was lifted away, there was a gush of flames as fresh air touched the blanket swaddling the body of an infant. The construction workers were familiar with the hazard: building in Rome usually meant building on burned-over premises, even when the fire had been the result rather than the cause of the previous structure's collapse. The beast handlers cursed and hopped and threw sidelong glances at their master . . . but none of them complained aloud. Vonones' temper at present was like a sheet of glass: it was apt to break without warning, and the jagged shards resulting were extremely dangerous.

At the moment, the Armenian watched while two of his own staff shoveled ash from the area of the stairwell onto a sieve—intended for concrete preparation—shaken by four of the construction gang. Ash that looked like smoke and smelled like corpses drifted down the breeze, while anything larger than mid-sized gravel caught in the wooden meshes. One of the men emptied his shovel onto the grate and swung back to rubble to refill it.

"Hold up," Vonones said, sharply enough that the sieve crew froze also, an unintended result but not unfortunate. Dust continued to drift and settle. The animal dealer stepped closer, regardless of the way his sandals and the lower edge of his tunic turned gray. He shifted to his left hand the whip he carried—an enigma to the construction workers, and the one overt sign of the terror Vonones felt at revisiting the site of the sauropithecus' former lair. Very delicately, he reached onto the sieve and plucked from the wood and plaster and bits of bone the object he had come to retrieve.

The men with shovels poised expectantly. One of the construction workers leaned over for a closer look. He drew back abruptly with a grimace. "By Apis' dong!" he blurted, "it's a spider!"

"No," said Vonones in a voice congealed by terror at what he was doing.

The creature he held had four legs rather than eight, and in size it more nearly approximated a large crab. The limbs and body were scaled, not segmented; and where they had been shaken free of ash, the scales were blue. In death it was shrunken so that the clawed feet and hands hugged its own caved-in chest and the flesh of the face was pulled back from the tiny, glittering teeth.

Vonones had not gotten a clear look at the larval monsters in the loft, even this one that Lycon had crushed against the wall as they broke free. His memory of the adult, from the hours he had seen it caged in the distant past, had filled in what he thought was a picture of the offspring. In fact, this flat-bodied creature was far less humanoid than the mother-thing, and even more disturbing.

Vonones dropped it into the leather sack he had brought for the purpose and pulled the drawstrings tight. He handed the container to one of the men with a shovel. It was not obvious that his right hand was shaking, but the staff of the whip trembled like a palm tree in a windstorm.

"We've got what we came for," the animal dealer called, overriding the tremor in his voice by sheer volume. "You can down tools. We're going back to the compound." He paused. "And keep your *eyes* open," he added, without specifying the reason for vigilance—because he did not care to make his fear concrete in his own mind.

The workmen obeyed with a noisy enthusiasm, tossing their equipment into the builder's cart which had been hired along with the construction gang. Vonones' own employees were more circumspect; and when they handed over their tools, they took from the wagon the nets and lassoes which their master had ordered them to carry on the march back. The four archers who had watched the proceedings with arrows nocked fell in at the front and rear of the forming column.

"Good work, chief," one of the guards called.

Vonones nodded without really hearing the words. Any one of the offspring would do, Lycon had said, and the beastcatcher was quite certain that the little creatures were tough enough that the body of at least one would exist despite the chances of fire and tumbling stone.

The Armenian dealer had been far more doubtful of success: his memory of flames clawing the sky was vivid and had been strengthened by his subconscious desire that all the events of the night be washed as clean as quicklime.

But of this Vonones was certain: Lycon would have whatever he said was needed to capture the sauropithecus if that thing were in the Armenian's gift.

CHAPTER TWENTY-SIX

The temple had been dedicated to a female deity, very possibly Venus in one of her manifestations. Roman gods, unlike those of the Greeks, had tended to be very circumscribed in the extent of their powers. Jupiter Greatest and Best was no more the same—spirit—as Jupiter Stayer of Armies than the Claudius who built the Appian Way was the same as the Claudius who ordered the invasion of Britain five centuries later ... and indeed, the latter connection may have been the less tenuous.

That was changing, had changed already since Roman armies had stormed through Greece—and Greek ideas, held as haughtily as the eagle standards of Aemilius Paullus, had taken Rome in turn. The newer temples were Graecicized and eclectic, universal as the emperors wished their rule to be universal. Above all, the cult of the reigning emperor. Scarcely less prominent, the Goddess Rome who personified not a city but the imperial rule. And even the foundations to deities whose names would have been familiar to the Romans who broke Hannibal, Jupiter and Venus and Minerva were cast now in a foreign mold.

A side effect of the distaste for the localized spirits of ancestral Rome was that this small temple and a hundred like it were falling into ruin ... and that suited Lycon's present purpose very well indeed.

"Lycon, you're too old for this!" Vonones said, wringing his right hand with his left, his thumb polishing knuckles mottled with the pressure of their grip of the whipstock.

N'Sumu looked around, shifting his feet instead of depending on the rotation of his neck to give a panorama of his surroundings. His nostrils did not flare—they did not move when he breathed, either—but he said, "It's very close, I tell you, its smell is all over. Standing here like this puts us at its mercy."

"Well, I'm not going to get any younger, am I?" said Lycon as he tied off the thongs that closed his body armor of iron hoops. It was of military pattern, giving enough play to his torso that he could at need cast a net, but solid enough to stop a well-thrown spear. Whether or not it would stop the claws of the lizard-ape, pricking through the interstices between the bands of iron, was a question which could be answered only in the event.

Looking over at the tall Egyptian, the beast-catcher added, "It doesn't have any mercy, Master N'Sumu. Let's say 'at its whim,' shall we?"

"Lycon, nothing that's happened is a reason for *you* to kill yourself," the Armenian went on. "You were the best, and you're very good—I know. But there are younger men we could pay to do this and do it better."

"Do exactly what?" N'Sumu demanded. His hands were generally hidden beneath his toga, but at intervals one or the other palm would flash into sight as the Egyptian saw something . . . or thought he did.

"Put it down to whim," said the beastcatcher, before the helmet he lowered over his head hid his smile.

Unlike the thorax armor, Lycon's helmet was a gladiatorial style. It was a bronze basinet, an ogive rising to a peak and surrounded by a flat brim a hand's breadth wide. The face, instead of being open as in a military helmet, was covered with a grill of heavy bronze rings—sturdy enough to turn a swordcut if not a thrust by a good blade with a strong man behind it. Lycon hinged the grill closed and latched it. His face disappeared. The full moon highlighted the polished bronze rings so that the shadowed flesh beneath became as insubstantial as air. The beastcatcher lifted his net, one identical in design to that which had been fretted to bits in holding the immature sauropithecus.

"You won't need that to capture the beast," said N'Sumu, nodding toward the short sword belted at the beastcatcher's waist.

The brim of Lycon's helmet lifted in agreement. Unemotionally, his voice slightly muffled by the grillwork, the beastcatcher said, "Guess you've got a point there." He did not move to unbuckle the weapon.

The night was very still, surprisingly still, perhaps because the low arches of the Appian Aqueduct passed directly behind the temple and effectively separated the old building from the northern nine-tenths of the city. The temple stood on a

low pedestal, with four columns across the front
supporting an extension of the roof and a similar
number of pilasters along either side of the enclosed sanctuary. The triangular pediment was decorated by a face and an inscription, both presumably those of the original founder of the temple;
but the bas relief was not classifiable even as to
sex, and the words were shadows made illegible
by discolorations of the underlying stone. The columns had simple Doric capitals, but their shafts
were unfluted and the soft stone from which they
were carved had pitted badly, especially where the
circular section had been joined by iron cramps.

It had never been a prepossessing structure. Now,
with the roof half fallen into the sanctuary and the
polarized light of the full moon accentuating the
flaws pitilessly from above, the temple had the
feeling of something to be found on the Street of
Tombs outside the city walls.

Five streets met in the plaza which the temple
fronted. Two bent around the front of an unusu-
ally large apartment block whose ground floor shops
opened onto an inner courtyard. The lowest level
of the brick facade was pierced only by two
doorways: a normal-sized one giving access to the
apartments in the upper stories, and a great stone-
arched driveway through which goods wagons as
well as customers could enter the courtyard.

The third floor—above the shops and the dwellings of the shop keepers—seemed to be given over
to the suites of the wealthy. At that level, a loggia
was corbelled out over the street. Planting boxes
on the tiled roof of the loggia indicated that the
inhabitants of the fourth story drew some benefit
from the structure as well. The fountain serving

the area was built against the wall of the apartment building, between the two doorways, instead of being sited in the center of the plaza. The fountain was something over eighty feet from the doors of the temple across from it.

N'Sumu looked around again, his eyes opaque, and hugged himself in what was clearly a response to the shudder which did not appear on the surface of his rich bronze skin. "You're unbalanced," he said aloud in angry wonder. "It could attack at any time—from *anywhere*—and you stand here in the open."

Lycon's helmet turned to the Egyptian. "It had a chance to kill me under the Amphitheater," the beastcatcher said softly. "It passed me by. I think I'll have to give it a reason to change its mind about leaving me alive."

"It didn't pass *me* by," N'Sumu snapped. He hugged himself again, and the agitation which never seemed to enter his tone showed itself in the sudden volume with which he spat out the words. "It knows that it's safe if it can kill *me*!"

"Does it know that?" asked the voice from the bronze grillwork. "Then you'd best get out of danger, hadn't you?" The helmet nodded toward the leaves of the sanctuary door, behind Vonones and the bronze man.

Vonones reached for his friend, hesitated, and then transferred the whip to his left hand to grip Lycon with his right. "Goddess Fortune be with you, my friend," he said, and he sounded as if he wished that he could truly believe in any god, even Chance.

Lycon chuckled, and it might have been the helmet's constriction which made the sound that of a drowning man. He clasped Vonones' arm, hand to wrist, then released the merchant and shook himself. The bronze and the iron armor had the same pale sheen in the colorless moonlight. The beastcatcher touched the net slung over his left shoulder, but he did not transfer it to his hand for ready use as he stumped off across the plaza.

N'Sumu watched the armored Greek with a stride as careless as that of a male lion at the height of his powers. The eye Vonones watched in profile flickered from sandy opaqueness to the abnormal, glittering clarity which was nonetheless normal for N'Sumu. "Do you know what he intends to do?" the Egyptian demanded without looking away from Lycon's back. The beastcatcher was nearing the apartment building opposite.

"I think so," said Vonones. "I'm afraid I do." Then he added, "Let's get inside."

There was a large party of animal-handlers in the courtyard of the apartment block; most of them trained in the arena rather than the field but the best that could be assembled in Rome on the present schedule. Vonones had as little confidence in their ability to capture the lizard-ape *in time* as he did in the hope that Lycon's armor would preserve him for more than one swipe of the beast's talons. A creature which could unlock a cage with its claws was unlikely to be seriously deterred by protection which did not cover the throat or the great arteries of its victim's thighs.

Such benefit as the sword could bring would be effectively posthumous; and even that was doubtful.

N'Sumu opened the sanctuary door whose corroded hinges had proven more of an obstacle than the padlock which Lycon had struck off in preparation for this night. Temples were centers of ceremony, not worship. In all likelihood, this sanctuary had not been opened in eighty years, ever since the Emperor Augustus had refurbished and rededicated it and scores of similar temples in superficial homage to the ancient values which his programs were undermining.

The door had double leaves which pivoted inward. Before they had swung open a hand's breadth—too narrow a slit to pass even a creature as lithe as the sauropithecus—the Egyptian paused. A beam of light, tinged slightly with blue and seemingly as palpable as a jet of water, gushed into the sanctuary and flooded the walls, floor, and ceiling. Only then did N'Sumu open the door leaves the rest of the way so that he and the Armenian could enter. The light appeared to have come from somewhere on his chest; but his toga was unmarked and unremarkable, and Vonones had only memory and the afterimage to assure him that the light had existed at all.

"If you're worried about it getting in b-before us," the animal dealer said with the hint of a stutter despite his attempts to control it, "it could be behind those." His whip nodded toward one of the door leaves, then the other. At the moment, he was more afraid of N'Sumu than he was of the sauropithecus itself.

"No, it couldn't," said the Egyptian as he stepped into the sanctuary. There was no reason not to hide what had happened, because neither Vonones nor Lycon would survive the capture of the phile. They knew too much, and they had made dangerously accurate extrapolations from what they knew. Still, the emissary saw no reason to add that the light would have stained itself bloody red had it played over the crouching form of the creature they sought.

The walls of the sanctuary were not pierced by windows, but several square feet of roof tile had blown off in past years to let in a dim column of moonlight like the sun drawing water through a break in the clouds. Vonones' eyes adapted to see in a room ten feet square and perhaps thirteen feet to the ridgepole. The cult statue had been replaced at the time the temple was reconstructed; but the replacement was of wood also and had decayed thoroughly during decades of neglect. Splits along the grain of the wood had cracked off much of the paint from the limbs and features of the goddess, and the torso had not been painted at all: a robe would be draped over the figure in the unlikely event of a ceremony at this shrine. The statue had less character in the moonlight than did the water-marks on the interior stucco of the walls.

The Armenian looked upward sharply, as the fact of the moonlight made him consider the opening through which it fell. But the Egyptian—and almost certainly Lycon, when he chose the location, though he had not said anything about it—had already considered and rejected that concern. Though the tiles were gone, the framing members of the roof were spaced too tightly for the beast to enter between them. That it could tear its way through beams which rain and the sun's heat had gutted of their strength was probable; but the delay would leave it at the mercy of whatever force it was that N'Sumu controlled.

That thought aroused a more serious question. The animal dealer shifted so that he could see past the bronze-skinned man and out through the hand's-breadth slit to which N'Sumu had again closed the sanctuary doors. Lycon's armored figure had disappeared into the apartment building where he claimed to have stowed the remainder of his paraphernalia for this operation. The distance between the temple and the entrances to the apartment block had seemed short when the three men had been standing outside the sanctuary—a clout shot for an archer, certainly. But it was not archers involved this time . . . not that an arrow could be more than an instrument of revenge, for only if the lizard-ape were gripped by someone sure to be its victim would it be unable to dodge the missile.

Aloud, Vonones said, "Master N'Sumu, will you be able to strike the creature down from this distance?"

The Egyptian did not look away from the facade of the building opposite. "I should be closer," he muttered. "Perhaps he'll lead it this way." He turned his head and added more sharply, "You understand that I can't afford to hit your friend Lycon instead of the beast?"

"Yes, of course," said Vonones, who misunderstood.

"The sauropithecus will give me only one opportunity," N'Sumu explained, "just as it did the first time. If I waste that chance, it will certainly deal with me before it finishes off your friend."

In a neutral voice, and returning his eyes to the empty doorways of the apartment block, Vonones said, "I see what you mean." He did, and he was more uncomfortable than ignorance had permitted him to be. His whip nodded in time with the angry pulse in his throat.

"Lycon," he added sharply, and the whip bobbed and held.

The man in armor stepped into the plaza, not from the arch to the courtyard as Vonones had expected but from the stairwell entrance giving onto the apartments above. He looked around, the motion and implied hesitation exaggerated by the rimmed globe of his helmet. His right hand touched the pommel of his sword, despite the fact that he already held a net with that hand.

N'Sumu noted the movement and said aloud, "You understand, Gaius Vonones—and your friend does—how the Emperor would react if his prize were killed instead of being captured?" He continued to face the opening and Lycon on the plaza beyond, but his eyes glanced sideways once and again to determine the Armenian's expression.

"Yes, I think I understand my lord and god as well as a barbarian from Nubia can be expected to do," Vonones said in a savagely controlled voice. The tremble of the whipstock increased, but the Armenian kept his eyes trained on the figure in armor. "And I think I understand Lycon as well."

As if he were a juggler on the stage, the figure in moonlight tossed something in the air. He tried but failed to catch it, betrayed by the lighting and the full-coverage helmet. His hobnails sparked visibly against the cobblestones of the plaza as he deliberately scuffed the object against the wall of the building before he picked it up again.

"Where did he get *that*?" N'Sumu snapped, his eyes once more beads of stone. He had kept his hands on the door leaves, blocking them to a safe approximation of being closed. Now in angry amazement, the Egyptian drew the doors further ajar.

"I gave it to him," said the animal dealer, satisfied for the first time in—far too long—by N'Sumu's obvious discomfiture. He had not known until that moment what it was that Lycon intended for the crushed remains of the lizard-ape's offspring. "From the site of the fire. This one, at least, was covered by masonry and not cremated." As Zoe and the children had been cremated, Vonones thought, and their ashes strewn in the Tiber—safe from further defilement by the creature Lycon had hunted. . . .

In the plaza below, the little corpse flew into the air again and slapped audibly against the brick facade before it fell back. This time the boot was planted squarely on it and ground against the pavement.

"If he kills it," N'Sumu said, his anger an aura as it could not be an overtone in his voice, "he and you and every member of your household will be killed in the most savage ways the Emperor can imagine. Does he *know* that?"

"*I* know that," said Vonones. The figure in the plaza had paused and was fumbling at the iron-studded apron which protected the thighs beneath the hooped body armor. "Perhaps," the Armenian said with a tinge of hope which irritated him but could not be suppressed, "the beast is nowhere around after all."

"I tell you, you mud-sucking primitive, it *is* nearby!" shouted the bronze-skinned man as the man in armor began to urinate on the lizard-ape's dead offspring and the adult launched itself from beneath a sewer grating.

The slotted stone cover was still lifting with the

impetus that had thrust it aside, though the creature it had hidden was a dozen feet away with its
foreclaws locked on the bronze helmet. A set of
male human genitalia were spinning through the
air much as the infant sauropithecus had done
moments before. The screams of the present victim were muffled by the grillwork over his face
and the blue-scaled killer clinging to it as both
went over in the momentum of the attack.

N'Sumu was through the temple doors and out
past the columns in front more quickly than he
had ever moved before. Despite that, the pudgy
animal dealer was racing across the cobblestones
of the plaza just behind the Egyptian. There was
no sign of the beast-handlers who should have
poured out of the courtyard in response to Vonones'
shouts if not the screams of the victim himself.

The sauropithecus hunched, locking its hind legs
at the victim's right armpit just beneath the iron
shoulder flaps. It kicked downward with its claws
interlocking like a battery of flensing knives. All
the muscles of the arm, from shoulder to wrist,
were carved off and flung away. The right hand,
still clutching the bundled net and with a skein of
bare tendons twisting behind it, sailed off on a
separate trajectory. The body armor and helmet
rang discordantly as they and the man within them
struck the pavement.

Lycon cast his own net from the third-story balcony and vaulted the rail to follow it. He had
stripped off his armor, though the victim he had
chosen to bait the lizard-ape into view wore another identical set to save the time otherwise to be
lost in exchanging the awkward hardware. When
the beastcatcher gave up his helmet and body

armor, however, he did not lay aside his sword. It was naked in his left hand as he dropped.

Lycon had a jump of two stories and the height of a balcony rail—twenty feet and more to stone pavers. The shock, if he landed correctly, would not be incapacitating—and the risk of landing wrong, of the base of his spine smashing down as his feet skidded on slick stone, was not a factor in Lycon's choice of plan.

For choice, he would have jumped with the net gripped in his hand. He had seen how quickly the lizard-ape moved, however, and he was unwilling to risk the chance that the bulk of his own body would warn the beast while the net itself could descend unremarked as a shimmer of moonlight.

Even in the killing rage that had ripped it from safety into the open plaza, the sauropithecus was aware of its surroundings. A portion of its brain had registered and ignored Vonones with the whip he carried—and had registered N'Sumu as what he was, not the persona he feigned on this planet. The creature had once been captured by the emissary; that would not happen again. Its hind claws buried themselves in the thigh of the schoolmaster Sempronianus—the decoy Lycon had provided to lure it from the sewers. Then, using its own hip-joint as a fulcrum, the creature twisted the victim's armored head and torso up as a buffer between itself and a bolt from the emissary's upraised palm.

Instead of trying to drop the net on its target, Lycon had given it a spin on an axis centered upon the snarling head of the lizard-ape beneath. The brass weights, verdigreed and deliberately unpolished, arced the edges outward as the net fell. The beast, warned by the flicker of shadow on the moonlit brick, tried to unlock its claws and leap from the schoolmaster's howling body.

The silken net, cast with an expert's touch, settled about slayer and slain like flame over oil.

The emissary, thirty feet distant and as shocked by the turn of events as the creature he hunted, screamed a curse in no human language as Sempronianus went silent in a haze of green which should instead have bathed the sauropithecus.

The beast was quick, but the net had dropped quickly enough. While the man who cast it was still in the air, the pattern of silken meshes touched the creature which was trying to spring away. The interrupted spin snatched the weights inward at a velocity which rose geometrically as the radius shortened. The lizard-ape, doubled in on itself like a chicken trussed for the market, somersaulted to the pavement as Lycon crashed down beside it.

The beastcatcher took the shock on his flexed knees, his balance perfect as it had to be. His hobnails bit and held: the slightest angle between them and the stone on which they sparked would have slid Lycon to the pavement with an incapacitating crash. The sword in his hand dipped under its momentum, touching but only touching the stone. Then the sword rose again and Lycon stepped forward, his grin as cold and inexorable as the edge of the steel in his hand.

With more than bestial intelligence—and more than human cunning—the lizard-ape had slid one arm through the meshes and gripped the silken cocoon from the outside. Instead of vainly attempting to push the net aside, the creature pulled against the anchoring thrust of its legs. The cords, even silk, gave as the black eyes glared murder and Lycon's sword ripped downward.

There was death in N'Sumu's eyes also. The emissary, running with the awkwardness of a wildebeest but covering ground as swiftly as that clumsy antelope as well, was a stride short of physical contact as his lethal palm turned to Lycon's back. Vonones, six feet behind N'Sumu, had already committed in the fashion instinct had warned him he would have to do. The merchant had not permitted himself to think about it, nor about the certain results, until the lash of his whip curled about the Egyptian's wrist. Reflex set Vonones' feet while N'Sumu's skidded out from under him as his palm lifted.

A pigeon roosting under the eaves sixty feet in the air disintegrated in a green flash while N'Sumu, Lycon and the beast crashed together like inexpert handball players.

The sauropithecus was least affected by the collision, but the net still wrapped its head and lower body. It slashed at what it could reach, willing to die so long as first it could kill. N'Sumu's scream changed in mid-note as the claws which had just been pulled out of Sempronianus' body now raked the emissary. Then Lycon thrust, finding the scales tough but no match for his sword or his resolution.

N'Sumu, not the lizard-ape, cried out again and tried to roll away. The emissary's right hand may have been trying the caress the terrible damage to his face, but Vonones could not afford to take chances now. He jerked on the stock of his whip. N'Sumu's palm twitched back from its chosen course like a fish played on a heavy line.

Lycon withdrew the short, heavy blade of his

weapon, a smooth reversal of the thrust that had fleshed it, until the arm of the sauropithecus shot out with the quickness that had torn a tiger's throat apart. The claws clicked and held on the slight waist of the blade, an inch beneath the crossguard and the flesh of Lycon's hand.

The creature grinned. There was a slot in the taut, scaled skin over its ribcage like a cross-section of the blade at its widest point: a finger's length by a finger's breadth, and the beastcatcher had felt paving stones grate against his point to end the thrust. He smiled as if he or the scaly thing were a mirror image of the other; and he drew back on his sword against the thing which gripped it as if a hand and claws could be harder than a steel edge.

The claw points left deep gouges as they slid along the metal until the blade's double edges had severed all the tendons in the scaly hand.

Lycon had thrust from the half-sprawled, half-kneeling position into which N'Sumu's impact had thrown him. Now he stood and backed a step while he looked down at the creature half-bound by the net he had thrown. One clawed digit gleamed like a sapphire brooch from the cobblestones, a few inches from the hand from which it had been cut. The ichor which pulsed from the lizard-ape's torn chest was too nearly transparent to color the scales beneath it, but the creature's belly shone liquidly in the bathing moonlight.

The beast's arms were still moving slightly, but it was not trying to squeeze life back in through the fatal swordcut as a man would do, as most men would do. It was reaching for Lycon, the way Lycon would have reached for it were he on the stones with his belly torn away. And they smiled at one another, the killers, until the light went out of the eyes of the one with blue scales and the other stumbled because his knees no longer needed to support him.

Vonones did instead, catching his friend from behind and easing him backward while the sword rang disregarded on the pavement.

"Won't bring Zoe back," whispered the beast-catcher. "But I beat it, and it knew it there at the end. It knew that I'd won."

Dead, the netted lizard-ape was as formless as a shrouded insect found hanging from a spiderweb: unpleasant for its associations, but quite harmless now. The other two figures sprawled in the plaza were moaning.

Vonones had assumed the man wearing armor was dead, as anyone who had received such injuries deserved to be. Shock seemed to have pinched off the blood vessels which should have nourished the man's right arm and leg—now bones and ragged tangles of flesh like offal from a slaughteryard. The effect of the bolt which was meant to stun the sauropithecus had worn off of the human victim N'Sumu had struck instead.

Lycon grimaced at the writhing thing. The beastcatcher felt drained but normal again, as normal as could be expected. He picked up the sword he had dropped.

"What about the men in the courtyard?" the Armenian asked, nodding toward the archway but keeping his eyes on his friend.

"Sent them away, out the other side," Lycon said. The blade of his sword glistened with the clear gelatin-like substance which covered it.

"Didn't want them to interfere when there wasn't any good they could have done anyhow." He thrust quickly, expertly, between the body armor and the grill of the gladiatorial helmet. The plaza echoed as the iron hoops arched and fell with the death throes of the man they had failed to protect.

"That one?" Vonones wondered with slight curiosity. The merchant's palms were sweaty now that he had taken sides against the Emperor's desires, without recourse and without hope.

"A schoolmaster," Lycon said as he wiped blood and ichor from the blade on Sempronianus' tunic. "He volunteered to act as bait, though he may not have been aware of that at the time."

And then both men looked at the other figure, the man who had called himself N'Sumu . . . the *thing* that had called itself a man named N'Sumu.

Vonones swore, more in wonderment than fear but with a tinge of fear as well. While Lycon and the two—others—were tangled on the ground, the sauropithecus had kicked down with its hobbled legs at the same time its arm slashed upward. None of the multiple claw-tracks were deep enough to be fatal, but they had snatched away the wool and linen of N'Sumu's clothing, and they had gouged deeply through the bronzed integument which previously appeared to be skin.

That it was not skin was as obvious as the fact that the face which claws had bared beneath the bronze mask was no human face. The jaws were twitching convulsively as N'Sumu breathed, but they moved from side to side instead of up and down. In that, the visage was insect-like, but for the rest of its conical smoothness it was more reminiscent of a moray eel. The teeth were pegs with flat grinding surfaces, and they appeared to be arranged in multiple rows within the mouth.

The real skin was dark though not black, indeterminate in the moonlight but seemingly closer to purple than brown. The blood that welled from the gashes in it was very dark indeed.

"What under heaven?" Lycon murmured as he knelt beside N'Sumu and began, with his sword-point, to extend a tear in the bronze overskin down the length of N'Sumu's right arm. Beneath that false skin was a pattern of interconnected nodes, a large one on the inner angle of the elbow and another which covered the palm of the right hand.

The sword had been blunted by use and the pavement. Vonones touched his friend's arm to restrain him and finished undressing N'Sumu's hand with the pen-sharpening knife he carried in his wallet. The false skin was resistant to direct pressure, but it parted like a maidenhead once the cut was started. One of N'Sumu's fingers was actually a part of the integument.

What remained when the small knife had picked away the counterfeit was something slimmer than human, with three fingers and an opposable thumb. Lycon stared at it and stared at the whole sprawling body in the light of present revelation. He could not imagine that N'Sumu had ever seemed human. A praying mantis the height of a man would have seemed less strange.

Vonones lifted the node away from N'Sumu's palm. Interconnecting it with the similar flat bulb at the elbow and a score of lesser nodes were a series of tendrils, thin enough to have an orange sheen in the moonlight where the thicker lumps of the same material were dull and colorless. The node had the wet flaccidity of a spleen with barely enough structural integrity to keep from tearing apart under its own weight. It had not been attached to N'Sumu's body or to the bronze overskin by any evident means beyond friction and the slight tackiness of its surface.

Lycon nodded and touched the skein of tendrils with his sword. The roughness of its edge gave it purchase on the material which stretched briefly, then fell away like gossamer. "If that's why he could—do with his hands," said the beastcatcher, "then we don't want. . . ."

The severed ends of the material steamed. For an instant there was a spicy odor, as if cassia had been flung on a hot stove. "There's more," said the Armenian, and the two men huddled together to flay the moaning figure of N'Sumu. The head was the worst part. Even with the portion the sauropithecus had ripped from the mask, the full reality was more disturbing than either of them had imagined.

"We should finish him," Lycon said in a low voice. He had not felt queasy in the present way since the afternoon on a mud bar he had cleaned a crocodile which had grown to three tons weight by devouring villagers who fished and washed in that stretch of the Nile. "He's . . . he's as like the other, the lizard-ape, as he is to us."

The animal dealer lifted his jaw in agreement. There was a particularly dense pattern of nodes ringing N'Sumu's head and neck. If the blob on his palm had been the charm which permitted the "Egyptian" to stun and kill, then these might well have something to do with the skill with which a mouth so inhuman mimed human speech. The little knife clipped each nodule out of the pattern of tendrils, then lifted it separately to the pile of offal on the stone.

Aloud, Vonones said, "Do you want to live, my friend?"

"What?" Lycon asked. "I. . . . Yes, I do."

"So do I," Vonones said, flopping N'Sumu's left arm aside to make the task of stripping it easier. "And Master N'Sumu here is going to make that possible. He's going to capture the lizard-ape alive just as he told the Emperor he would."

The Armenian smiled brightly, but it was not for some minutes that Lycon understood what his friend meant.

CHAPTER TWENTY-SEVEN

The veils were drawn back above the hollow of the Flavian Amphitheater so that the sun could flood in on the mid-afternoon main turn in the arena. The sand had been raked smooth over the area, as large as a freeman's farm in the dim, grim days of myth and Romulus. Blood did not show, not even from the ivory chairs of the imperial entourage on the lowest of the viewing levels. Domitian, shaded himself by a panel of gold-shot scarlet silk held by a pair of slaves, leaned forward in anticipation. His tongue touched his thick, cruel lips, and his fingers twitched as if they had a throat between them to squeeze. Crispinus, unshaded and smelling a little of sweat through his heavy perfume, watched the Emperor sidelong with a false smile and the inner awareness that imperial whim could cause any of the fifty thousand spectators to be thrust down into the arena.

The section of German guards carried spears and shields whose blazoning cost more than a share-cropper's annual profit. The plywood cores of the shields were perfectly functional, however, and would provide the necessary protection should a beast somehow get through the spiked iron grill within the arena proper and up the eighteen-foot wall above which the tiers of seats were ranged.

There was just a possibility that the shields would be needed this afternoon.

"Lord and god," said the tribune Lacerta, who had seen—or seen flashes of—the lizard-ape on the loose, "I really think the danger of this creature's speed is such that—"

There was a bellow from the expectant crowd, though there was nothing unfamiliar about the beast that snapped and snarled its way onto the sand through a short covered passage from the cells below. It was a tiger, young and powerful, with a sheen on its coat indicating the good condition of the muscles beneath. The tiger's belly sucked in sharply behind the rib cage: the beast had been fed only lightly for the past day and a half, leaving it hungry without breaking its spirit the way a week of starvation would have done. The beast whirled, clawing at the goads of the men advancing behind the movable grate in the passage. Then it sprang fully out into the arena and roared at the surrounding spectators.

"That fellow Vonones did a splendid job with the cat, didn't he?" observed the Emperor as he considered the tiger with the eye of a connoisseur of blood sports. "Philon!"

"Lord and god?" replied the secretary who sprang to attention with his stylus poised over a wax tablet.

"A diploma for the animal dealer, Claudius Vonones," Domitian said, "freeing him for port duties throughout the Empire for a period of five years. That will let him bring us more entertainment as good . . . if he's wise."

"But lord and god," pressed Lacerta, "this creature, this sauropithecus, is amazingly fast and can leap—truly, I saw it—at least thirty feet. I fear it may be dangerous for even you to watch it in the open like this."

"You'd put *me* in a cage, Lacerta?" the Emperor asked, turning to the Guard officer with a look of chilling speculation on his face. "Or do you think I should hide in my palace while a unique animal kills a tiger in front of—" he gestured toward the packed stands, the fifty thousand men, women and children who had managed to acquire tickets for this most special of occasions "—half of Rome?"

"My master and god," Lacerta lied, straightening with a taut face and freshly-beaded sweat on his forehead, "you know that I did not mean such a thing."

The Italian officer remained braced to attention, his eyes turned toward the arena and his mind focused on images of his own death. He did not relax, even minusculely, until he heard Domitian say, "Jump thirty feet? I wonder if it will leap onto the tiger as soon as the arena door—"

Another door in the high arena wall swung down, and the crowd thundered over anything further the Emperor would have said—even as the event embarrassed his hopes.

The sauropithecus did not leap into the arena. Indeed, it could be seen clutching at the movable grating until a slave with a torch thrust it out onto the sand in stumbling despair.

"It doesn't look like a lizard at all," said Domitian

loudly, and in obvious displeasure. "Or an ape, so far as that goes."

"I thought you said it was blue, Lacerta?" Crispinus called, shark enough to be a part of any offered kill. "That thing's really a purple in good light."

"Head like a fish, not a lizard," put in another courtier.

The guard tribune was shaking. He had parlayed his brief glimpse of the sauropithecus in action into sole credit for the beast's capture, aided by the seeming unconcern of Vonones and Lycon to tell Domitian himself a story that meant riches and power for its heroes—or hero: the Egyptian mangled unrecognizably, another of the capture party torn to collops, and—in the tribune's version—Lacerta himself pinioning the beast while its claws cut deep grooves (artistically rendered by a tinker with mallet and chisel the next day) in his armor.

"It's exceptionally cunning," Lacerta said, repeating what he had been told, "and I have no doubt that it's luring the cat closer." He had a great deal of doubt—the creature looked very much as if it were running around the iron palings in a blind panic—but surely the gods would recognize a prayer, whatever its form? To the hope expressed as a certainty, the tribune added the lie, "That's what it did when it killed the first tiger."

This tiger was certainly fooled. It did not like the crowd noise or the direct blaze of sun on sand, but unlike some of its kin it did not react by cowering against the bars until barbs and torches drove it back toward the center. It hunched, midsection first rising, then falling, as the paws wriggled for purchase in the sand and the tail twitched.

The orange of its fur overwhelmed the black of the stripes overlaying it in the dazzling sunlight. The great head shifted to follow the scrambling so-called lizard-ape. The whole body shifted; and the tiger sprang for its prey.

Almost a hundred feet separated the cat from the bipedal monster with which it shared the arena. The tiger covered the distance in three magnificent bounds which drew gasps of delight from even the jaded familiarity of the onlookers.

The prey leaped up onto the grating. The creature had been RyRelee, emissary from a Class 5 planet of the Federation—and more recently, before it lost its false skin and the battery of biomechanical devices which permitted it to kill and stun and process information in hundreds of human languages, had been N'Sumu the Egyptian wizard. Now, in the last moments of its life, it was the lizard-ape. It caught a cross-bar scarcely eight feet above the ground, and the tiger smashed it back to the sand with both hind paws firmly planted.

The purple-skinned corpse did not even twitch as the tiger used it as an outlet for its own fury.

"Not very satisfactory," said the Emperor in a tone so menacing that it was scarcely necessary for him to add, "Philon—Marcus Cloelius Lacerta here. To the arena this afternoon. Another tiger, I think."

The tribune whirled around with a scream frozen on his face. Two of the Germans whom he had until that moment commanded gripped him expertly, effortlessly. Their spears fell ringing to the travertine paving, unnecessary now that the threat from the arena had failed so markedly to materialize.

"It's a pity, you know," said the Emperor. He extended his thick lips in a pout. "I was looking forward to seeing a real killer."

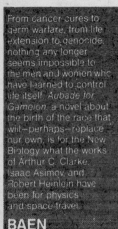

The Newest Adventure of
the Galaxy's Only
Two-Fisted Diplomat!

THE
RETURN
OF
RETIEF

KEITH
LAUMER

When the belligerent Ree decided
they needed human space for their
ever-increasing population, only
Retief could cope.

$2.95

BAEN
BOOKS

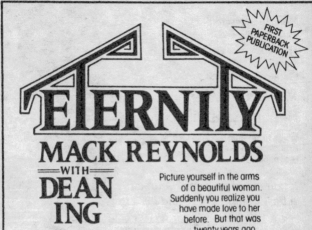